Linda Boulanger

Dance With The Enemy
By Linda Boulanger

Cover Design/Interior Design:
Tell~Tale Book Covers

Published by TreasureLine Publishing

ISBN: 978-1-61752-159-1

Also available in eBook publication

PRINTED IN THE UNITED STATES OF AMERICA

For my sister, Leigh Bridges, and my brother, Dean Gamble, who both lost their lives to cancer during the writing of this book. Forever loved, forever missed.

Chapter 1

Labored steps took the warrior toward the gathering hall with only the men pressing in behind moving him forward. He cursed himself for having downed the tankard of ale customary among the men before they headed to the building on the other side of the town center where the women waited. Every year, from the time he turned eighteen and was allowed to participate in the Dremis festivities, he'd looked forward to the Ball and the week that followed. This year was different. For the first time in eight years, he wished he could be excluded.

With his insides churning, the warrior forced his feet to move, one before the other. His throat worked to swallow, the dryness of his mouth far greater than anything he'd felt, even going into the worst battles. He stopped just outside, blocking the door, and ended up the brunt of more than one warrior's disgruntled murmur. Shaking his head, he stepped back and watched his best friend and jousting partner take hold of the handle. He turned away, fearful he might lose the meager dinner and drink he'd had. Three steps back, he stopped. His eyes glazed over as he turned toward the opened door, raising his chin and drawing in a deep breath. She was there. He could smell her.

Shadowed eyes dancing over the crowd of women dressed to entice, he wondered why they bothered. The warriors that trailed in with him were hungry, driven by need born of lengthy denial. They needed little encouragement.

It was the same every year. There were those men who would find themselves thrown into a maddened frenzy by the assailing scent of a particular woman, one chosen for them and altered to make her irresistible to a particular warrior when she came of age. The King's finest warrior groaned. He would have given anything to have never found himself in that life altering group. Yet there he was, with the madness taking over, pulling him toward his destiny.

With ease he swept past the women vying for his attention, the increasing intensity of one scent keeping him focused. He pushed away a blonde pawing at his arm. Others stepped before him, only to jump aside to avoid the same fate. Eyes wide with madness, he looked around, cursing the Masters for their silly rituals, making the warriors hunt through the crowd of women, both Marked and Unmarked, until they found their own. It did nothing but turn them into animals, almost guaranteeing the quick conception of the next generation—children who were bound to be stronger and more intelligent than those who had come before them, thanks to the genetic superiority of their parents. He supposed that swift guarantee was what the Masters wanted.

While he searched, he wondered if his Chosen knew him—had her senses gone on high alert as his had, letting her know she'd been marked as his? It wasn't like every woman there didn't know *why* she was there. It was the season when those who had come of age were sent by their families. The Marked would be paired with one of the elite warriors from families whose blood was as royal as their own. The others hoped to find favor with one of the lesser warriors, still a privilege guaranteeing a life of prestige. Some would take on the title of second, becoming a mistress to a warrior who had fulfilled his duties and secured the bloodlines with the birth of a mightier future generation and now sought fulfillment of a different kind. They would be honored since their children would carry royal blood, even if not considered one of the elite. Others became Ladies of the Court, providing pleasurable companionship to the men of royal lineage who either had no Marked or whose chosen mate had not yet reached the appointed age. Even as one of many women, it was still a station garnering favor and comfort within the walls of the King's castle.

For years, that was the position Tahruk had found himself in, fulfilling his lusty desires without consequence. He had assumed it would be the same that year, until he entered the hall and caught her scent. Never again would he mock a warrior for falling under the spell luring them into the frenzied world of madness as they went about locating the woman marked for them.

Looking over the sea of women, he cursed his luck. The rumors were correct. They looked better this year than any he could recall. Hopefully his Chosen would not disappoint, though at that point his need was simple, requiring a feminine body with or without the benefit of looks. He merely wanted a woman in his bed. It had been too long. The latest training rituals taking them right up to the Dremis night had kept them far away from the women and had him famished from a need that drove deep.

Where was she? His frustrated gaze fell on a golden-haired vision leaning against the support post across the room. Arms crossed over ample breasts, draped in the finest of gold silk, she watched him without pretense. He knew she knew what she wanted… she wanted *him*.

As he moved toward her, the others quickly stepped

aside, their disappointment evident in sighs and hung heads. They all knew where his long stride was taking him.

He smiled as the scent of his woman grew stronger with each step toward the golden goddess possessing everything he liked in a woman. A tall and slender frame, fair hair that spilled over her shoulders like spun gold, light eyes that danced with mischief—the Masters in their omniscience would have known and paired him accordingly. He licked his lips in anticipation, pride puffing his chest at the thought that his Marked was the finest of them all.

As he closed in, a small, dark figure darted past him, causing his direction to switch abruptly only steps from the blonde temptress. His nostrils flared as he peered into the wave of feminine forms.

"Where are you?" The words were a low growl in his throat that erupted as he plowed through those that moved too slowly. The blonde goddess was reduced to nothing but a fleeting fantasy, forgotten as his mind became all-consumed with the maiden who was to be his and his alone… if he could find her.

Every turn he made, the woman marked for him seemed to be just beyond his grasp. Was this part of the game? The crazed intensity of the unusual mating dance made him light headed. Him! The King's finest, outmaneuvered by a woman. All sense of reasoning fled from him. His only need was to get his hands on her. *Now.*

"Freeze!" The boom of his deep voice did exactly that. Men and women alike, no one moved… save one. Not more than an arm's length from him, the small figure, covered from head to foot in black silk, bolted from the crowd and darted toward the door.

"Stop her!" He moved after her, impeded by the

immobile women who had not so long ago tried to entice him. He thrust them aside with no care for any who stood between him and his Marked.

Three different men tried to get a hand on the shadowy figure, slowing her only slightly before she gained access to the door and ran free. The warrior smiled as he too slipped into the darkness beyond the hall. Did she not realize she had just made finding her easier? Not only would her scent be unmixed with the others, she had just entered his domain. The outdoors was where the warrior felt most comfortable, especially in the land where he had grown up and played throughout his years.

Nose skyward, he sniffed before turning his head to the right just in time to see the dark figure slip into the brush beyond the square. What a pity the rough thicket would mar her delicate flesh. She hadn't chosen wisely. The dense growth would surely hamper her movement in the long skirt as well. All the better for him. He nearly purred with anticipation.

"You can't escape," he called with his first step crunching the underbrush. It never dawned on him to wonder why she would even want to.

Chapter 2

Her chest heaved with every breath, straining against the bodice of the silk gown. Silk. Supposedly spun by the gods, it was meant to entice as it fell in revealing layers over the satiny skin of young ladies waiting for the men for whom they were chosen. To Elenya it only impeded her escape through the thick brush. She pushed the hood of the cloak-like garment from her head, releasing a magnificent mass of red tresses that matted against the trickle of sweat running down her back, now bare from the unusual cut of the dress.

What a waste. She thought of her trip to the courts as well as the expensive fabric and the excitement that had surrounded picking it out, fashioning it into a body-covering masterpiece that represented her future, her dreams. Her family shouldn't have bothered, her destiny decided many years ago by higher authorities anyway. The only thing she'd needed to entice her warrior was her scent. Or was it his scent? She wasn't sure, knowing only that she'd been marked, ceremonially injected as a small child with his blood mixed with a chemistry altering concoction that was to create an inseparable bond between them for all eternity.

Even aware that her future was assured, Elenya was no different from the other girls who dreamed of a lifetime dance with one of the elite warriors of the court. It meant a life lived in the luxury of the circle of the highest once she came of age.

Only the moment Elenya realized the Masters had matched her with Tahruk, she knew that would not be the case. Tahruk! Why? Their families had been enemies for generations. There had to be some mistake. She knew she had to find a way, to find someone who could make it right. Her only chance was to get to the house of the Masters.

Ignoring the aching in her legs and lungs, she refused to pay heed to the burning of the cuts and scratches inflicted on her limbs by the cruel sticks and whipping grasses. She would not cry over the sounds of her beautiful black dress ripping as she ran. She glanced down at what now looked like shredded rags. Careful! Taking her eyes off the terrain could make her lose her footing and then it would all be over. She could hear him not far behind. Only her slight size and the intensity of her need to fulfill her fool's mission aided her ability to outmaneuver him through the dense brush.

Elenya longed for the smooth sandy beaches of home where life had seemed so promising as she'd played beside her sisters and within earshot of the voices of the elders who had appointed themselves protectors of their prophetic fulfillment: *her*. It's where she had learned to run.

Thoughts of her past vanished as the house of the Masters came into sight. Elated that her uncanny sense of direction had led her right to it after seeing it only once, she grew concerned about the freshly harvested field that lay before her. While making her way easier, her pursuer would also be unhindered.

A man opened the house door causing hope to surge, hurrying Elenya forward. He had to be one of the Masters.

"My lord! My lord!" she screamed, and watched as figures, night gatherers, rose from all about—men she hadn't realized were there. Panic tried to cripple her as they began to close in. She dodged them, sometimes barely missing their groping hands, and stopping only when she had thrown herself at the feet of Daruh- the head Master.

It wasn't until her arms wrapped around his legs that she dared a glance back at the warrior crossing the clearing at a more casual pace. As he neared, she could see the anger burning in his eyes, their dark depths glowing within his sun-bronzed face. A shiver ran through her, shaking her whole body, and still she was unable to break away from his gaze. She felt the pull of the marking as she watched him run a hand through his night-black hair. Gritting her teeth, she fought against the urge to rise and go to him.

"Tahruk? What is the meaning of this?" asked the voice above Elenya's head.

"I wish to know that as well, Lord Daruh." As the warrior spoke, his chin tilted upward and he sniffed the air.

Daruh looked at his brethren before addressing the other man. "She… the woman is yours then?"

Tahruk nodded, his glare shifting down to the beauty who attempted to scoot around the strong legs of her refuge. His eyes roamed over her, anger making the dark depths of his own eyes shine as he took in her honeyed-cinnamon hair, small stature, and sun-kissed ivory skin. His gaze settled on the softness of her pink lips and he clamped his own mouth tightly closed after his tongue had flicked across its contours. He watched Daruh's hands lock on her arms and lift her to stand before him. She tried to look over her shoulder. Again, the unmistakable pull warred against her fear.

"Look at me," Daruh commanded, his voice caring while still demanding obedience. He smiled as he wiped some of the grime from her face. "Why would you do this?"

When she didn't answer, he added, "What is your name, maiden?"

Her voice trembled as did her body. Gone was the brave woman who had fled her warrior. "I am Elenya Avenille of the Aleone Drille," she answered quietly, listening for certain response from behind.

Having recognized her by her appearance as the Aleone woman, hearing her speak it pushed the warrior beyond reason. "Aleone!" Tahruk's roar had Elenya pressing herself against Daruh, his strong arms encircling her small frame.

Daruh silenced the younger man with a raised hand, though the outburst was understandable. The disdain felt by the two Drilles, one for the other, had been passed down from generation to generation.

"There must be a mistake…"

"No." Daruh stopped Elenya's verbalization of the thought that echoed through many heads. "The Masters do not make mistakes. You must go with this man and fulfill the obligations imposed by the marking."

"I… I am afraid…" Elenya whispered before looking over her shoulder at the stiff form of the warrior for whom she was chosen. "My lord, please. You see how he looks at me."

"He will not harm you, child. He is honor bound, as are you." Daruh raised a brow as he spoke the words, making sure the young warrior understood as well.

Elenya hesitated then nodded before looking up at the stars. She pulled in a shaky breath and turned toward Tahruk. Head bowed, she went to him, not bothering to fight her tears. Her dreams were shattered, the broken pieces washing away with each teardrop that fell onto the hand that grabbed hold of hers.

Honor would have her pay for the sins of her ancestors. Simply by being born, she had been chosen to dance for a lifetime in the arms of her enemy.

Chapter 3

Nearly a century before...

The wooden gavel fell against the square slate, cracking through the already heavy atmosphere. The King brought it down three more times before the crowd could be quieted after the reading of the guilty verdict.

"Because of the crimes you have committed," he continued, "you shall be hanged at daybreak in the Centrehead Square, a sentence that is irrevocable. Further, since your crime was inflicted directly upon the King's family, your Drille shall be exiled, sent to the far Eastern shores of Riandus."

The King's steely gaze softened only slightly as it shifted from the accused criminal to the man's mother—the daughter of his oldest sister. He'd been about to make the exile permanent as well, though the depth of sheer anguish on the woman's face caused him to reconsider. He had to give her hope.

Ah, Damalenya, he thought. Even more so than his own children, this woman he loved as dearly as a daughter possessed a spirit closer to his own. Her will to have everything go her way, regardless of the rules mandated by those in authority, seemed to have been passed down to her children. And her beauty, perfection that far surpassed all others, made everyone fall over themselves to fulfill her wishes. Even him.

As she sat on the Diaz wrapping a strand of her long hair around her finger, the old King was struck with inspiration. “Your Drille shall remain there, in exile, until a sign is received. A sign recognizable to all.” Damalenya sat up taller, her hands falling to her lap, her neck stretched taut as she listened. “The sign shall be a daughter, born with eyes the color of a perfect rock spring emerald and hair the exact same coloring as Damalenya’s.”

The crowd gasped. Though the green eyes had been seen on occasion throughout the years, never since the princess’ birth had another possessed hair in such a rich shade of honeyed-cinnamon. Damalenya dropped her chin, her shoulders slumping in the same direction. Only those close to her recognized the change in the position of her hands as she clasped them together and closed her eyes while she offered up a soundless plea for divine intervention.

Young Mordin Andorak had watched the sentencing in silent fascination. As a grandson of the King, he was related by blood to the accused. Only his father had been the King’s eldest, not the daughter of the King’s brother, as his cousin’s mother had been. A boy of eight at the time, Mordin would have been considered too young to attend the proceedings had he been anyone other than the future king.

He’d had no idea the part he would play in seeing the sentence come to pass. Though, when they’d come to him earlier that day and told him the child had been born—a baby girl with hair the exact color of Damalenya’s and eyes that showed promise of changing to a beautiful emerald green—he'd thought of the courtroom and his cousin who had given his life in the name of love over seventy years earlier. Had it been worth it? He wouldn't know. His love had been chosen for him, coming in the form of a bond forged by the marking in a marriage arranged by the Masters.

Taking off his crown, Mordin ran a hand through still thick, though no longer dark hair as he continued to think. If he was being honest, he'd have to say he loved his Chosen well enough—the sharing of blood assured some feelings beyond simple lust. After all, there was something about having ones blood running through the veins of another that demanded at least a modicum of bonding. For a man, it created possessiveness as well as a drive.

But the heart?

He'd found love once—a love orchestrated by life, not the mingling of blood, when he'd fallen for one of the Daughters of Damalenya just weeks before the Dremis that brought his Chosen. Had his father not recognized the signs and stepped in, he might have found himself in the same situation as his cousin who sent Aleone into exile—a man who compromised one of the Zanak women marked with the blood of another man. All in the name of love.

Young and naïve, Mordin had thought he would dissolve the ritual of marking when the time came for him to take the throne. Yet there he stood, crown in hand, having effected no change whatsoever.

He thrust his guilt aside, instead taking up his quill and sending a note to the Masters urging them to act diligently and to wield wisdom in choosing the blood serum they would administer to the Aleone child. He had no say in the markings, could only hope that his request would be used as a guide and that somehow, someday, all wrongs would be made right.

Chapter 4

18 Years Later

The End.....for now!

Beautiful young eyes strayed from the paper, glowing with satisfaction at the words she'd just penned. The smile that haunted Elenya's lips lent a false sense of contentment to her flawless features. She closed her journal, caressing the cover, tracing the indented image of a young girl gazing up at the stars in a night sky. Her fingers knew every bump, every crease, every line of that cover. The journal had been a gift from her grandmother, and she'd been writing in it since she was old enough to write, old enough to understand who she was. And who she was loomed before her, ready to create the story that would fill the blank pages of the rest of her life.

The firstborn daughter of Madrik and Senya Avenille of Aleone, Elenya was a direct descendant of the royal family through her mother. The fact that Senya's lineage came from a former princess, the daughter of a past king's sister, mattered little. Her blood was still royal, from a line known for producing exceedingly beautiful women with distinguishing emerald eyes and hair a rich combination of cinnamon and honey. The decree, set by the King many years before, declared their people would remain in exile until a child, a girl, was born with a particular mixture of that cinnamon and honey. That girl had been her.

After that, a simple injection had marked her for a match with a man also from the royal lines. The serum, perfected by the Masters centuries ago, contained a vial of her future mate's blood taken when he was three and mixed with other unrevealed components. The celebration of her third birthday, some unknown years behind her husband-to-be, was observed with a grand ceremony. She remembered the joy, all eyes on her, hailing her as her Drille's salvation. She'd been honored, lavished with attention, and gifts had poured in from other Drilles. The trinkets and monetary gifts represented adulation in their extravagance that dizzied her as a child. She knew she was special, even above others marked that year within the kingdom of Dorengar.

There was an awfulness that accompanied the marking as well, something she didn't like to think about, though the eve of her departure from Aleone seemed to open the floodgates, those memories refusing to be held back. It wasn't until the ceremony was nearing the end that the beast of reality reared its ugly head. Her small body strapped to the stone altar at the front of the gathering hall, she lay still, terrified as one of the Masters lifted the syringe high in the air, blessing it, blessing her before plunging its length into her outstretched arm.

Even at three she'd been taught about the marking, though no one had told her about this part, how she would be gagged and tied, her parents held back by guards as the liquid poured from that vial into her. She remembered the heat flowing through her tiny veins. She'd tried to scream, a silk cloth keeping the sound inside while the room began to spin above her head. A blurred face peered down into hers, one of the Masters. His lips moved, she'd heard sound, though his words were unintelligible, seeming to come from the far end of a long tunnel.

When her body stilled, the convulsing stopped, she found herself veiled in peace. She remembered turning her head, a slow, labored movement. Her vision swam before settling on her parents standing where the guards still blocked them from her. Her father, red faced, had to be physically restrained while tears fell from her mother's green eyes, streaking otherwise perfect porcelain cheeks. Elenya had never seen her mother cry.

"Mama." The word was whispered when the cloth was removed from her mouth. A single tear had trailed down her temple, dropping to the table beneath her head.

Everyone within the hall stood quiet, sobered, having forgotten this part of the marking during their exile. Or maybe not wanting to remember. It seemed so barbaric, especially when it involved such an innocent, young child. And for what? So that royal bloodlines would be assured, for the perpetuation of the superior race of warriors the Centrehead desired to defend its kingdom lines? Even in exile, the families of Aleone had followed certain rules to assure that matches were made only among the pure and strong. They had planned and prepared, doing so without the need for barbaric markings or marriages among total strangers, young maidens pulled away from their families to face the unknown alone. Elenya found it hard to believe the majority of the women who were sent to the Dremis felt honored. To her, they were little more than glorified breeding stock. She hated the continual reminders that she should be proud that her marking had restored Aleone's grace with the Centrehead.

She was also told there was no way she could have remembered the marking, that she was too young. But she did remember. The whole event was imprinted vividly within her head as plain as the raised scar on her arm from the injection that marked her. And written in the pages of her journal. It was all a part of who she was.

A wistful smile tugged the corners of her petal pink lips as she rose and crossed the room to look at her reflection in the gazing ball. That little girl stared back. Only she was a woman now, looking very much as her mother had the day of her marking, some fifteen years before—years that had transported her to the time she must go to meet the man whose blood she shared.

She laid the journal on the table and reached for the carving that sat beside the globe, her fingers caressing its smooth curves even before she looked at it. Another smile flitted across her face, this one genuine, though whether it was from romantic thoughts of the entangled wooden figures she held or for the one who had given it to her was anyone's guess.

"Soon enough that will be you, just as I'd imagined when I bought it for you." The deep voice resonating quietly into her chamber caught Elenya off guard, as did the rose tossed casually through the air to land beside the figure she'd just sat back down. She looked at it for a moment, fingering the single thorn left on the stem, before wheeling toward the window, her face aglow with candid welcome.

"Shemek!" She rushed toward the young man lounging against the wall just inside her window, a lazy smile lifting the corners of his mouth, and her heart. "I wondered when you would come. I was concerned... there are so many guards. Oh, Shemek! I'm so glad you're here." Her delight was unmistakable as she threw herself into his arms.

Shemek held her close, her head resting against his fast beating heart as he stroked the length of her loose, dark red curls. "You're shaking, Ya." His use of her childhood nickname made her want to cry. She held it in, for her and for him, smiling instead as he tipped her face up to his. "What's wrong? And don't tell me you're cold." He knew her too well. Even with the night breeze coming off the water, the air of Aleone remained balmy. She wasn't cold. Her trembling came from the fears of a young woman about to embark on the unknown. Having to leave the only man who had ever held her heart made fulfilling her duty to her people that much harder.

As Shemek stared down at her, he longed to hear her tell him how she felt. They both knew they were words she would never say regardless of the volumes spoken from her soul shining behind the green eyes that bore into his.

"You'll be fine!" He broadened his smile, pushing her back to take her hands in his. He brought them to his lips. "Ya, there's no way he will not fall madly in love the moment his eyes fall upon you. You'll see. He'll lavish you with his affections, shower you with finery, and you'll forget all about this crazy world where we live."

Elenya scrunched her nose, her lower lip jutting out just as she'd done since she was a small child. She stepped away and turned her back on her old friend. She didn't want to forget. This was her home, they were her people. She loved them. She loved him... She went to the table where her journal lay. Tomorrow she would begin to write in a new book, but tonight, she only wanted to remember, to feel Aleone. She picked up the rose and brought it to her nose, breathing deeply.

"Can you sneak me outside, Shemek?" she asked, dropping the flower and turning abruptly to look at him. They both knew he could. Shemek was a master at getting around undetected. "I want to see the stars above Aleone

one last time." Her voice broke. She closed her eyes willing the tears to subside.

Shemek didn't try to comfort her, didn't speak. Instead, he dimmed her chamber's light and slipped his hand around hers. With the stealth of the warrior he had become, he led her out the window, through the shadows, and into the night.

They stopped far down the beach at a secluded spot secure from the view of any wandering villagers. Elenya breathed deeply, relishing the familiar salty sea essence of Aleone air. She kicked off her shoes to caress the sand, imprinting the feel of it between her toes. No, she didn't want to forget. She tilted her head up, taking in the stars in the night sky, just as the girl did on her journal front. How different would they look in her new life? Would she be able to see them from the Centrehead, to know Shemek was staring at the same stars back home?

"You're… you'll come see me, won't you?" She waited for his answer, her gaze snapping to him when it didn't come. The moon was bright enough for her to clearly see the pain etched in the lines of his face. "My sister, Shemek… Surely my family will join me eventually, wherever I end up. Marry her and join them if there is no other way. Join me."

Again Shemek didn't answer. Elenya moved quickly, dropping to her knees before him, grabbing his hands into her own and pressing her forehead to them. She looked up, imploring him with her eyes, her lips grazing his knuckles as he'd done to hers not so long before. "Please, Shemek." Her words wrapped around him in a whisper on the night winds.

"Elenya." He grasped her upper arms, pulled her up to

face him. "Tomorrow you begin anew. What you have now…" He motioned around with a circular gyration of his hand, then shook his head. "No, Elenya. You must say goodbye for good. Why should your sister give up her future? Why would I break your sister's heart for my own, especially knowing that seeing you with the man whose blood you carry would pain me more than never seeing you again? I feel certain it would drive me quite mad." He shook his head again. "No, Ya. This is the end."

Elenya couldn't keep the tears from her eyes, or stop them when they spilled onto her cheeks. "Yet, I'm supposed to happily give up my life." Her words screamed of self-sacrifice.

Shemek nodded. "Like the stars, you'll shine for all of us. *You* are Aleone's hope, our future. Your sacrifice has opened gates kept shut against us. It's what you were born to do." He pointed at the sky and Elenya looked up, the stars orbed spears through her tears. "They shine alone, yet every night they still shine and are greatly loved by those who watch them from afar. Even for those who know they will never touch them."

Fresh tears coursed down her face and Shemek wiped at them with his thumb, though it didn't help. Then he surprised her by doing something he'd never dared to do before. He lowered his head to hers, covering her lips with his own.

Heat swept through Elenya nearly rivaling that of the marking. Breathing became difficult, her legs weakened and Shemek caught her, pressing her into him as his lips continued their silent demand.

They were both shaking when he finally pushed Elenya away from him, knowing that kissing her violated Drille code. Since she was marked, and especially since she was

Aleone's *chosen*, it was an offense punishable by death.

She continued to look up at the sky as he led her away, her heart lighter as they walked back toward her family's home. A smile played across her swollen lips. Tomorrow she would leave, a piece of Shemek seared into her heart. He had risked his life by kissing her, and though she was sure he meant it as a kiss goodbye, she also knew it had to have affected him. Somehow, someway, he would find her again. And even if he didn't, she knew a part of him would always love her. That was enough to allow her to look forward to a new dream—the one she'd been walking toward since the day she was marked.

Yes, life as she knew it was over, but now Elenya saw it for what it truly was—a continuation. She would rise with the sun tomorrow morning, setting out toward her new life. And in the evening she would gaze up at the stars that now represented for her a different kind of hope. She thought of the words she'd written in her journal and knew they were truer than she'd imagined. This was only the end… for now.

That next night, leaning against the railing, her honeyed-cinnamon curls whipping loose from their tie, Elenya breathed deeply, eyes closed as she enjoyed the misty sea spray against her face. She felt at home aboard the King's vessel sent to retrieve her from the shores of Aleone, though it was finer than any she'd seen in her eighteen years of life.

She looked up at the stars sprinkled across the sky and smiled. Without concern that anyone would see her in the dim light, she pulled the corked bottle from beneath her cloak and stared at the rolled parchment inside. She recited the memorized words she'd written on the page, then flung the bottle as far from the bow as was possible for her slight form.

For a brief moment, hope won out over fear and she allowed herself to look forward to what was to come, to believe in the dream she'd asked for through her penned words. With one last glance at the stars above she turned, ready to sneak back to her quarters to prepare for the moment when she would fulfill the very reason she was born.

Chapter 5

Tahruk slipped his arms into the soft fabric of the dove gray tunic he would wear to the gathering. With a poorly contained tremble, the corisan's seemingly small hand inched forward to smooth the lines over his charge's thick biceps, only to be pushed away. Tahruk's countenance was darker than it should have been for one preparing for celebration.

With clipped movements the warrior wrapped a near-black sash around his waist and tightened it with a sturdy jerk. He despised this yearly ritual, hated the fact that the Masters chose whom the elite would marry. Not that he should care. He'd never had any need for love, observing marriage as merely a means to fulfilling his obligation to sire children. Besides, his *Chosen* had eluded him for eight years. Few men reached his age of twenty and six without being bound by some maiden at the Dremis gathering. Perhaps the Masters had forgotten him.

He smiled, only the corners of his full lips twitching upward to match the wickedness of his thoughts. Either way, his bed would be warmed by an unknown maiden, one as fresh as the new clothing that hung on his powerful frame. Hopefully she would be one of the women brought in specifically for the pleasures of the warriors whose *Chosen* had not yet arrived. He wondered… he'd heard this year's grouping was far more alluring in their innocence than in most years, though tonight he craved a maiden perhaps knowledgeable even though unskilled. Too often the young women, dressed to whet the appetites of the too long denied warriors, were fearful, untaught—combinations that did not go well together. Tahruk had never minded, really. Under normal circumstances he very much enjoyed his part of easing a reserved maiden into her new position as a Lady of the Courts. He was known for leaving ladies skilled in the art of love, a proficiency appreciated by visitors and need-laden warriors fresh from training or the fields of battle.

Why then did he not feel the weightless anticipation that usually accompanied preparation for the ceremony? Though true that he despised the ceremony's reasons for being, he was usually able to look beyond the fanfare to the reward. And then to the three weeks of rest that followed. Tonight, though, he wore a brooding veil that refused to lift.

Your enemy will soon walk by your side.

The odd words darted through his mind, pinging within Tahruk's head while he pulled on his boots. He knew the exile had been lifted from his family's enemy and their *Chosen* was said to be in the midst of the Dremis maidens. Again Tahruk wondered why her presence should concern him. Since her marking some fifteen years ago, their exile had ceased and her people had begun to venture to the Centrehead, though not yet in the masses that were sure to come with her union.

He supposed his concerns lay in her match. Depending on whose blood she carried, her family may very well be spending a lot of time near Zanak—his family Drille. It seemed likely since the majority of Drilles were centered about Dorengar's Centrehead that she would be living close by. He sighed. Their families would be forced into becoming civil neighbors after being at odds for nearly a century. The Courts would demand it, especially with Princess Damalenya's line continuing their cause, claiming the death of the Aleone man should have served as punishment enough and that the exile as a whole was unjust.

Damn their claim! Zanak had been wronged. Life had been lost there too. The woman, marked for someone else, had given birth to a child, a scrawny boy with hair the color of honeyed cinnamon. And soon after, their woman had died, the child quickly following her into eternity. How could they not believe the punishment was just? And what did it matter to him? He would not be paired with the daughter of his enemy. As absurd as the reasoning for these pairings seemed, to aid in the reproduction of their superior race, idiocy in the matches did not appear to rein. Thankfully.

The dark gray pants of soft leather received a rough thrust into black boots before the warrior straightened, towering over the man sent to assist him. He paid little heed to the corisan, bellowing instead for Nema, who breezed in, pride simmering in the depths of her eyes nearly as dark as Tahruk's blue-black ones. She looked him over, her neck craning toward the ceiling to take in all of him.

"A finer man among the elite has never been, my lord." Her voice cracked, garnering a sharp scowl from the young warrior. The woman, older than his mother, chuckled, nonplused by his dark demeanor. Without even bothering to hide it, she brushed away an errant tear. "Your *Chosen* will be honored to carry your blood, and your children."

Tahruk huffed, pushing back a strand of the night black hair as it escaped its leather tie. "Were my *Chosen* here to see me… perhaps. Though, if she were, I would surely know," he ground out between clenched teeth.

"As you say." Nema pointed to a chair near the garden door of Tahruk's chamber. "Now sit so I may properly bind your hair. You have a long night ahead of you."

He stared at her for a few moments before complying, both of them continuing in silence. The warrior's thoughts returned to the feeling that gnawed his insides. If Nema was right, tonight would change the course of his life.

"Why do you smile, Nema? You look as guilty as a cat whose mouth is full of yellow feathers." His eyes locked with hers in the reflection of the gazing glass before him. "What do you know?"

"No more than you." Her gaze was steady, lips thinned after she answered.

"My senses tell me nothing." One fine brow shot up.

"You have already said as much," she countered.

Tahruk watched, knowing her shrewd senses were on alert. Could she know, even before he knew himself, that his body sensed the presence of his *Chosen*? "Your intuition tells you otherwise?"

The older woman who had always been a part of his life, who had acted as his nursemaid and governess when he was young, sat at the family table, and took the same liberties as any other family member—she didn't answer at first. Instead she stared out the garden door, appearing to look beyond the blossoms.

Tahruk's heartbeat quickened, his mouth drying as he watched her, relaxing only slightly when she shrugged her slender shoulders.

"We all wait in anticipation, my lord. Each year, you go to the ceremony while we idle away the hours, hopeful your *Chosen* will be among the maidens and the match will be superior. Until she arrives, it will be so."

The warrior stood, drawing the older woman's gaze

back to him. She smiled. He returned the gesture before pulling her to him. "You are a terrible liar, Nema."

Her cackle rose into the air as she pushed him away. "An old woman is unfit for the arms of a mighty warrior when fair maidens await, my lord. And you shall much sooner find your answer there than here." She shooed him toward the chamber's door with a look over her shoulder. "See, the Dremis moon has begun to shine. Make haste, lad."

Tahruk turned in the doorframe to see the moonlight beginning to creep in through the garden door. Only Nema, who knew him even better perhaps than his own mother, understood the flash of emotions that played across his handsome face before his warrior's mask dropped firmly into place.

"Do not wait up, Nema, for the lady I bring home will surely not be my own," he practically growled. He looked at her one more time, then turned, a confident stride removing him from her presence where he pushed out into the night, wishing the moonlight would wash away the churning he felt inside.

Chapter 6

Arms lifted, Elenya allowed her gown to slide into place. The silk whispering down her body made her shiver and the corisan assigned to help her giggled behind a discreetly lifted hand. She leaned in to whisper to the innocent maiden.

"Tonight you will know the feel of a man's hands instead, my lady." Her voice was as silky as the material she'd slipped over Elenya's head. "That first touch is something you will not soon forget."

Another tremor shot through Elenya, though for different reasons. Eyes lowered, she remained quiet, hopeful the other woman with her heavily kohled eyes and lips tinted a deep red would understand the subject was not one she wished to discuss. Looking the part of a harlot wasn't something she desired either, even though it seemed many of the other maidens preparing for the ceremony did. It all seemed so silly considering she'd been bound to one of the elite warriors since she was three.

With a touch none too soft, the corisan lifted a brush to Elenya's honeyed-cinnamon hair and began the tedious task of dressing the thick crop of curls that fell down her nearly bare back.

"It's a pity this gown was designed to cover your lovely hair, my lady." She ran a strand of Elenya's tresses between her fingers. "This exact hue has not been seen since the days of Princess Damalenya, I'm told. In fact, had your mother's hair been slightly darker, she would have been the *Chosen…*"

"Ceeda!" The voice of the head mistress stopped the woman's wagging tongue. The heavyset woman strolled toward the pair, her curled fists burrowed into what had once been her waist. "Folklore is best left to the story tellers, not the corisans of the Dremis maidens."

Elenya stared at the images of the two women in the reflective glass, the green spheres of her eyes darting back and forth between them. The older woman's mouth barely shifted from the tight line, only a brow lifted above one eye to emphasize her statement. The impact of her words, however, was as clear as if she had shouted. Elenya's corisan bobbed, her dark hair falling over a bared shoulder as she curtsied to the head mistress. She kept her eyes averted until the older woman turned and the sound of her footsteps could be heard on the far side of the room. Only then did she look at Elenya's reflection and roll her eyes.

"Close your mouth, dear. Even in a position as high as yours, such a look is unbecoming on a lady."

So is your smirk, Elenya thought, though she did as instructed, more out of surprise than anything. She was glad this girl did not belong to any of the families she would most likely be paired with. She was certainly nothing like the Lady Larina who had accompanied her on the trip from Aleone. Larina had been every bit a lady, even given her position as one of the Ladies of the Courts.

That was something else Elenya was thankful for—that her marking assured her a single mate. She would never have to serve as mistress to the lot of the King's warriors and honored visitors, though being separated from Larina had left her lonely and hopeful women like Ceeda were an exception.

Her mind went immediately to Cerissa, another woman she'd met on the trip from Aleone. They'd picked her up along with others at one of the two stops made to take on additional Dremis maidens between her home harbor and the Centrehead, and Elenya had developed an instant disliking of her. The interest the other woman had taken in her made her uncomfortable. And Cerissa's incessant attempts to flirt with the crew who were specially trained to turn off their emotions where women were concerned to protect the innocence of the Dremis maidens, was especially offensive. Her mother would have said Cerissa was on the prowl, with her tresses of spun gold that draped down her slender frame in a riotous cascade begging a man to run his hands through them. Never before had Elenya seen eyes a more beautiful blue, nor had she realized such an ethereal vision could exude such an air of one seeking mischief. It seemed obvious to her that Cerissa had every expectation of making a good match even though Elenya quickly learned she had no royal blood running through her veins. No one seemed to know exactly where she came from. In fact, when Elenya had inquired during one of their onboard gatherings, Cerissa had attempted to embarrass her by telling the group she was a Goddian warrior commissioned to protect precious cargo aboard. She'd looked directly at Elenya when she spoke the words. Unnerving to say the least.

The lines of Elenya's tinted lips thinned. The Goddians were a group of mythical women hailing from a non-existent territory. They were trained as stealthy combatants, sent into areas where the presence of men would have alerted the enemy. Cerissa, a Goddian! To have to share a warrior with a woman such as that… Elenya would rather die.

She sighed knowing she had no more say in the matter than the Ladies of the Court did. Even as a marked woman, her warrior could decide to take a second—a woman to warm his bed after his obligations with his Chosen were taken care of. It wasn't supposed to happen that way. The mingling of the blood was designed to create a bond that heightened his desire to stay faithful to the one marked for him. Too often, the men strayed, taking seconds or becoming regular visitors to the halls of the Ladies of the Courts, something they'd grown accustomed to. Again she found herself hopeful Shemek's words would come true. She desperately wanted the man whose blood ran through her veins to have feelings for her beyond those created by the marking. She wanted more than desire quenched only by their coming together as one.

The thought had Elenya's cheeks reddening with an intense burning.

"The Dremis Moon hangs high, ladies. Time to assemble in the Great Hall." She jumped when the head mistress clapped her hands and called the women together. The warriors had returned from the last of their training only that day. They were anxious, many optimistic their Chosen had come of age. Others were interested only in a warm body pressed next to theirs.

Elenya rose, hopeful the man whose blood she carried was one of those steeped in expectancy. She wished her heart was not so heavy. With held breath she fell in line, only to let the air out slowly in an attempt to ease her nerves. She knew her angst was for nothing. In a few hours it would all be over anyway.

The thought did little to lessen her fears.

Chapter 7

Elenya stood with her hand covering the flesh exposed by the cut of the front neckline of her dress. She waited, her heart beating so strongly she was sure everyone around her could see it. With deep, steady breaths, she worked to slow her breathing for fear of hyperventilation. Shouldn't she be excited for this moment, not fighting off waves of fear and nausea? Her whole life had been about this one moment when she would meet the man she'd belonged to since she was three, the man whose blood flowed through her veins.

With the arrival of the King's warriors, her angst grew. She found herself nearing all-out panic when they were released into the midst of the maidens and the madness began. Those whose Marked had arrived were forced to find the woman chosen for them. Elenya watched. She'd been schooled to know her warrior would know her through her scent, or rather his scent mixed with hers through the mingling of their blood. Only, the resulting frenzy that seemed to heighten already aroused animalistic needs terrified her, especially when she realized what the warrior searching for her did not—that she'd been marked with the blood of her family's enemy.

As the leader of the King's elite forces made his way toward her, she ignored the pull of the marking and darted away from him, making her way out into the night, into his territory. One thought rose above all others—somehow she had to get to the Masters so they could right this wrong. There was no doubt in her mind a mistake had been made. Surely fate would not force her into a lifetime dance with her enemy.

Tears threatened for the first few steps into the wooded area that lay between her and the house of the Masters. With a mental shake, she pushed them away, knowing the acknowledgment of any weakness would hamper her success, and that was something she couldn't afford.

Scanning the landscape before her, Elenya kept one ear tuned toward the sound of the body crashing through the shrubs and vines behind her. He was much too close for her to ease her pace, forcing her to move even faster. She did her best to ignore the tearing of her dress and the lashes to her flesh that stung worse with each successive contact. If she didn't make it…

No, she refused to let herself think like that. She had to make it. She just had to.

As she broke through the clearing that separated her from the house of the Masters, Elenya urged herself to move faster. She knew the warrior was close, and would now be unheeded, just as she was. With his speed, if she didn't continue to push herself, he'd be on her before she could reach her destination. A surge of elation coursed through her when she saw a figure step out of the house. Unsure her voice would cooperate, knowing it must, she screamed, garnering the attention of other men within the field that she hadn't realized were there. As they converged on her, Elenya propelled herself forward with a final burst of energy and threw herself at the feet of the only man who might help her. She looked up into his face, praying he would not let fate foist this faux pas on her.

With a pull that she could not deny, Elenya glanced

around from behind his legs where she'd scooted, and winced at the ferocity of the look on the warrior's face. Even from several steps away, she could feel the anger burning inside him. Her heart plummeted, knowing there'd been no mistake. Was there any hope that, someday, the blood flowing through her veins might be enough to unite their hearts? She doubted it, even as the heart attempting to beat its way out of her chest was gripped with a yearning far beyond anything she'd ever felt in her life. Not discounting the fact that she was young and inexperienced, she still felt the flutters and knew what they were. Within her belly, a quivering bundle burst into a million fiery fingers that moved outward, making it even harder to keep from moving toward him.

Cursed marking, she thought as the Master lifted her to stand before him, forcing her to look at him, to answer his questions. Several moments passed, the conversation coming to a close and Elenya finding herself trudging behind the warrior, her hands encircled by his firm grasp. It was then the tears began to fall, the haze of disbelief still engulfing her along with a grief that was surpassed only by the foreign urges that continued to awaken within her.

Stumbling for what had to be the fourth or fifth time, Elenya was swept up into the warrior's arms, cradled against his chest, her ear nestled against his beating heart. A few more steps found her drifting into oblivion, a sweet sigh escaping her parched lips. For the first time since she'd arrived in the Centrehead, Elenya felt a sense of belonging. Too bad it couldn't last, she thought as the comforting darkness engulfed her.

Chapter 8

The next morning, Daruh woke with a stiff neck and sluggish limbs. Sleep had not come easy for the old Master with thoughts of the young maiden troubling him throughout the night. He was not so old to have been unaffected by the plight of the youthful beauty. He only hoped the night was kind to her. He prayed the rumors he'd heard of the young warrior, *her* warrior's ways with a woman, were true. She was the kind of woman who needed to be coaxed in loving, not forced into submission in a man's bed. Surely her womanly instincts had taken over allowing her to subdue the hatred and anger burning in the depths of the younger man's eyes. Cursed be it that these inexperienced young ladies were simply handed over to barbaric men! Daruh fought down his anger. Why would the Masters before him have made such a match?

Masters! They were supposedly men bred with superior intellect, but were they really or were they merely men, wizened by expanded age? Where was the all-knowing master plan?

He pushed his self-deprecating thoughts away in the wake of another thought, a stirring he had not felt in many years. The maiden… her green eyes turned up to him pleading for his help, her half-clothed body pressed first against his legs and then against his chest in refuge. Soft, red curls had flowed down her back and over his upper arm when she'd turned toward her warrior... He had forgotten how a woman felt.

He turned his thoughts back to Tahruk. If he dared hurt her, Daruh swore he would…

He'd what? The maiden belonged to the warrior, not him. And, although Tahruk was honor bound not to harm his Chosen, there was little anyone could or would do if he ended up walking a less than honorable path.

Chastising himself, Daruh knew he'd better put down such thoughts. Worlds were not governed by men whose emotions ran unchecked, though hearts *had* been tamed by the face of a gentle beauty time and again throughout history. Perhaps the Masters before him had not been wrong. Perhaps…

Daruh smiled as he slipped out of bed. Perhaps it was already time to pay a visit to the home of the newly united couple. No doubt the girl would be meeting the elder Sharanis soon. A supportive figure might temper the moment for all involved.

Chapter 9

The morning greeted more than one restless sleeper. Tahruk stretched before rolling over to prop himself for a better view of his sleeping bed partner. He didn't bother to cover his own nakedness, concentrating instead on the thoughts running through his head as he looked down at the tousled beauty. Her shape beneath the covering stirred him as it had the night before.

He revisited the way she'd looked beneath her torn garments. Her lack of resistance when he'd removed them had surprised him, especially after the chase. She had stunned him. Not so much that she ran—though he'd certainly been taken back by her actions. What surprised him more was the intensity to which it had excited and enticed him, adding to the animalistic needs heightened by the marking. He'd been near crazed when he'd caught up with her. Only the presence of the Masters had saved her from an unpleasant first coupling.

The long walk home from the Masters' house had calmed the raging fire and anger burning inside him. That, and the tears that dissolved her defiance. He rubbed his hand, still feeling where the moisture had landed while he led her into the dark night. A woman's tears had always tried his patience before, though each droplet had eroded his anger like an elixir, softening his warrior shell. When she'd stumbled, exhausted by her fruitless attempt to escape, he'd swept her up, cradling her limp body in his arms instead of forcing her to walk the rest of the way back to Zanak under her own power.

It must have been the effect of the marking. There was no other explanation for the behavior of a warrior not easily molded or swayed. With a deep breath, he hardened his heart. Marking be damned! Her people had still wronged his, their punishment a mere slap on the wrist compared to what they deserved. He fought his desire to let his lust and her beauty cloud that reality.

When her green eyes opened to find the angry warrior staring down at her, a noise somewhere between a squeal and a yelp squeezed past her tightly drawn lips. He laughed when she started to bolt away only to realize to do so would expose her nakedness shielded by nothing beyond the thick coverlet. She reversed her actions and attempted to burrow deeper into the bedding.

Lips twitching, Tahruk hooked his finger in the top of the covering only to find her small, soft hand quickly clamped around his. He arched a dark brow. "You would deny me that which is rightfully mine?"

She shook her head. "No, my lord. I would never dream of such, though one might think the cover of night would provide better preservation of dignity."

"And *you* would know all about doing what one must to preserve the dignity of another, *my lady*." His snort caused her to attempt to flatten herself away, his face remaining mere inches above hers. "What do you plan to do with the cover of the coming night? Use it to run from me once again?"

He watched a spark of anger light up her green eyes, was enticed by the way she scrunched her nose and pursed her full lips, the lower one jutting out just a bit. Desire rolled through him, though her next words were a vocal slap momentarily pushing down his building need.

"Your people have a way of making others behave as they should not, resulting in sacrifice by the innocent."

"You know nothing of my people. Besides, the blame falls with the man. Our woman made a dreadful mistake," he ground out between clinched teeth.

"She seduced him, forcing my people to pay for the actions initiated by *your* woman." She glared at him. "I ran because I was certain a mistake had been made this time as well. I feared your treatment of me."

"And did you believe Master Daruh's words? Did you hear him when he spoke of *my* honor?" With a calculating glower, he watched her facial expressions, knowing he was chipping away at her false bravery. It was a tactic he often used on his opponents on the fields of battle.

The movement of the covers as her other hand snaked from beneath to push the red curls back from her forehead caused Tahruk's nostrils to flare. Again she attempted to press away.

"The Dremis night can be a fearful place to the inexperienced…"

"You seemed to have plenty of experience in what you did last night."

The derision in his voice made her flinch, though anger quickly replaced the sting. She lashed out at him, assailing his chest with her fists, her strength no match for his.

"How dare you accuse me of such," she growled as he settled atop her, straddling her still covered torso. Her wrists caught above her head with a single hand, he pinned her beneath him.

"Settle, hellion!" Never before had he had a woman fight him like she did. And this one was *his* woman! The irony of the situation caught him, causing him to laugh. She attempted again to buck him off, her efforts only enticing him more. "There is no doubt you have a warrior's blood running through your veins, Little One."

"It *would* have to be *yours*." The words came from between clenched teeth.

"You could have done much worse. You will at least enjoy the status of the Sharanis name—our families united properly after all these years." He moved to lie beside her again, a firm hand on the coverlet above her belly keeping her in place. "And you will enjoy being in my bed."

She stared at him for a moment before shaking her head. "Knowing what happens to a marked woman who does not preserve her innocence, how dare you take mine and then claim I had prior knowledge. If you think I will now willingly submit…"

"Your innocence has not been compromised! There would have been little enjoyment gained from taking advantage of the sleeping."

"Sleeping?" Understanding began to take shape and she groaned before closing her eyes. "I don't remember…"

"You remember nothing, because there was nothing. Your Dremis night ended when you mocked me once again by falling asleep while I tended the scrapes you received by your ill thought out run."

They lay silent, the same thought running through each of their minds. They had not fulfilled their commitment to the marking which could hinder the procurement of an heir. If she didn't conceive, and quickly, he may be forced to take a second. Elenya thought of the bottle she'd tossed over the side of the ship that brought her to him, a bottle filled with foolish dreams.

Tahruk stared down at her, visually tracing the lines of

her face, her beauty drawing him in. He felt a surge of pride pushing his heart to thump faster and harder. She really was exquisite. And she was his. His blood ran through her veins and his touch would be the first, the only touch she'd feel.

He leaned toward her, only to pull back when he saw the fear in her eyes. He frowned as he found himself wanting to cradle her in his arms and whisper tender endearments to her, telling her it was okay, that she would be all right, that he wouldn't hurt her. Damn her! Why should he care? She was his enemy, and she'd mocked him. Twice!

Only he did care. Even beyond a physical desire, something pulled at him making him want to take care of her, to teach her, not force her. He wanted her to discover the wonders that awaited her, to show her how much they could enjoy one another…

His concerns faded when thoughts of her body's reaction to his flooded his senses, setting off its own reaction. With startling swiftness, his mouth locked over hers in a less than gentle kiss, one she could scarce refuse, even if she'd wanted to.

Elenya was unprepared for her reaction to the feel of his lips on hers. She wasn't sure what made her body arch toward his or how her hand found its way into the thick crop of his night-black hair. She'd never felt this form of need.

That wasn't true.

A vision of Shemek flitted through her mind, only to be pushed away by thoughts of the warmth that had spread through her as Tahruk had gazed down at her at the Master's feet. He'd been angry and she'd still had to fight the desire to rise and go to him.

The pull of the marking. That was all it was. That was

all *this* was, the whole thing.

He released her as abruptly as he'd pressed himself upon her, flooding her with a pool of emotion, including a certain self-loathing at the strength of her desire for her enemy. She looked up into his face washed with triumph.

"I am not your servant," she hissed and tried to roll away.

"No, but you are *mine* and I am *not* finished."

Elenya froze when he pulled her back and began to trace the bones of her neck, sliding his fingers up to follow the path of her jaw line. Even her breath stilled when he brushed the tips across her bruised lips.

His lips twitched, a brow raised. "You enjoy my touch."

Elenya shook her head, enticing him to further action. Soft caresses danced down the back of her arm leaving his mouth free to explore and her breathless, ready to cry out when he stopped a mere feather width from the top of the sheet.

He laughed. "You feel how the madness drives and frustrates…" His tongue darted out to sear her flesh just where the roundness of her still-covered breasts began, and her held breath whooshed out. His lips pressed harder, her heart hammering against them.

Cursed man! Resisting the pleasures of the flesh was going to prove to be such bitter-sweet torment. Even the savagery resonating from the man who controlled her did little to assuage her desires. If anything, it added, intensified, causing her to strain against the bedding in an attempt to push herself toward him, her own unfamiliar need propelling her.

It was at that moment, the moment the warrior's

descent commenced, that the door to his bedchamber opened. Elenya screamed. Tahruk roared. An older woman swooshed in, seemingly oblivious to the scenario playing out between the couple.

"Mother!"

"*Mother*?" Elenya quietly echoed Tahruk's growled word while fighting against him to properly cover herself as *Mother* deposited a load of clothing on a nearby chair before turning to face the bed.

Tahruk released his hold on Elenya's back. He pulled his hand from beneath the sheets and reached behind him to draw the coverlet over his own nakedness. *Mother* seemed unaffected.

"I informed you last night that I would stop by this morning with something suitable for your Chosen…" She shifted her gaze, smiling as she looked directly at Elenya who was sure she failed miserably in her attempt to return the kind gesture. "For you to wear, my dear. None of it will fit properly but will suffice until your belongings are brought over."

Her belongings. Here. More finality to her plight.

"Thank you." The words squeaked from Elenya's tight lips.

Mother frowned, looking at her son.

Elenya cut her eyes to see Tahruk's face and jumped at the ferocity of his glare set on his own mother.

"You're scaring the dear girl, Tahruk." She pressed her hands to her hips, frowned, and made a tsking sound, ignoring the warrior's ire. Her smile returned when she looked back at Elenya. "Introductions to the household in one hour, dear. A bath waits in the outer chamber."

Skirts rustling, the older woman moved to the door, stopping just shy of her exit. She didn't turn around as she spoke. "Fear and conquest have no place in the bedchamber, my son. Leave it for your enemies on the battlefield. Take heed, for she will either loathe you or adore you by how you make her feel… in here." She tapped the side of her head.

The door closed quickly behind her, leaving a silent room. Again shifting her view to her warrior, Elenya noted the flared nostrils, this time for a different reason.

Tahruk growled and rolled away from her side before slipping from the end of the bed with cat-like stealth. His movements were clipped, forceful as he wrapped a covering about his waist. Single words and short phrases narrating his belief that women were cursed creatures and the bane of mankind's existence punctuated his exit from the room.

Elenya remained beneath the covers, motionless except for her shallow breaths and her heart that was beating way too fast. She'd been unable to tear her gaze away from the sinewy lines of the warrior's body. Wanton thoughts filled her head alongside the vision. Heat crept into her cheeks. She'd never seen a man before. Not like *that* anyway. Never *in all his glory.* It was a sight that would be forever imprinted in her young mind, and in her heart.

Chapter 10

"You'd best get up, Missy, unless you expect to disobey your mistress."

Elenya craned her neck to see another woman slightly older than Tahruk's mother standing in the doorway. What a busy place this warrior's bedchamber was! She frowned, sure the room had seen its share of women. Like most men, the man she was marked for would not have remained idle waiting for her to come of age.

"No need to scowl. You don't want to wrinkle that unblemished forehead of yours." She pointed to her own brow, beginning to show signs of aging, and winked. Elenya tried not to laugh, but failed. "That's better." The woman also laughed and moved, uninvited, into the room to retrieve the robe from the pile of clothing Tahruk's mother had left on the chair. "I've a tub filled with hot water waiting for you. Join me and let's see if I can find the fair maiden beneath those layers of wounds and grime, the one who has already hooked her talons into the young master's heart."

Elenya snorted, though a smile won out at the woman's words. How could it not when the tone was so light and playful? She took the offered robe and waited for the woman to leave before rising to slip into the soft fabric. She hoped the parade of people in and out of the bedchamber was not a customary occurrence. Being within a strange house was already proving to be a more trying experience than she'd hoped for. At least the women seemed unfazed at having a daughter of Aleone in their midst, though maybe somehow they didn't know.

Self-mocking laughter tumbled from her as she wrestled her curls free of the robe's collar. Her hair coloring alone spoke volumes, alerting all who saw her of her true identity. With an upward glance, she offered a silent prayer that they were indeed allies, then went to find the older woman and the promised warm bath.

Fresh scents lured Elenya to a lovely room toward the front of Tahruk's quarters. A quick look around told her it was most likely a sunroom and she wondered if it always doubled as a bathing chamber or if this was uniquely for her. Unlike her warrior's bedchamber, this room had felt the touch of a woman. The décor was light, and she found herself delighted and awed by the garden that seemed to spill into the room, adding to the already ripe fragrance. Elenya smiled, imagining herself as a garden pixie. Her sisters would have loved to have played that game of make believe with her.

The smile faded at the thought of her sisters and the vast distance that separated her from them, leaving her empty, wondering if there was any chance they would ever join her. A single tear slipped down her cheek. Even if her family came, life would never be the same. What would happen when her Drille collided with his?

"You're far too young to carry so much weight on your pretty shoulders, love." The woman spoke from the corner where she busied herself with what Elenya supposed was a mixture of fragrances for her bath.

Elenya wiped away the tear, pressing her lips together to still their quivering. In reality, the weight of the future of her people had always rested squarely on her. So much hope and fanfare had surrounded her preparation for what everyone expected to be a preferred match. She was, after all, the prophesied one, and her marking meant the annulment of the exile. All wrongs should have been forgotten. Elenya should have been guaranteed favoritism.

At least that's what her family and the leaders who had visited from the Centrehead from time to time throughout the years had led her to believe.

"Climb into the tub, child. I'll be there in a moment. I have but one more…" The hissing sound Elenya made as she lowered herself into the great tub caused the woman, draped in finery with her blondish hair loosely pinned, to turn abruptly, leaving her partially finished concoctions.

"Too hot?" she asked moving to Elenya's side.

Elenya shook her head. "The scrapes. They burn."

The woman made a tsking sound. "Wasn't the best decision you made, to run." She moved back to her concoctions, returning quickly to fill the tub with something from a small bottle. "This will help." She ignored Elenya's frown. "Breathe in. I'm Nema, by the way."

Elenya did as she was told, breathing deeply, allowing the heavenly scent to soothe her body both inside and out.

"Thank you, Nema. It's lovely and it does help. What is it?" Elenya felt herself relaxing.

"My own mixture of herbs and florals. Perfected years ago to salve the wounds of battle. For you, I mixed in your lord's favored essence of Oleander."

"Oleander!" Elenya was already rising from the tub.

"Be still, child." Nema laughed. "The essence alone

isn't harmful at all. In fact, it's quite soothing. As long as you don't eat the deadly blossoms, which I really don't expect… No, the master would have my head should harm come to you."

"I fear my lord cares little beyond the need created by the marking and his obligation to procure an heir. I can't say I blame him for his contempt of my people and the fact that he is being forced to mix his blood with them. But they are my people, my family. We have paid fully for the wrongs committed by those before us." She sighed. "You know that I am from Aleone, do you not? My marking was to have ended my people's struggles. Yet… why would the Masters have paired me with the enemy? I don't understand."

Nema didn't answer, handing her a bar of Oleander scented soap instead after having her wet her hair. Elenya, thinking the conversation over, closed her eyes and willed her body to relax in the tub that was… man-sized. Goose bumps sprung up at the realization it was a tub the warrior had most likely enjoyed many times. She tried not to think of the way his hand had felt on her bare back or how warm his mouth had been, pressed against the flesh of her chest. Lost in thought, she jumped when Nema began to talk, making the other woman chuckle.

"The Masters know what they're doing. You'll see, once the two of you adjust to this pairing. It may take time because he's extremely loyal to his family, your lord is. But I sense that in you as well. It's why you ran. While not wise, it was honorable and your lord knows that. Believe me when I say that you excite him beyond his need to quench the fires of the marking. I'm surprised his duties where you're concerned remain unfulfilled."

Elenya's brows shot up. Her cheeks flared. "How…" She bit at her lip and slumped into the water.

Nema chuckled again, moving in behind the tub where she began to wash Elenya's hair. "Had you fulfilled your obligations, your lord would not have been so tense," she answered the unasked question, her fingers increasing their pressure against Elenya's scalp in her attempt to work the perfumed concoction through the maiden's thick hair. "Tahruk may be tightly wound, but nothing relaxes a man more so than..."

Elenya covered her ears, earning another cackle from Nema. Talk about the act between a man and woman was certainly not a subject she was used to discussing, especially with a stranger. The kiss she'd received from Shemek and the feelings accompanying it had been the extent of her education before she'd come to Zanak, though the fires her warrior had ignited within her made Shemek's kiss seem more like a spark inadequate to start even the driest of kindling.

Elenya's eyes popped open when a strange tingling vibrated through her, and her vision filled with the object of her thoughts. His brazen precociousness seemed to pull her in instead of pushing her away as she watched him stroll in from the garden entrance. Her eyes danced over his bare torso and the knee-length leather pants carelessly laced about his waist. He looked every bit the god-like creature she and her sisters had made up for her, a sight that made her heart stutter then go into double time. She shivered and wondered if Nema noticed.

"Leave the lady to a peaceful bath." Nema motioned for him to depart. Instead he moved further into the room.

Elenya quickly crossed her arms, covering breasts that were barely visible beneath the sudsy water. Tahruk's mirthful hoot as he stood beside the tub, peering down, only served to tighten his Chosen's lips, though Elenya had little choice but to look at him when he placed a finger beneath her chin and lifted her face up to where he could look into her eyes. When he ran his thumb across the thin line of her mouth, her lips softened, parting slightly.

"Much better." He stared at her a moment longer before his dark eyes snapped to Nema with her hands still entwined in his new mistress' hair. "I'll stay," he informed her before moving to a chair near the cold fireplace. Plopping down, he reached out to capture an opened blossom from a nearby potted rose and tossed it toward the tub. Without thought, Elenya caught it and brought it to her nose, inhaling the fragrance and cutting her eyes toward Tahruk, now lounging with one leg draped carelessly over the chair's arm. Yes, he was every bit as beautiful as she'd imagined. On the outside, anyway.

"Rinse." Nema's voice cut into her thoughts, the older woman's hands urging her deeper into the water. "We mustn't delay lest we distress your mistress."

As Elenya slipped beneath the water her thoughts flitted to Tahruk's mother. She hadn't needed to enter her son's bedchamber. She could have simply sent Nema, especially knowing her son as one might expect a mother would. She had to have known her presence would probably anger him. Yet the house mistress had been concerned enough for Elenya's well-being to risk his wrath. The thought filled her with hope. Perhaps his mother really would be an ally against the man whose very stare threatened to devour her.

Tahruk's absence when she resurfaced showed that Elenya knew as little about that man as she did the heart of a mother toward her son. To her surprise, several more rose blossoms floated in the water around her.

Minding her own business, which seemed to be getting Elenya ready, Nema seemed nonplussed by what had gone on, instead moving away to grab a wrap for Elenya. "Come, love. Let's get you ready. Lady Neria doesn't like to be kept waiting. I'll have to dress your hair wet as it is." Helping Elenya dry and dress in the finest of silks, she had begun to work on the maiden's hair before either of them spoke again. Elenya's loudly expelled breath prompted the skilled hands to stop. She turned the girl around.

"Speak, lass. It does you no good to hold it in."

Averting her gaze, her voice trembling as she spoke, Elenya asked, "Will it be so bad?"

Nema's brows drew down. "Bad?"

The thick strands not fully pinned nearly toppled as the maiden nodded her head. "You know. The consume…" she sighed and shook her head. "I'm… afraid." Elenya sniffed, blinking back tears.

Nema shushed her, not wanting moist eyes to mar her beauty. And what a beauty she was! The elders had done well for the young master. She smiled, looking deeply into the green eyes so filled with concern. How much should she share? Her own experience had not been so bad. It had not turned out favorable, in a sense, but… her Chosen had been gentle, skilled at the art of love. She knew it was not that way for many a maiden, though. These men were warriors, trained to participate in barbaric acts from an early age. The men of Zanak, some of them at least, were rare, possessing both qualities.

"It's fortunate you were delivered into the young master's bed, love. Do not fear him, and all will be well."

Pulling the young woman into a firm hug, she missed the deepened apprehension on Elenya's face.

Nema pulled away and smiled. "Come, before I am

blamed for keeping you from your warrior for too long."

Elenya tried to share her cheerfulness, though her angst kept it in. She wished she could slip into her role within her new family as easily as the tinted leather sandals were slipped on her feet. With a last blossom placed in her hair, she was led out on her journey for proper introductions.

As she faced her mistress and the slew of family members and servants, Elenya wondered how many of them knew she was not truly a new mistress within the house. Not yet, anyway. Tahruk's eyes, devouring her from where he sat to the side of the garden dais, told her his desire was to consummate the relationship as soon as possible, and certainly it would happen quickly once darkness curtained the house of Zanak.

She'd undoubtedly be meeting the elder master of the house before then. Looking at all the strangers around her, she was thankful he'd been held up at the training center. From what she'd heard of him and his loyalty to Zanak, there was no way he'd accept her into his family with open arms. How glad she was that he'd been absent when Tahruk arrived home with her.

Heat crept into her cheeks as she thought about lying against Tahruk's chest and how good it had felt nestled in his arms after the long run. Only when he'd laid her in his bed and begun to remove her clothing had her wits returned. With a gulp, she turned toward him, unable to resist returning his hungry stare. She longed for him to offer her another glass of wine as he had the night before. Almost as much as she longed for his touch.

Chapter 11

The introductions were followed by a short tour and a casual lunch. As they sat on the patio off the main garden, Elenya enjoyed the fragrant color pallet, so different than what she'd experienced back home. They had their own scents and sun-painted landscapes—a soothing array of blues and greens mixed with the browns of the beach—there was no comparing the two.

She did enjoy the way the Sharanis' Drille seemed centered around the gardens, with the individual wings that jutted off the main part of the complex having the added luxury of their own smaller, private gardens. She thought of the roses in her bathwater and couldn't help but smile. A ventured look in Tahruk's direction had her breath hitching and her smile fading away on a dreamy sigh.

"What has prompted your amusement, my lady?" When she didn't answer, Tahruk leaned toward her. "Shall I tell you what would amuse me?" His eyes settled on the soft mound of her breasts peeking from the neckline of her gown.

Elenya placed a hand on her chest and nearly choked trying to swallow her last bite. Tahruk laughed as he stood, amusement dancing in his eyes. "Come with me. I wish to have you to myself for a while."

Hesitating a second longer than she should, Elenya finally took hold of the offered hand, her tongue darting out to moisten her lips as she stood. She cut her eyes to look toward Nema, unsure exactly why, and tried to find comfort in the other woman's smile and nod. Nema's words from earlier echoed in her head. She must stay calm and do nothing to irritate her lord—a task that would be difficult with the tension running so high between them.

"Settle," he commanded as he slipped her hand through the crook of his arm. "We haven't much time before my father's return. Not nearly enough. I only wish to walk. With you. *Alone.*" The final words were spoken to reseat a handful of family members who had begun to rise when they'd heard the couple planned only to walk.

Elenya did her best to settle down, as bid, yet her legs refused to still their quivering as he led her from the security of the family gathering.

"Where are you taking me?" Nerves caused her voice to squeak.

Tahruk patted the hand clinging, vice-like to his arm. "You needn't worry so much. Not yet."

Elenya tried to pull away, only now he held her hand to his arm so she could not.

"You would do well to treat me with the respect I deserve, my lord. You act as though you've forgotten who I am," she grumbled.

"And who would that be?"

"I am the fulfillment of prophesy and my blood is every bit as royal as yours." She paused, turning fiery eyes on him. "I am a Chosen."

"Perhaps it is *you* who has forgotten. You do remember that it's *my* blood that runs through your veins, right? You are *my* Chosen." He quirked a dark brow at her and spoke his next words with slow emphasis. "*You* are *mine*."

Heat crept quickly to stain her cheeks, anger seething just beneath the surface, though Tahruk's laughter kept her silent. Had she met him without the marking, she was quite sure she would hate him.

He squeezed her hand slightly as they continued in the same direction. "I'd like to take you beyond the wall, though I wonder… Should I be concerned you might run again? I can think of better ways to expend my energy with a fair maiden than chasing her through the woods." He lifted a brow as he spoke his warning. "Should you run, I will catch you and no Master, not even God above will be able to protect you." They stopped before a large wooden door in the compound wall at the far end of the hallway leading to Tahruk's wing of Zanak.

Elenya pressed her lips tightly together, contemplating the warrior for a moment before shaking her head. "No, my lord. My actions last night were most unwise."

"Ah! Intelligence does reside beneath that lovely mass of curls."

Elenya tried to pull away again, her nose scrunched in offense, a frown crinkling her forehead and chin before she noticed his eyes. They held only mirth.

No. Not *only* mirth. She could see the tempered desire there as well. He chuckled when her eyes rounded and kissed her quickly as she continued to stare at him. They grew even rounder when the muscles of his arm flexed beneath her hand as he opened the door. She gave his arm an involuntary squeeze, her fingers gliding over the rippling mounds as he pulled her through.

Tahruk gritted his teeth and covered her hand with his own to still her caress. "Do not press my need, Little One, lest I quickly take what I should have taken in the forest last night." Two more steps and he stopped to press her against the outer wall, forcing her to look up at him as his body molded against hers. He ran his hands down her arms, and in her foggy state she noted the scrapes were nearly gone. She tried to form a mental note to thank Nema for her healing concoction, though coherent thought was proving difficult. Especially as Tahruk's hands clasped with hers and he brought them to his chest which was pressed against hers. They were so close. So…

Her sharp intake of breath as his fingers raked across the top of her breasts only served to propel him onward. Unable to fight against the marking, Elenya welcomed his caresses, her lips parting willingly when his mouth covered hers.

Cursed marking! She seemed unable to control herself, writhing against him, welcoming his hands on her, attempting to help as he tried to gain access beneath her gown.

Cursed dress! She remembered the feel of his lips on her neck and wrenched her mouth from his to press his head down.

"Heaven help me," he murmured, his mouth against her throat.

"My lord. Release me from this anguish. Please," she pleaded.

Her words must have surprised him as much as they did her because he pulled away. His breathing heavy and labored, he searched her face.

"Tonight," he whispered before again devouring the sweetness of her soft, pink lips.

"My lord. My lord! Pardon. Excuse…" The young man stopped a few feet away from the couple. Bent over, hands on his knees, he gulped air.

"Well?" Tahruk growled and stepped away from the wall, keeping Elenya against him with the gentle press of his hands on her back and neck. His lips continued to explore with soft kisses between temple and ear. His gingerly manner with her contrasted greatly with the glowering look he gave the runner.

"Begging your pardon, my lord. I was told to inform you of your father's early return."

"Early ret… Hell and damnation!" He tensed, thrusting Elenya away from him and grabbing her hand. "Come. We must hurry."

"My lord. One more detail." The runner raised his voice to make sure he was heard by the couple already several steps ahead of him. He straightened to follow. "He entertains a guest. Master Daruh."

"Daruh! What business does *he* have here?" He looked at Elenya, a vision of her clinging to the Master's legs flashing into his mind.

Elenya cried out as his hand clamped even tighter around hers.

"Send Nema to my quarters," he barked at the runner. "Tell her to be quick."

"Your corisan has already been dispatched…"

"I said to send Nema!" Tahruk growled.

"Yes, my lord," the young man called to the swiftly moving couple before beginning his own journey in the direction of Zanak's service entrance.

Tahruk didn't slow down when Elenya stumbled, tripping after an attempt to look back at the runner.

"You will do well not to allow your eyes to wander, ever." He kept her upright with a hand slipped hastily around her waist, and met her scowl.

"And you shall do well not to assume nor accuse

falsely!" She broke away, beating him to his quarters by only two or three steps, enough to have completely missed the surprised smile that lifted the corners of his full lips.

Nema was right. This sometimes docile woman-child had a spunk that enticed him beyond the pull of the marking. In that, the Masters had chosen well for him.

She turned to him at the door and he caught her jaw between his fingers and thumb. "Do not forget who you are, Little One. Regardless of whether our bodies have yet to become one, *we* are already united. You carry my blood. You are *mine*!"

"Is that how you treat your treasures? Unhand the lass, young master, lest she grow fearful of you. She is not your enemy."

Elenya's brows shot up when Nema's words cut through their moment. She reached for his hand, pulling it from her face where it fell hard against her chest. Her heart beat fast against his palm.

"Is that the feel of your enemy, my lord?" She shook her head. "How can we be enemies if we truly are one?"

Tahruk scowled down at her, his emotions fluctuating between anger and lust. His jaw tightened, causing his cheek to twitch. Her eyes wandered down to his cheek, then to his lips and back up. Even his drawn brows and thinned lips did not cause her to flinch this time. Instead she pressed his hand tighter and moved closer to him. Her face remained turned up to his.

Nema cleared her throat. "Your father, my lord."

The corners of Elenya's lips twitched. The fire burned bright in her eyes.

"Vixen!" he growled at her, taking a kiss before he pushed her away. "Prepare her, Nema. I'm sure we have little time."

"In that you are correct, my lord." The older woman nodded her head at the flustered young man before taking the hand of the equally muddled maiden.

Chapter 12

Elenya frowned at her own behavior. She was becoming someone even she didn't recognize, her feelings intensified by the increased tension that seemed prevalent since Tahruk's father had returned to the Drille. There was an edginess that crept in whenever he was mentioned, especially when coupled with her name and their impending meeting. Surely he could be no worse than his son.

The thought of Tahruk's mother and her sweet countenance brought a smile. If her husband was the ogre these people's actions led her to believe he might be, surely the woman's nature would not have been so genteel. She hadn't seemed overly affected when his return was discussed during the noonday meal. Even Nema chuckled a bit when she talked about *the old bear*.

"Your belongings have arrived, miss," Nema told her before directing her down an unknown hallway. "Let's get you into a dress more fitting the occasion, shall we?"

Elenya glanced down at the silk gown she was wearing. She had fine dresses, though Aleone's finest obviously didn't compare to that of Zanak. She bit at her lower lip wondering how to explain that the dress she wore was as lovely as any she'd ever possessed. And to confess such to a… to a servant? Was Nema actually a servant? She had served Elenya, and yet she'd sat at the family table during the meal. And in a position of authority. She called

Tahruk *young master* and *my lord* and yet spoke so boldly to him, almost as a mother might.

"What is your position here, Nema?"

Nema surprised her by answering with a cackle. "Ah, lass. It's complicated. Something to discuss another day. For now it must suffice for you to know I am here for you." She stopped before an ornately carved door, pushing it open with the palm of her hand to expose an exquisitely decorated room. "Your personal chambers," Nema told her, motioning for her to go inside. "Your lord has been awaiting the arrival of his Chosen with great anticipation, though he'd never admit to such." She laughed again. "Don't let him fool you. He has his father's bite and brawn, yet carries his mother's heart just as much. Give him time and you'll see."

Much of Nema's comments went unheard. Elenya was too lost in the beauty of her surroundings, even ignoring the inner voice that told her the rooms were only hers because she was Tahruk's Chosen, not because he had prepared them for *her* specifically. Still, they were hers. He didn't have to care *for* her to take care *of* her. Love seldom played a part in these matters. They had one purpose and one only and that was to assure the strength of the royal bloodlines. That was why she'd been born—to fulfill that honor, and these beautiful rooms were part of her reward for being chosen.

A moment of sadness filled her heart. She thought of the bottle carrying her dreams that she'd thrown into the sea. Secretly, she'd harbored the hope she'd find love.

"My lady?" Nema waved a hand before Elenya's face, pulling her back. "The dress?" she inquired when Elenya continued to stare blankly.

"The dress. Yes. I, uhm…" Her young shoulders

drooped. She looked at the floor and sighed. "I'm unsure I have anything so fine as to fit the occasion any better than what I'm wearing…."

"Have I inherited a beggar then?"

Elenya spun toward the door at the sound of Tahruk's growl of annoyance.

"My lord!" Elenya and Nema chimed in unison, though Elenya's voice was laced with shame where Nema's carried clear anger.

"Does she look or smell the part of a beggar? And even if you had, you are without lack, possessing abundance enough to care for whatever needs she may have. It's your duty besides." The older woman pointed a long, thin finger at the warrior, her eyes narrowed as did her lips. "Leave us so I may tend to your Chosen. Go!" She had crossed the floor while she spoke, and with her palms against the massive chest, she pushed. He didn't budge immediately, his eyes on the maiden who stood, head still bowed, in the center of the fine room. With a last grunt, he turned and walked away, his heavy footsteps and mumbles echoing in the hallway. Only one word was clear to Elenya. Aleone. It was spoken with disgust.

"One should not question the wisdom of the Masters," Nema muttered. "Now let's see those gowns.

Elenya shook her head. "It doesn't matter. I shall remain as I am."

She missed Nema's frown as the older woman moved to stand before her.

"Lass." The softness of her voice brought Elenya's head up at last to where her tear filled eyes met Nema's. "Oh no, love. Don't be saddened by the young master. His tongue speaks what has been fed into his head, not what he feels in his heart."

"What does he feel, Nema? Lust brought on by the scent created by my sharing his blood? I'm nothing more than breeding stock to him, and once that job is done, then what? He's being forced to mix with a people he despises. He's a man used to being in control and that has been removed from him." She sniffed back her tears. "What he will feel in time, if he doesn't already, is resentment. He's right. I'm a burden that he's bound to by someone else's choice. A poor choice no one can change."

Nema was shaking her head even before Elenya finished. "Your road may not be easy, but it's one you can walk, and you will. You are wrong about the choice and your lord's ability to care." She cupped the youthful face in her aging hands, pushing away the tears with her thumbs. "You are everything he needs, not only for him, but for your people and his." She paused for a long moment before pulling Elenya into a hug. "Now let's get you ready. What do you have that we might use to wow that old bear that lords over this family?"

Elenya closed her eyes, her head still against Nema's shoulder, her thoughts shifting quickly to the apprehensions she felt knowing she would soon meet this bear. She'd begun to wonder if he would make her warrior seem a kitten and feared he would be a wall to her and Aleone, even if she could break through with his son.

Nema worked on the maiden, both physically and psychologically as she hastily prepared her for the presentation. By the time she was ready, Elenya exuded something of a more confident air. Whether she actually felt that or simply seemed to, it would serve her well in coming face to face with Renaine.

The older woman smiled, feeling her own confidence

that if anyone could settle the old bear into accepting this union it would be this young beauty who had already captured the heart of her enemy warrior, whether she realized it or not. Nema was certain. She'd lived enough years to see many a mighty man fall to a fair maiden.

Chapter 13

The air crackled, the attraction nearly palatable when Nema presented Tahruk's Chosen to him. She stood back, watching the couple, each drinking in the fine details the other offered. Tahruk had changed his attire as well. His dark hair, caught back with a leather strap that matched his form-fitting calf-colored pants, stood out against the white tunic covering his torso, all highlighting his bronze skin. Elenya's eyes danced over him, her appreciation unmasked.

A slow smile spread across the warrior's handsome features and he held out a hand to her. Without hesitation, she went to him, a vision floating across the floor in her sheer ecru gown layered over shimmering gold silk. A wide, gold sash accentuated her tiny waist.

Nema had piled the maiden's red curls high on her head. Spiraling tendrils framed her lovely face, adding focus to the high cheekbones and fine arch of her brows. A cluster of longer strands snaked down her exposed back with a few stragglers strategically placed to the front. Tahruk's eyes went to the flesh exposed by the gown's low neckline.

"You approve, my lord?" The maiden's voice was a husky whisper when she asked.

Tahruk reached for her, his arm snaking around her waist as he pulled her to him. Her eyes widened and she sighed when he began to caress the flesh above the silk folds of her bodice.

"Oh, my lord," she breathed in a whispered pant, her head falling back, offering him an irresistible taste of her satiny neck. "Perchance we may put off this introduction a bit longer?" Her accompanying moan made him chuckle. He enjoyed this bit of wantonness he saw in the innocent beauty before him, forgetting it was most likely due to the effects of the marking.

"No, Little One." His words against her neck made her shudder. "My father's wrath is not worth even you." She frowned and he laughed—a hearty sound deep in his belly. "Besides, I promise I will take my time with you, and that time will be most rewarding for both of us." He sealed his words with a kiss to the rounded swell of both breasts, one after another, before rising to capture her lips.

"May this day pass quickly then."

Her nearly inaudible wish had him raising a brow and she blushed. He kissed her cheek before looking to Nema.

"There are no festivities planned after the evening meal, my lord. You are expected to dine with the family, of course."

"Of course," he answered Nema, though is attention had returned in full to the maiden. He gently tilted her chin up, kissed her lightly on the nose, and whispered against her mouth. "When nightfall comes, I shall fulfill your desires."

"Yes, my lord." Her tongue flicked out to touch his lips eliciting a loud groan from him as he crushed her to him.

"My lord!" Nema said quite loudly, knowing if this did not stop now there would be no turning back for the couple. The desires of the marking having gone unfulfilled were too strong.

"Hell fire and damnation!" Tahruk growled pushing Elenya away and turning his back. He breathed deeply for a moment then instructed the women to meet him in the corridor outside his quarters.

Tears welled in Elenya's eyes. "Did I do something wrong?" she asked once they were outside.

Nema could not hold back a quiet chuckle. "No, love. You did everything just right."

The door to Tahruk's chambers opened removing Elenya's opportunity for further clarification. Nema winked at her as the maiden took the warrior's offered arm.

Chapter 14

Elenya stood in a veiled room staring out at the finest hall she'd ever seen. Her family's great hall seemed quite neglected in comparison to Zanak's.

Her attention focused on the view from the curtained alcove, Elenya jumped when Tahruk returned to her side. He seemed not to notice as he fidgeted with the belt and gold neckwear engraved with the code of Zanak that indicated his elite status.

Nema entered from the other side of the alcove, followed by Tahruk's mother. Lady Neria's smile, as kind and lovely as Elenya remembered, wavered only slightly when she looked from Elenya to her son. There was concern, though Neria's radiant smile returned when she turned back to Elenya.

"I have something for you, dear." The rectangular box she took from atop a tasseled pillow held by Nema was made of wood carved with a lovely floral motif. Neria ran a hand across the carving. "This was presented to me before I became matched to Renaine." She and Nema exchanged a peculiar glance. "It's been passed down many, many times, from generation to generation." She looked again from her son to his Chosen. "I am honored to present this to you and welcome you into the Sharanis family, Elenya."

Elenya gasped when the box was opened to reveal its contents. The stunning display of diamonds, rubies, emeralds, and yellow sapphires had her staring, wide-eyed. Neria removed the gem covered neckpiece and held it in place as Tahruk fastened it around Elenya's slender neck, pressing his lips just above the clasp.

Elenya shuddered. Her fingers playing over the piece, she spun toward the warrior, her face awash with girlish wonder. Tahruk nodded his approval and she smiled before turning back to Neria whose face mirrored hers. "It's heavy! Thank you, my lady." She curtsied low before Neria, the woman's gratitude overwhelming her. Elenya knew the presentation of this family piece was an outward indication of the woman's acceptance of her.

"Rise, my dear." Neria held out a hand and helped her to her feet where they embraced.

"The master is ready," A herald told them from just outside the curtain.

Lady Neria released Elenya and nodded. She turned to her son, their eyes locking momentarily with some message Elenya wished she could read. Another nod from the house mistress and she and Nema were gone.

Elenya turned to her warrior, angst raising her brows.

"Come." He offered his arm, though no explanation.

Touching the jeweled neckpiece with her free hand as Tahruk parted the curtain, Elenya closed her eyes for a moment in an attempt to tamp down the fear that tried to settle in her middle. She was Tahruk's Chosen, she reminded herself, and his father must simply accept fate, even if her family was the enemy Drille. She raised her chin and stepped out behind the warrior, wishing she felt the confidence she tried to exude through her stance.

Outside the curtained alcove, Elenya was once again taken with the beauty of the hall. Lush tapestries of deep gold, greens, and burgundies lined the walls. Similar coverings lay beneath their feet. Long, wooden benches, highly polished, carved with scenes matching those in the tapestries, lined the aisle leading to the dais before them.

Two people rose from the dark brocade-covered chairs in the center of the raised surface as the couple began their journey down the aisle. Elenya recognized one of the men as the Master whose legs she'd attached herself to, begging mercy for the mismatch between her and the Zanak warrior. Worry knotted her insides—concerns that he somehow knew their relationship had yet to be consummated and he had come to absolve the ties. Whether that was possible or not, Elenya didn't know. Either way, his presence caused her heart to sink just as her dreams surely had in the bottle thrown overboard.

"Fretting is unbecoming upon a woman of Zanak." Tahruk's warning echoed softly beside her.

Elenya's head snapped toward him, his words reminding her again that she must not forget who she was.

He glanced at her then looked back toward the front affording Elenya the opportunity to study him a moment longer. Her eyes roved over the defined lines of his raised chin, the set of his full lips, the power and prowess of his finely honed physique—it all portrayed confidence. He was not only of royal blood, he was elite, the King's best, and she was his Chosen.

She turned her attention to Master Daruh, noting his smile fixed on her was friendly, and she allowed her confidence to grow. For the first time she looked at Tahruk's father, the house master. He was a near perfect replica of an older version of her warrior, though his slightly lighter blue eyes seemed more scrutinizing, his forehead wrinkled from what she assumed was an ever-present scowl. His mouth turned down, pulling even more so the closer they got. As she took him in, nervousness caused her to prattle. She spoke to Tahruk through barely moving lips, speaking about the first thing that came to mind. "My lord." She cut her eyes toward him, and once he looked at her, continued, "Were you pleased that I did not run when you took me out?" She had no idea what had made her think about that now. Timing was something she was going to have to work on.

Tahruk fought to contain a sudden burst of laughter, attempting to maintain reverence before his father. "I am. Though I believe you were too preoccupied to consider running. Rather enjoyably so, I might add."

Elenya's face burned red. Still, she managed to swallow loudly and continued speaking. "Yes, my lord. You are correct. And I am quite certain I shall enjoy further exploration of this new form of diversion."

Mere steps from his father, Tahruk groaned. "Ah, but the true diversion stands lovely at my side."

Elenya had no time to react to his words. They had reached the dais requiring immediate action on her part. She released Tahruk's arm and dropped into a low curtsy where she remained, awaiting the house master's words.

"Rise," he commanded, his voice deep and even. "Come forward, child."

Elenya bristled at the reference to her not yet being a woman, though she obeyed, hopeful her shaking legs didn't show through her skirts. With a deep breath, she turned to watch Tahruk moving to stand beside Daruh. Both men gave her a single nod.

"My lord." She bobbed again directly before the leader of Zanak, noting his attention was captured by the neckpiece.

His brows furrowed. "What is your name?"

The harshness of his voice caused her to jump, though chin up, she answered as boldly as she could muster, "I am Elenya Avenille of Aleone." When he did not answer, she added with a sense of bravado beyond what she felt, "Chosen of Tahruk Sharanis of Zanak. Marked by the Masters in all their infinite wisdom… my lord."

Behind her, gasps echoed at the indicated challenge of her words. Elenya's insides quivered, though she held Renaine's gaze.

Renaine broke the stare, his eyes falling again to the bejeweled neckpiece before his nose flared and he sniffed the air.

"And yet my son has not seen fit to fulfill his duties with his *Chosen, marked by the Masters*." His tone mocking, he quirked a brow at her.

Dislike fuelled the tone of her retort. "We had an… unfortunate beginning, my lord."

Renaine's snort was drowned out by a voice behind her. "Proving my brother is a fool for not taking you and exacting the punishment you deserved for your little foray last night."

Elenya swiveled, as did the others, their attention claimed by another warrior every bit as stately as Tahruk and Renaine. The other man stared at Elenya with desire so blatant she felt the need to fold her arms over her chest.

He laughed. "Perhaps *he* isn't attracted by the scent of the enemy."

"Redahn!" Lady Neria rose to her feet, a hand held up to her by her husband was the only thing that stopped her movement from the front bench.

The low growl from the other side of Renaine turned heads toward the warrior accused of slacking his *duties*.

Daruh quickly moved to stop Tahruk's advance, holding him back with a hand on his chest and another around his upper arm. Hatred burned in her warrior's eyes as he glared at his brother.

Elenya began to step toward him, feeling the pull again, only to be stopped by a hand on her arm. She turned to glare at Renaine, wrenching her arm from his grasp.

"You are a bold woman, Elenya Avenille of Aleone, though your decision to flee from my son has already prompted questions of your loyalty. What have you to say in your defense?"

Eyes narrowed, she threw a scathing glance at Redahn following another snort from him. Turning back to the house master, she brought her chin up deliberately and squared her shoulders. "Upon the confirmation from Master Daruh that no error had been made, I immediately submitted to my warrior, my lord, with every intent to… fulfill my… obligations and duties to the Zanak Drille. Only," She lowered her head and her voice, "exhaustion overcame me last night and… visitors at daybreak prevented certain… fulfillment… this morning." The words were broken, spoken haltingly, her cheeks flaming. "Still, I am honor bound to do all that is expected." She forced her gaze up no further than the house master's chest and clamped her teeth together in an attempt to stifle her unease while she waited for his command.

At last, Renaine nodded and looked at Tahruk. "I trust, my son, this… *issue* will be amended post haste. We would not want it said that Zanak does not honor the directives of the Masters, nor do we wish to prove ourselves disloyal to the King." He looked from son to maiden. "At least she is not hard to look upon. It will make fulfilling your obligations easier…"

The unladylike snort that interrupted the house master prompted Tahruk to a hasty answer of assurance to his father before he moved to Elenya's side and turned her away.

"My son." Renaine's voice halted them a few steps from the dais. "We shall dine one hour earlier tonight for your convenience."

"Perhaps you should take the time between then and now to tend to your *obligations,* Brother. 'Twould be a pity for one so fair to fall into the wrong hands before you could attend to that little detail." Redahn stretched his hand toward Elenya and Tahruk jerked her to his other side before squaring on his younger brother.

"And I would be honor bound to relieve such a scoundrel from his ability to breathe should the Courts not do it for me," Tahruk told Redahn who, although mighty in his own right, could not have taken on the jealous elite warrior and emerged the victor.

"Boys!"

It was Nema who stepped between the two men. She pushed Tahruk back toward Elenya and took Redahn's arm. "Come," she urged him, tugging on him to follow in the other direction.

Tahruk ushered Elenya down the long aisle at such a fast clip she might have fallen had the pace itself not kept her upright. At the end of the aisle he shoved her into the curtained alcove and followed her in to pin her against the back wall. His hands began to move possessively over her even as his mouth sought hers. Her skin prickled. Surely he did not intend to take her right there.

"My lord!" Her voice was a mere squeak as his lips moved to her throat.

"You are *mine*," he growled, straightening, though

never releasing the pressure that held her to him. "No matter what, my blood runs through your veins. *Mine*!" His hands rubbed along her bare arms, moving to the exposed flesh of her back and down to press her even tighter to where there was no mistaking his desire. "My seed alone shall spill into you." His lips again on hers, he whispered, "With me, only me, shall you become one."

Voices approaching had him stepping away. He stared down at her, his breathing ragged, labored. Elenya trembled in his arms.

"You are *mine*," he repeated, before disappearing through an opening on the far side of the alcove.

"I have always been yours," she whispered, staring at the space where he'd been. "We are already one."

Always her guide, Nema appeared seconds later. "Come with me," she told the maiden, taking hold of one of the arms that hung limp at her sides. "Let's pay a visit to the family seamstress. We may as well take advantage of the short time we have."

Elenya simply nodded and allowed herself to be led away, unsure the turmoil inside would allow ladylike words to spill forth should she speak.

Chapter 15

The remainder of the afternoon was spent at the mercy of a woman with graying hair swept into a haphazard bun that served as holder to many of the tools of her trade. She unnerved Elenya to an irrational degree, most likely escalated by the sense of injustice that simmered just under the surface when she thought of how ill the men of Zanak had treated her. Exactly how they should have acted, Elenya didn't know. Had her own words not labeled her as glorified breeding stock? Why then was she angered when the father spoke of her coming together with his son as a *duty*? And why when she thought of the fulfillment of that obligation did her heart race and heat rise to her cheeks? These men—the man whose blood she carried, his father… and that brother of his! What had they called him? Redahn? His manners toward her were deplorable. With her fists clenched, she glared at those around her, feeling herself nearing the end of her endurance, especially when a knock rattled the door and Tahruk let himself in.

"You nearly knocked me down!" The seamstress huffed from behind the opened door.

"Then you should bar your door next time or plan to stay out of the way." He sent her a look that had her scurrying back to the silk draped maiden standing on top of the pinning stool. Tahruk's eyes roamed over Elenya, taking in her crossed arms and frown as well as the untamed yards of material that covered her. He turned to Nema. "She seems ill prepared so close to the dinner hour. How am I to collect her in *that*?"

Nema's chuckle had them both glaring at her. "Seems tension reigns all around," she spoke to a dressmaker's figurine in the far corner. "I think we shall all be better off once this night is behind us."

"You try my patience, Nema."

The older woman shrugged at the warrior's bark. "I must say you have maintained far greater restraint under the circumstances than one might have expected, my lord."

Elenya frowned. Nema was the one person she thought had understood her and her predicament. Now she was praising the warrior for his ability to maintain his composure. She threw her hands up and stepped off the stool, all heads turning toward her.

"What?" she snapped at them before stomping toward the screen where she'd left her own clothes when she'd arrived. "You people act as if I am not even here. And when you do acknowledge me, it's… it's only… you treat me as if… Oh!" Again her hands went up. She gave them another dour look, then mumbling, she disappeared behind the screen.

Tahruk stood dazed for a moment then stalked across the floor ignoring both the older women's demands for him to halt. Forehead and chin both wrinkled in contemplation, he followed the path of his Chosen.

"This space is not nearly big enough for the both of us, my lord." She whirled to face him then stood, one fist on a shapely hip, the other hand holding up the bodice of her gown not yet where it should be. Chin up, lips pressed tightly together, she glared at him when he failed to retreat.

She snorted, the loose red curls swishing about her bared shoulders as she shook her head. "Suit yourself, but if you're going to stay you may as well be of service." Turning away, she thrust her arms into the sleeves, what little there was of them, then stepped back and pulled her hair away.

Tahruk groaned, closing his eyes against the sight before him. He fought down the urge that flared at the vision of the expanse of flesh flanked by the open back of her dress. It took every ounce of restraint he had not to push the sleeves back off her arms as he imagined the dress pooling at her feet, the feel of her silken skin beneath his hands... He already knew how she tasted, how she smelled...

"The buttons, my lord," she commanded, her voice steeped in impatience. The toes of her stocking-clad foot thumped against the floor to reinforce her sentiment.

"You would do well to hold your temper, Little One."

"And you would do well to help me so that this blasted night may commence." After a charged moment passed without his reacting, she added with a less than demure nod to her head, "Please, my lord."

"Hellion," he mumbled, stepping forward, his fingers beginning to work at the buttons. Re-holing the dainty embellishments proved more difficult than their unfastening—a task he much preferred.

A trip back to Tahruk's chambers was still required for Elenya to quickly change and have her hair properly dressed by a corisan who proved little better than the one assigned on the night of the Dremis celebration. Unlike her predecessor, this girl held nothing of the overt boldness of Ceeda, instead exhibiting a mousy fearfulness that had an already frustrated Elenya taking the brush away from her and finishing the task herself. She'd always tended to her own needs back home. Why not here?

Home. The thought swept through her with sorrow. Nothing seemed to have gone as expected here, and the comfort of her childhood seemed more a fading dream. She longed for the gaiety of evenings spent with her family, the security of her mother's arms, Shemek…

"Where is the maiden I found in the dressmaker's shop—the one with the fire in her blood and exasperated words threatening to spill from those lovely lips?"

Elenya's eyes snapped to Tahruk's reflection framed in full by the length of the gazing glass. Straightening her sagging shoulders, she pushed the last of the jeweled pins into her knotted hair while she studied him. Like Shemek, he was dark haired, his skin bronzed from the hours spent outside training for battle. Both men were toned, muscular, though unlike Shemek's younger body Tahruk had the physique of a fully developed man. He was quite magnificent, really.

His movement away from the door frame startled her and Elenya jerked her eyes from his advancing form only to be drawn right back. He stopped directly behind her, taking his time to study her reflection.

She jumped when he reached for a strand of hair she'd left loose to cascade over her shoulder. He smiled. "I like it when you leave part of your hair down," he told her, his voice growing suddenly husky as he began to stroke her shoulder, his fingers trailing up her slender neck and along her jaw line. "You look quite lovely, my lady."

Elenya hadn't realized she'd been holding her breath until he bent to press a kiss to the back of her neck and it whooshed out, accompanied by a nearly silent moan.

"If it was anyone but my father at the head of our table, Little One, I would bar the door and ravish you until we were both sated," he whispered against her ear, eliciting another shudder from her innocent body.

"You seem quite sure of your abilities, my lord." Her raised brow earned a laugh from the warrior, though he didn't bother to answer. Instead he stepped back and produced a jeweled box from inside the leather pouch fastened around his waist.

"Have you chosen jewels for this evening?"

Touching her own neck, Elenya gasped remembering the neckpiece she'd removed at the seamstress' quarters. Eyes wide, she bit at her lower lip while she stared at the warrior's reflection.

Tahruk laughed, seeming to know exactly what she was thinking. "Rest assured Nema will have taken care of that old piece. Its weight alone makes it impractical, unlike this…" He opened the box to reveal a piece that made her gasp. The combined peach moonstones and pearls were absolutely stunning.

"Oh, my lord. It's lovely, though it must have cost a fortune."

Tahruk waved away her concerns and worked to remove the necklace from the velvet lined box. Laying it around her neck he latched the heavy gold clasp then squatted beside her, his reflection even with hers in the mirror. "Moonstones are the stones of new beginnings." He fingered the piece around her neck.

"And the pearls?" she whispered, her gaze remaining locked with his in their reflection. Having lived by the sea her entire life, she knew the answer. Still, she wanted him to speak it.

"Ocean magic," he told her, swallowing hard. "They

symbolize integrity, purity, and grace. They're also said to infuse the wearer with a sense of commitment, love, and readiness." He paused for a moment. "It's a rare piece indeed, though its price does not compare to what *you* have paid to play pawn in the Masters' game."

Elenya tilted her head, her eyes imploring his as she turned to look directly at him.

"I am well aware of your sacrifice." He stared back, then chastely kissed her and rose to his feet. "You seem to bring out a softer side in me, my lady, though if you tell anyone I shall deny it vehemently then punish you severely. Now come." He extended a hand to help her up. "Let no man be accused of keeping my father waiting."

An odd mixture of disappointment and relief warred within Elenya as her warrior led her to the family gathering. She was confused, conflicted. On one hand, she felt rescued by this imposed delay, the thought of their coupling still sending tendrils of fear through her.

On the other hand, she yearned for him, to feel him close. There was no denying the charge between them when he took her in his arms or when his mouth covered hers. His lips and hands seared her flesh with a promise of greater fulfillment. Even now, just thinking about it, fire spread rapidly, engulfing her insides.

He turned to her as they stepped into the dining hall, his eyes moving over her. She jumped when he stretched his hand toward her, his knuckles caressing her cheek before he circled her lips with a fingertip. The sensation was a sensual tickle that drew her closer to him, her head tilted up asking that his mouth replace his hand.

He smiled. Eager to fulfill her wish, he cradled the back of her head in his hand, coaxing her head back farther.

Her lips parted when his mouth met hers and his tongue probed. He wasted no time, his desire to taste her overwhelming them both.

"Would have thought your chambers a more suitable location, Brother. Unless, of course, these public displays of yours are merely smoke screens hiding a true lack of desire to fulfill your honor bound duties."

"Redahn," Tahruk growled, pulling back just enough so that his forehead rested against Elenya's. His breath tickled her mouth where their kiss had left her lips moist.

As the others joined them he slipped an arm around her shoulders and led her toward the table where no one sat until Renaine had taken his place at the head of the table and lowered himself into the honored seat. Lady Neria sat at his right, Tahruk at his left with Elenya securely by his side. Redahn's presence next to his mother, directly across from her, was a cause for unease.

Other family members, including sisters Elenya had met earlier, their husbands whom she had not, were seated accordingly down the rest of the long table. Elenya's brows drew down as she watched Nema slip into the seat next to Redahn.

"Your Chosen is troubled by many things, my brother. It appears more than your… *inadequate attentions* are giving her cause for concern."

Elenya didn't honor Redahn with so much as a glance, turning instead to look at Tahruk. His eyes down, she noted his jaw flexing—a sign she had already learned indicated his anger. Her brows drew deeper.

"Perhaps a *better man* could relax the lines from that pretty face…"

"Enough!" Tahruk exploded from his seat, his fist crashing against the table as he leaned toward his brother.

Several of the women screamed, some of the men stood. Only a hand from a rising Renaine against the warrior's chest saved Redahn who had pulled back as far as his chair would allow. Tahruk had been a finger away from grabbing the front of his tunic. It was anyone's guess what would have happened next, though assuredly it would have involved violence and spilled blood.

Tahruk continued to glare at his brother even after Renaine had pressed him back to his seat.

"Aleone has caused dissention within the Zanak Drille for decades." Renaine leveled his stare at Elenya. "I do not intend a foolish decision by the Masters to tear my family apart."

Elenya's eyes widened and locked with Renaine's. She tried to swallow, her suddenly parched throat making the task impossible.

"Do not take your ire out on the girl, my lord. The maiden has no fault here. She had no say in the match either."

Heads turned in the direction of the speaker—Nema. Her glare leveled on the glowering Renaine, Elenya was surprised he did not silence her. "To disavow the Masters' choice would make us no better than those before us. What happened between Zanak and Aleone must be left in the past."

Whispers and snorts sounded round the table.

"Leave her be, my lord. Soon enough the strength of her scent will be but a memory and your boys can settle." She paused, then quietly repeated her sentiment. "She harbors no fault here."

The table was silent, most of the occupants staring down at their plates. Elenya noted Redahn's annoying flick of his thumb against the corner of his napkin. She glared at him before cutting her eyes toward Renaine, whose stare shifted between her and Nema.

Beside her, Tahruk seemed fixated on an undefined spot on a distant wall. His brows drawn, he tapped aimlessly at the full lips that had covered hers not so long ago. An unexpected wave of desire rolled through her. *Want me*, she thought, then chided herself for her wantonness when the man hadn't even defended her honor against his father. She pressed her lips tightly together and lifted her eyes to Renaine's. Silent moments followed before he cleared his throat and looked at his oldest son.

"As instructed earlier, I intend for you to tend to your duties, post haste, my son, before the girl makes the lot of us insane."

"Will be my pleasure to do so, Father."

Indignant gasps and snorts sounded from the women while the men chuckled and whispered amongst themselves. Elenya's face burned, a reminder she mustn't forget it was only the animal nature caused by the marking that had propelled her warrior into such rapt desire for her earlier. Renaine was right. Once *duties* were fulfilled, this foolishness would subside.

The atmosphere of the family gathering never fully recovered, even as the meal progressed, which made everything more difficult than it need be for Elenya. She reached again for her glass of wine, only to feel her warrior's hand clamp over hers. She frowned at him.

Tahruk shook his head and leaned toward her, speaking quietly, "I fear you have already had more than is fitting, my lady. Not to mention the lot of the group is awaiting our retirement."

Elenya looked around, surprised to find conversations

had lapsed into silence, broken only by a word or sentence here and there. Platters were empty, glasses relieved of their contents. How had she missed the restlessness that had set in? Or had she ignored it? Perhaps the tension that shrouded the six at the head of the table had made her oblivious. Few words had been shared. Little had been consumed beyond the glasses of fine wine that her warrior was now telling her she could partake in no more.

Elenya stared at her half-filled cup yearning for one more gulp of the smooth liquid to calm her nerves. It was fine. Much better than the weak drink her family allowed her.

Tahruk stood and extended a hand to her. She placed her palm against his and ignored the quiet snort from across the table as she rose to stand beside him.

"Father, Mother." Tahruk nodded at each. "With your permission, we shall take our leave."

"About time." Redahn clanked the metal of his thick ring against the wine cup as he mumbled the words.

"Be silent." Renaine's deep voice and command made them all jump, though the warrior at Elenya's side relaxed his ready-to-spring stance.

"Permission granted, my son. Godspeed in your mission." The older man stood and placed a hand on his son's right shoulder. Tahruk bent his neck to receive the kiss his father placed on top of his head—a sign Elenya recognized as a blessing offered to his son. She glanced to Lady Neria and then to Nema, barely able to return their smiles before Tahruk took her arm.

"Come, my lady. Good evening, Mother. Nema. Brother."

Redahn had been mostly quiet throughout the meal beyond his outbursts. He had interjected some when they'd talked about training, general family concerns, and the injury he'd sustained in the last battle that had kept him from the training fields. Elenya had avoided eye contact with him though she'd felt him staring at her throughout the evening. Now, looking at him, her vision blurred slightly, though not enough that she missed his hungry sneer. She shuddered and wrapped her warrior's arm in a loose hug that restored her stability as he led her from the table.

Elenya had to walk quickly to keep up with Tahruk's great stride that brought them to his quarters at a much faster pace than she would have liked. She was quite certain mere seconds had passed before he was closing the door to his private rooms behind them. Begging herself to relax, she fought down the dizziness that surrounded her.

Tahruk took her immediately to his bed chamber and pulled her to him. There was no pretense as to why they were there, especially when his mouth came down hard and hungry on hers. It made her head spin faster, her vision swam. When her knees buckled, he swooped her into his arms, giving her no time to think, even if she could have, before he deposited her onto his bed.

Tahruk sat on the edge of the bed, his body twisted at the waist, strong arms pressed on either side of his Chosen. His breath caught, desire flared as he took in her beauty, starting with the thick curls that covered his pillow. What a glorious crop of shimmering, cinnamon-honey red. He ran his fingers through the curls, the action releasing a mixture of Oleander and her scent—his scent within her. He groaned with wanting. *Slow*, he reminded himself. He felt her hands, warm and light through his thick tunic, run up his chest and slide down his arms.

He rubbed his thumb in a gentle circle against her

temple, his eyes fixed on the fullness of her soft mouth, and moistened his own lips in anticipation. “Ah, Little One. I…”

Her hands fell from his arms, plopping limp against the bed.

“My lord…” she whispered, fighting against heavy lids. For the first time he realized she lacked focus when she tried to look at him.

Concern clouded his thoughts. “Are you ill?” He leaned closer, his nostrils flaring when she shook her head.

“I’m… I’m so… just so tired.” Her eyes closed for a long moment. She sighed then attempted to open them again. Her lashes fluttered and closed. “Your wine,” she said in a breathy tone. “I believe it stronger than I am privy to at home.” Again she tried to look at him, gave up, and rolled onto her side away from him. “Forgive me, my lord. I must rest.”

Tahruk stared down at the fully clothed beauty in his bed. “*Forgive me*?” he repeated, disbelief working his jaw. Frustration and fury welled within, culminating in a deep, guttural growl. Stiff movements propelled him from the bed, his fists clenched by his side.

“Hell and damnation!” he roared. The maiden stirred only slightly at the outburst. He stared at her. For two days the fires of lust that burned within him had been denied. Not doused or dampened, merely denied. In truthfulness, they’d grown stronger with each passing moment. The more he was around her, the more he wanted her. All of her.

Contemplation battled within him. He could attempt to wake her and take from her what he wanted, needed. He had every right. She was his, marked by the Masters as his for the very purpose of assuring the strength of the royal bloodlines. Breeding. It was that simple. It was her responsibility as much as his to assure that happened. She was honor bound to submit to him.

Hands opening and closing, Tahruk inhaled deeply. His chin crashed into his chest as the air whooshed from his lungs. *Damned*, he thought. *I'm damned either way*. His need was overwhelming, and yet… damn if he wanted it to be a forceful taking the first time with her.

He sighed. He shouldn't care. It wasn't as if he'd chosen her. Her people were the enemy, were they not? That was a fact that could not be denied. He'd seen it barely masked within his father's eyes. Generation to generation, they'd been taught, reminded of the trouble Aleone had caused them.

But the more time he spent with this daughter of Aleone… She rolled onto her back and he watched the rise and fall of her chest with each breath. He felt the stab inside his own chest. His brother's face as he leered at her flashed through his mind. He'd said something about her falling into the wrong hands. The thought of Redahn's hands on his maiden angered him every bit as much as it had when his brother had spoken the words.

"You are mine and I will have you!" He spoke through clenched teeth as he stepped back toward the bed, then turned abruptly and stormed from the room.

Chapter 16

Long, even strides took the warrior from Zanak compound and propelled him toward the Great Hall at the center of town, his need moving him beyond reason. To hell with the Masters and their foolish rules. He didn't care that one of the first instructions he'd received as a boy was that once a warrior was paired with his Marked, he was to remain uncoupled with another woman until after his Chosen was determined to be with child. He supposed it was to increase the chances of fertility, though to Tahruk it seemed as absurd as the marking ritual itself.

Of course, most of the warriors whose marked maidens had presented had already consummated the relationships and many would be boasting of their virility soon as bellies began to swell and new generations were born. He swore aloud as he neared the hall. His very presence there would indicate to all that everything was not right in his world. For a brief moment he contemplated potential fallout. What would be said of him, his ability to woo and subdue? He had a reputation within the walls of a maid's bedchamber every bit as great as the one he boasted of on a battlefield. Would blame fall on his Chosen then? Would she be considered cold, inadequate? Or would cause center on the fact that they hailed from enemy Drilles, and no matter how badly some wanted it, sometimes wrongs could not be righted?

He didn't care about the Masters' plan, though behind-the-hand comments sent in the direction of his Chosen, her beautiful face crestfallen—the thought constricted his heart. He fought against it. It was her fault he was here. Damn her and damn the wine.

"The mighty warrior returns so soon," a distinctly feminine voice purred, stopping him from pulling open the door.

He turned. It was her—the lusty blonde who had attracted him the first night. His eyes ran over her, top to bottom. She smiled as his focus returned to her face.

"As have you, fair maiden." Tahruk stepped into the shadows, closing the distance between them. "I'm surprised you haven't been swept up by a warrior unwilling to let you leave his side."

She shrugged then shook her head, the blonde locks swishing about her bared shoulders.

Tahruk focused on her sun-kissed skin, knowing she would be soft and warm beneath him.

"I'm not interested in just any warrior." She reached out and fingered the fasteners of his tunic.

He grabbed her hand and held it to his chest, staring down at her. "You know my Chosen has arrived?"

"Of course. I was there. Remember?" She moved closer to him. "I also spent time with her and the other maidens who arrived by ship." Pulling herself to full height, she kissed the spot where his neck dipped in. "The Masters did you a disservice, my lord. Your Chosen is no match for a mighty warrior whose legendary reputation must surely create cravings beyond those she could ever hope to satisfy." She pressed herself firmly to him.

"I am bound to her," he defended. It was a weak rebuttal and a throaty chuckle told him she was fully aware his being bound did little to lessen the desire he felt at that moment.

"And yet you returned. What were you expecting to find inside the hall, my lord?" Her hands had begun an intimate dance over his body. "Were you searching for me?"

He shook his head. "I already told you I would have thought you swept away long before."

Again she shrugged. "No royal blood flows through my veins. Though it could flow through my children's... I could assure a man of certain pleasures that would overshadow being wrongly paired."

Experience told Tahruk this maiden was looking for more than just a tousle. Was she suggesting he take her as a second? Many warriors had them. His mother was a second, sought after the Masters' choice for his father had failed to bear the required offspring. His mother, however, was as royal as Renaine's Marked. She was the younger daughter of his Chosen's family actually, and she'd stepped into the role without protest, bringing forth two males and four daughters.

He looked down at the maiden, breathed in her warm, musky scent. She was certainly fair to look at, soft beneath his hands. It would be simple to accept her…

Thoughts of Elenya refused to be pushed from his mind. How would she feel when she learned he'd already taken another, even before he'd had her? He fought his angst. The blonde was right. His Chosen was his enemy and she'd shown little promise in her ability to satisfy.

Chapter 17

The warrior settling in beside her caused Elenya to rouse. His bare chest loomed before her eyes and she swallowed hard before looking up into his face.

"Sleep well?"

Her brows drew down at the tone of his voice. Was it mocking? Angry? She almost thought she detected a hint of mirth. She rubbed her forehead, trying to recall what had transpired between them, but could not.

No. She did remember. She felt for her dress and, as she thought, she was fully clothed. Tears dulled her eyes.

"Forgive me, my lord. I…"

"Shh." He placed two fingers against her lips.

"Rest, Little One," he whispered. "Morning is practically upon us."

Elenya searched his dark eyes, though the moon that had yet to be drowned by the sunrise was not bright enough, nor did she know him well enough to try to imagine what he was thinking.

Her lips suddenly dry, she attempted to moisten them only to touch his fingers with the tip of her tongue. The warrior groaned. She started to pull back then stopped. Placing her palms on his chest, she felt his flesh quiver beneath her touch and leaned in to kiss the space between her hands.

With little effort he pulled her upward, his mouth

greedily covering hers, his tongue demanding entrance that she did not deny.

She breathed deeply then pulled away. “My lord? Have you been with another woman?” Silence stretched between them, emerald depths searching masked blues as they stared at one another. “You smell of a woman’s scent.” She was backing off the bed when his strong hand grasped her wrist and hauled her back to his side.

“The intensity of my need should answer your question,” he growled.

Elenya had no experience in such matters, she only knew her heart hurt and her pride pushed her to try to free herself from him. As she pushed against him, he rolled her to her back and pressed himself on top of her, holding her flailing fists above her head. He tried to kiss her, though a quick jerk of her head landed his lips on her jaw. He merely nibbled his way from there to her earlobe instead.

“Unhand me!” she demanded.

“I think not.” His voice rumbled against her ear. He pressed her back to the bed as her hips bucked against him in her attempt to free herself. He stifled a chuckle. It was fairly obvious that, in her innocence, she had no idea how much her actions enticed him.

“I will not be used in this manner,” she squeaked.

“I will use you in any way I please. Though I can scarce fathom why you fight me so when moments past it was you who tempted me. I would have let you sleep.” He was assaulting her collarbone with tender kisses. She cried out when his tongue darted out to trace the bone line.

“You have betrayed my honor,” she managed to say on a mere breath, her senses reeling.

Tahruk stopped. He reared back to glare down at her. Elenya froze as well, frightened by the look in his eyes.

Again she wished she could read him. All she knew was that the fight drained from her, and the only thing she heard was the heavy breathing that remained from their exertion.

"Honor!" he roared at last, releasing her and pushing away. "First you run, then you fall asleep. Twice, no less. Now you fight me and accuse *me* of betraying *your* honor?" Tahruk rolled from the end of the bed, his nakedness causing Elenya's breath to catch. She sat up in the bed, watching him. What a glorious vision his silhouette made against the pale light filtering in from the garden exit.

She looked away as he turned to face her. Fingertips against her forehead, she peeked through splayed fingers only to look away again. She hoped he could not see the redness creeping into her cheeks.

Her head down, she heard him sigh. "There was another woman."

Elenya tensed, her gaze still averted.

"*She* was waiting for *me*, expectant of my return." He paused, letting his words sink in. "She asked that I take her to my bed and make her my second."

Jaw tight, lips thinned, her head snapped up, her eyes locked with his before her face crumbled in humiliation. Biting her lip, Elenya clamped her eyes shut against the pain and spun away from him to collapsed into the pillows where she sucked air as best she could to keep the tears from falling.

His hands on her shoulders, he lifted her, pulling her back firmly to his bare chest. She could feel his breath on her neck and ear, though it only added to the misery that weighed on her own chest. She hated herself for feeling betrayed, hated herself for driving him to the arms of another even before their own relationship had been consummated. Honor said she could reject him for such and return to her people to live a solitary life since the marking would destroy her should anyone claim her innocence besides the man for whom she'd been marked. Her heart told her she would not. A loud sob tore from her.

"I could have taken her, Little One. But I chose not to," he whispered against the cinnamon-honey curls covering her ear. "I told her my bed was already filled with all that I would ever need."

Elenya reacted slowly, his words taking their time to register on her tormented brain. Finally, she turned toward him, twisting slightly so she could see his face.

Tahruk waited as her eyes again implored his.

"My lord..."

Her whispered words, lips parting softly as she leaned into him was all the permission the warrior needed. Not needed, *wanted.* He wanted her to want him. And she did.

With a gentleness matched to her innocence and to the lady she was, he kissed her, his mouth remaining over hers even as his hands pressed the silken material from her shoulders. The dress pooled around her waist, revealing a corset of the softest pink adorned with ribbons and lace.

The need burning bright in his dark eyes reflected back from hers. While his mouth again claimed hers, his hand explored the curves beneath the feminine garment. He was pleased with the barely audible sounds she made, sounds he more felt than heard, though her response to his touch quickened his urge. Experienced fingers deftly unlaced the corset before he pressed her, ever so gently, onto the bed. She trembled as he removed her remaining garments. Was it fear or expectation? Tahruk was unsure. He only knew it fueled his desire.

Like a tiger upon its prey, he moved atop her, stopping just long enough to kiss the tender flesh of her belly. *Soon,* he thought. Soon enough her beautiful body would swell with his child. *Their child.* He kissed her stomach again before need propelled him upward.

Tahruk cursed silently at the trepidation in her beautiful green eyes, noting the fear wrinkled brow. "Shhh," he attempted to whisper against her lips, though she turned her head, shaking it to let him know she wished for him to stop.

"No, Little One. You are mine and I must have you now. I cannot, will not stop this."

Elenya tensed completely. Her whimpering pierced his heart without softening his resolve to make her his.

"Elenya!" He spoke firmly, his voice still soft next to her ear.

She froze, her eyes connecting with his when he pulled his head away from hers. Her only movement was the rapid rise and fall of her chest pressing against his. Tears welled in her green eyes.

He kissed her softly, feeling the trembling of her lips. "They teach you nothing of what to expect, do they?" He kissed away an errant tear, not really expecting an answer. He continued to nuzzle her cheek with his own, wondering how to allay her fears. The likelihood of unpleasantness before enjoyment made it impossible for him to promise he would not hurt her. He pulled back to stare at her. "Trust me."

She looked up at him, a war of uncertainty evident in the tightness of her features. She finally nodded, her movement short and stiff.

He smiled at her. "Keep looking at me, Little One. Breathe as I do."

She did as he instructed, relaxing somewhat until he began to press himself more firmly against her. He felt her slipping away again.

"Elenya." He spoke her given name for only the second time since she'd come into his life. This time his voice was gentle and caressing—unlike the force with which he claimed her innocence, pushing himself into her with certainty and swiftness. There was no easy way.

With eyes that said *I will continue to trust you because you asked it of me*, Elenya lay still beneath him, her lips quivering as she fought to hold back the tears.

"The worst is behind you, I promise," Tahruk told her, his thumb caressing away a stray tear. "Now I will show you the rest of what they failed to teach you. Tonight you will know the wonders of being a woman."

And with those words he began to move, slowly at first, allowing her to get used to him, though his own restraint was quickly tested. Every place they touched seared him, leaving him certain their bodies were melting together, forming a singular pool of molten liquid that seeped into his veins and fueled him, pushing him to bring them both to greater heights.

Elenya quickly moved from fearful to willing, opening herself up to him, with sheer abandonment. She cried out as her young body shattered around him, her eyes widening when the force of his own release came with an unrestrained roar.

In the end, Tahruk's gentleness surprised him as had the intensity of what they'd shared. He continued to hold her close, kissing her, nuzzling her, not quite ready to break their union. Memorizing the feel of her beneath his fingertips, he reveled in her body's response to his. Never before had he imagined feeling such oneness with a maiden as he did with Elenya. She may be the daughter of his enemy, but he could not imagine a woman more right for him. The Masters truly had been wise in choosing her for him.

Tahruk stared down at the woman sleeping by his side. Propped on his elbow, he brushed a strand of hair from her forehead, allowing his fingers to enjoy the warm softness of her skin.

He chuckled at the depth of her sleep, thinking of the other times when she'd slept well in his bed. This time, no frustration remained on his part as it had before. Making no sound, he reveled in the sated look on her peaceful features, tried to remember what he'd heard—something about the glow of a woman in love. He'd rather think a woman well loved shone with a soft brightness, as did his Chosen.

He settled his head onto the pillow beside her, drinking in the scent of her tousled hair. It smelled of a sweet mixture of Oleander, her, and him. He released the handful of honeyed-cinnamon locks and moved closer to her. Elenya turned, her back to him, moving her body tightly against his. She sighed, a contented sound that made Tahruk smile. She was his. Her body knew it as well as her mind. Now he must work to secure her heart. He had no experience in such matters, but surely he could learn. As willing and eager as she'd been to learn the things he'd wanted her to, he should be more than willing to put forth the effort.

"Elenya Sharanis of Zanak. I shall have *all* of you," he whispered, his palm resting over her heart. The feel of her warm skin filled him with renewed desire. He fought it down. Time was theirs. He need not wake her now.

Chapter 18

Light, feminine moans and the warmth of silky flesh moving against him roused Tahruk from a peaceful slumber. Even before he opened his eyes, the scent of the woman marked with his blood flooded his mind with heady visions of their passion filled night. Full lips twitched, the corners curving upward as he thought of the fulfillment in their meeting. She'd surprised him, giving herself in ways he'd never expected. Or at least she had once her fears had been laid to rest.

A spark of anger threatened as he thought of the lies she must have been told by those she should have been able to trust to tell her about the wonders of a man and a woman. Never had he known a maiden to be so filled with fear. A tightening within his chest accompanied the pleasure he felt at having been the one to put her fears to rest. This tiny woman who carried his blood, would carry his children, had awakened a nurturing instinct within the warrior he'd never have believed himself capable of possessing. He'd begun to realize it well before their coupling, though after becoming one with her, it had bloomed full and strong. Enemy or no, he already knew he would protect her with all he had, even to the point of giving up his life for hers should it ever come to that. In a few short days, days filled with frustration and change, a transition had occurred. She was becoming his life. Was that part of the Masters' plan? Was that the true reason for the mixture and the marking?

He thought of his own father. Renaine was definitely not a man swayed by sentiment or emotion, and yet he'd refused to abandon his Chosen when she could not produce the required heir. To this day, she remained as one of the family, had taken part in the rearing of his children and the running of the household. Only now did Tahruk understand the look that still softened his father's eyes when they fell upon her. The old bear of a man had fallen in love with her just as surely as Tahruk's heart had opened itself to Elenya . He looked at the beauty nestled in his arms. What would he do if she failed to conceive? Would he be able, willing to fulfill that obligation with another?

No. Duty be damned, he could never imagine wanting anyone besides his chosen now that he'd had her. He would fight the Courts, flee with her if he must…

"My lord?" she whispered, running soft fingers over his deeply creased brow.

"Shhh." He pulled her hand down, kissing the fingers that remained to play over his lips. Their touch tickled, deepening an already ignited need. Elenya looked up at him with wide eyes, their questioning quickly replaced with understanding that brought forth a girlish giggle and made him laugh. She smiled and snuggled closer to him in a way that was all woman. Tahruk wasted little time covering her nakedness with his own body, groaning when the softness of her legs encircled him, pulling him tightly against her. What choice did he have but to take what she was offering? He sighed as their union caused her to arch against him and suck in an airy breath. He wouldn't mind waking like this every morning for the rest of his life. That, he was certain, wouldn't bother him at all.

Chapter 19

The young woman from Aleone weighed heavily on Daruh's mind through the early hours of the morning. Shortly before noon, he pushed his paperwork aside deciding instead to pay another visit to Zanak Drille. He wanted to find out what the elder Sharanis had heard about the instability to the Northwest anyway. With Renaine's match being one of the few that crossed kingdom lines, his Chosen hailing from the now unsettled Corigan, if anyone knew what was happening, it would be him. A quick stop at Zanak before lunch at the castle would serve Daruh two-fold.

Daruh was shown into the main garden when he arrived at Zanak where he found Renaine hovering over several maps and correspondences laid out on a table not far from the roses Nema tended. Odd as it was, he couldn't say he was overly surprised at Lady Neria's absence.

"What brings you to our corner of the Centrehead, Daruh? And so soon after your last visit." Renaine barely lifted his eyes from the scrolls before him when he spoke.

"Morning, Master." Nema's pleasant voice lifted in greeting as she walked toward the two men. "Should I ring for refreshments, my lord?" she asked Renaine.

Brows drawn, Renaine looked from Nema to Daruh then out toward the sundial in the center of the garden before shaking his head. "Perhaps Master Daruh would like to join us for lunch since we're so close?"

Daruh studied the other man for a moment, wondering if he was being asked or told. He shrugged. "I had planned to take my meal at the castle, though this will give us more time to chat." He glanced down at the maps in front of Renaine. "I was hopeful you might shed some light on the unrest befalling Travensworth's kingdom."

Renaine's eyes locked with Nema's before again turning to the Master. Out of the corner of his vision, Daruh could see her body tense.

"Would you mind letting Neria know we have a guest, Nema? We both know she doesn't like surprises." The shaking of Renaine's head was barely perceptible when Nema began to step toward him. Instead, with a curt nod, she turned to make her way from the garden.

Renaine watched her leave then went back to scanning the maps. "Women tend to worry needlessly when too much information is shared, would you not agree?"

Daruh sank into the chair across the table. He watched the man studying the maps. When he didn't answer, Renaine looked up, raising a brow.

"You disagree?"

"For some women, perhaps. Though I would think you might prefer Nema had firsthand, factual information. You know she's bound to learn about it soon enough on her own, and I can attest to the many tales that are swirling out there. She probably won't get the truth."

Renaine regarded him for a moment before nodding his head. "I'll take that into consideration, Daruh, though the truth may allude us all. Besides, I'm sure Nema's need for information isn't the real reason you're here."

Daruh chuckled. The Zanak men certainly couldn't be accused of beating around the bush. He looked out over the colorful pallet of the garden. "I suppose I was also wondering how the young couple was getting along. I didn't see them about when I came in."

"Nor has anyone else." Renaine's gruff chortle surprised Daruh. "My son's mother was not pleased to learn his chamber door had been barred against her unwelcomed entry this morning." His brief explanation of Neria's visit to Tahruk's chamber the morning after the Dremis had Daruh laughing as well. "Neria may be a social butterfly with etiquette beyond measure, but she knows little of the ways and needs of a man, I'm afraid."

Daruh nodded, thinking of the peculiar circumstances that thrust Renaine and Neria together. The two did seem ill suited in all but procreation. Together they had produced beautiful daughters and two of the best warriors the King's army had ever seen, at least until Redahn had been injured.

As if on cue, Redahn materialized before them. "Daruh." He nodded at the Master while settling into the chair next to his father. He leaned forward, staring at the papers on the table before relaxing, a lazy yawn spreading across his stubbled face. "I heard last night he was going to marry Venderlay's daughter to put an end to the squabbling," he tossed out casually, pointing to the map of Corigan.

The older men exchanged looks.

"Is Travensworth not betrothed already? I was quite certain his marriage had been arranged from his childhood." Renaine's comment was directed at Daruh though with a frown thrown in his son's direction.

Daruh contemplated the news. "Are you quite certain that's what you heard?" he asked Redahn.

Redahn shrugged. "It's what I heard. Some of Travensworth's men were in town last night." A closed-mouthed smile curved his full lips. "Though I can't say my attention was centered on them. I suppose I could have heard wrong."

Renaine raised a brow, his equivalent to an eye-roll, then shook his head before looking back at Daruh. There was no denying they'd both be paying a visit to town after their meal to see if the story could be confirmed.

"Lady Neria has asked that you be informed lunch is ready. She's serving in the dining hall, my lords." The young woman curtsied then bounded away, though not before blushing from the once over she received from Redahn. The young warrior shrugged at the scowl he received from his father. Again Renaine's brow rose at his son just before they took their leave from the garden.

The meal was nearly over when Tahruk surprised them, slipping in through one of the concealed doors leading to Zanak's hidden passages. His shirt, untucked and open, hung over hastily donned pants. He too was unshaven and had obviously not been awake long.

Without saying a word to anyone, he filled a platter from the sideboard then sat at one of the empty seats near the head of the table. "What?!" he asked after taking several greedy bites while all eyes watched his every move.

"Pray tell, son, where is the girl? You haven't harmed her, have you?" Neria blurted out, her words unleashing a low mummer running through the lunching party.

Tahruk stopped chewing, then finished his bite and swallowed. He looked from person to person. “Good God in Heaven. Are the lot of you mad? Of course she’s fine. Why would she not be? She simply had… a most eventful morning.” A chuckle sounded low in his chest, the sound shared by Redahn. The two brothers exchanged a knowing smile in a rare moment of unison before it dissolved, garnering Redahn a glare from his older brother.

“All is well then?” Renaine asked after giving his son a chance to chew another bite.

Tahruk slammed his fork to the table and pushed back his chair. “I suppose you want details of the event?” His snarling retort was accompanied by a rather ferocious glare that barely earned him Renaine’s raised brow. Others at the table were a bit more animated. Shocked gasps, faked coughs, and even a few covered ears were seen or heard.

“I’ll take the details,” Redahn offered.

“You’ll take *nothing* that belongs to *me*.” Tahruk rose with jerky movements. He looked around the table, mumbling about tasteless madmen, then stomped back to the sideboard to fill another plate. Daruh noticed his choices were made with much greater contemplation than before. It made the old Master smile.

“I do not wish to be disturbed the remainder of the day,” Tahruk announced after moving toward the concealed door. He glared specifically at his mother until Neria looked down. Then he trained his eyes on Daruh. “Since when has Zanak held such fascination for you, *Master*? Our business seems suddenly yours for some small and feminine reason. Perhaps it’s time you found entertainment elsewhere,” he grumbled before disappearing.

The old Master’s chuckle was met with obvious relief

from the parents of the disrespectful warrior. Moments later, Daruh announced his departure. Though Tahruk had not said much about the young woman, his actions were enough to make Daruh feel comfortable about her well-being. He would call on her specifically in a few days. But for now, he'd focus elsewhere as her warrior had suggested. He needed to shift to the priority of finding out all he could on the situation in Corigan. Though a smaller kingdom, her forces were strong and they were too close to the border of Dorengar to let any concerns lie unchecked.

Chapter 20

Tahruk fought against the dour mood that danced around him as he walked back through the hidden corridors. Only the thought of the young woman waiting in his bed kept it at bay. The morning had been far more fulfilling than he'd anticipated, at least until his grumbling stomach had demanded a trip to the dining hall. Too bad he'd been unable to ignore it. A mumble of disgust bounced off the stone walls of the corridor. How in the world his mother have even considered he might hurt his Chosen was beyond him. As unconventional as everything had been between them thus far, he wouldn't change a thing. He smiled, thinking about Elenya. She'd surprised him, surprised them both actually, and he was sure the pleasures would continue…

"Damnation!" He swore at the empty bed that greeted him when he slipped into his bedroom through yet another concealed door. A few deep breaths cleared his head enough for him to notice the opened door to the garden, though he frowned when he saw her. The eyes that greeted him were not those of a woman assured of her position within her lover's heart. She drew her shawl more tightly about her as he approached. Tahruk didn't say anything, just sat the platter of food on the rock beside her, then watched her trace an imaginary design in the water with bared toes. She seemed unaffected by the colorful fish living in his garden pond swimming by her feet. He supposed living in Aleone with the sea as her playground had made her more at home with these creatures of the water… definitely more so than most women.

And yet she jumped when he brushed the honeyed-cinnamon curls from her shoulder. His frown deepened and a tiny flame of ire sparked in his gut. Had he been wrong about her? Had all they'd shared that morning been nothing beyond requirement for her? With a snort, he wheeled around and marched from the garden, his heavy footfalls coming to a stop in the hallway just beyond his bedroom. "Damn," he swore again, then shook his head and turned back around. With a slow stride, he returned to the garden and settled into one of the wooden chairs designed for relaxing beside the pond.

Still frowning, he watched her, enjoying the way the light danced off the multi-colored strands of her hair, felt a stirring at the slight movement of her form beneath the wrap. Yet he was troubled. How could she possibly still have doubts? All uncertainty had had fled him the moment he'd asked her to trust him and she'd nodded her consent, submitting herself to him, even through her fear. The look in her green eyes—the tears that had formed when he'd claimed her innocence that were quickly replaced with wonder and a desire that matched his… Tahruk shifted in his seat to alleviate the discomfort caused by his sudden need for her. Were it any other woman sitting in his garden, he'd have simply taken her back inside, if they made it that far. He didn't want to do that with Elenya. Her needs, sexual and otherwise, were every bit as important to him as his own. Maybe more… a thought that surprised him and had him sighing out loud.

Elenya turned toward him, quickly looking away when

their eyes met and turning her concentration back to the water at the edge of the rock where she sat. With her own sigh, she pulled her knees to her chest and hugged them close before looking at him and then the plate of food.

"Thank you." Her voice was petal soft. So much so that Tahruk wasn't sure whether he heard the hint of a quiver or not. Damn it! What would she have to cry over now?

He watched her nibble some of the soft cheese before breaking off a small piece of bread. At this rate, it would take her days to consume the platter he'd fixed for her. Why were women always so insufferable, so difficult to figure out?

Nema would have chastised him had she been there, especially when his thoughts caused him to glower at the girl when he really didn't feel angry with her at all. He simply didn't understand her. Wooing a woman wasn't something he'd ever had interest in doing before.

Under his scrutiny, she seemed to withdraw more, finally pushing the barely touched food away. Tahruk pressed his lips tightly together. She had to be hungry. He'd been famished. Think, think… what could he possibly do to help her relax?

He chuckled, knowing exactly what would make *him* relax, though she'd probably recoil at any advances he might make. She reached for another piece of bread, broke it and tossed it to the fish. His mouth turned up with hers, even if her smile was for the silly fish and not for him.

"You miss the shores of Aleone?"

She nodded before taking another bite and flinging the rest to the water below. "I've never been away before."

Tahruk tried to remember the first time he'd been away from home. He was quite sure he'd been around nine or ten when he'd gone on his first three day preliminary mission. It hadn't bothered him at all to be away. But then, he'd known he would be returning once they were finished. At this point, Elenya had no way of knowing when she'd see her family again. Sometimes the family of a marked woman left their Drille, invited by their daughter's new family to start anew closer to wherever she settled, but it was up to them to decide whether they would do so. Land had been reserved on the far side of the Zanak compound in anticipation. All it would take was a simple agreement from Elenya's father and Tahruk would break ground. He'd have to wait until he received word from him, the circumstances between the two families in this case making all decisions most uncertain.

"Tell me about your family. I believe I heard you mention sisters to Nema. Do they favor you?" The warrior suddenly wanted to know more about her and hoped his interest would help draw her from her melancholy.

Elenya held up a hand with pointer and thumb pressed close together. "We're all similar in some ways, though very different in others." She smiled. "There are four of us. All girls, much to my father's vexation." He laughed and nodded. She smiled but didn't continue.

"Tell me about them," he coaxed.

It took her a moment before she started to speak again. "I'm the oldest, of course." She turned to stare off across the garden. "Denya is but a year younger than I. Taliana is three years behind her, and Vensi turned twelve the day after I left." Her voice caught and she cleared her throat to help her regain her composure. She continued, seeming to find comfort in talking of her family. Tahruk was pleased with himself for having thought to ask. Nema would have been proud of him.

"We all share the Princess' green eyes, though each of us has a distinct hair coloring."

"They didn't get the red then?" That revelation surprised him for some reason, and had him trying to imagine Elenya with different colored hair.

Elenya shook her head causing her red locks to swirl about her shoulders. She relaxed the shawl, letting it slip down to her waist and Tahruk swallowed hard. Even though there was nothing revealing about the full sleeved dress she'd chosen, he imagined releasing her from its confines and watching it slide from her shoulders much as she had the shawl.

"Vensi's is perhaps the closest, though she favors our mother. I'm told her curls have too much honey to be considered a match for the Princess'. We joke about Vensi's sweetness being nowhere but in her hair!" They laughed together, the sentiment tasting sweet on Tahruk's lips. "Taliana has the golden straw halo of a goddess, and Denya… her curls are as dark as the night. Much like yours, my lord."

She turned to look at him with her last words, her eyes wandering over his hair. Tahruk imagined her fingers entwined in the strands instead, her body writhing beneath his. Was she remembering as well? He was quite sure he saw her shudder before reaching for the shawl and wrapping it about herself again. He frowned as she went back to feeding the fish in his pond.

There will be time, he told himself as he fought back disappointment. She just needed time. Hadn't Nema said that very thing?

"Would you like to pen a note letting your family know you're well?"

Her head whipped toward him. "A note? Now?"

Tahruk shrugged. Why not? "I happen to know there's a ship leaving for Aleone tomorrow morning. It sits in the King's harbor now. Perhaps we could walk down and present it to the captain…"

Elenya was already halfway off the rock before he finished. "That would be wonderful, my lord!" The rise of her voice left no mistaking her excitement. She stopped beside the chair, bobbing a curtsy at his side.

Tahruk reached for her hand, watched her eyes widen as he pressed her fingers to his lips. She stood still, watching, waiting, the shawl clasped tightly around her with her free hand. He knew she questioned his expectations. With a gentle squeeze to her fingers, he released her hand. "Go." He tossed his head in the direction of the garden door. "There's a small writing desk in the corner of the room where you bathed. You'll find pen and paper inside."

He chuckled to himself after she left. As intimate as they'd been, and as freely as she'd given of herself during that time, he found humor in the fact that mentioning her bath could color her cheeks so. He felt a surge of warmth within the lower regions of his body and shook his head. Come to think of it, he'd had to fight hard to keep himself from sending Nema away and pulling the maiden from the water so he could consummate their union right then. Only the knowledge that his mother would be waiting and the fear in Elenya's eyes had kept him from sating his lusty needs.

He wondered if it was possible that she still feared him. Was that the cause for the uncertain way she'd looked at him? Did she still view them as enemies? They were, weren't they? Nothing had changed—the past events remained the same. Just the thought of Zanak's Chosen being compromised by the Aleone man left Tahruk seething. He leaned forward, his head in his palms. How could he care for a woman who shared the blood of his enemy?

Sitting up straight, he stared into the distance and shook his head. She shared his blood as well. Thanks to the genetically altering concoction she'd been given all those years ago, he was more a part of her than they were. Even so, no matter how he'd felt before or how deeply ingrained his distaste for Aleone ran, there was no way Tahruk could make Elenya pay for the actions of others. In his heart he knew the Zanak woman had not been innocent in luring the man's affections just as surely as he knew desire could make a man do crazy things. How well he knew that. He'd been doing them since he'd first caught his Chosen's scent only two days before.

Two days. It seemed like she'd always been with him.

Tahruk smiled as he pushed himself up from the chair. She may not have been with him, but he'd been with her since she was three. His blood flowing through her veins, they'd become one some fifteen years before he'd had the honor of truly making her his own.

With a loudly expelled breath Tahruk headed toward his room. He had a note of his own to take to the ship waiting in the harbor. His letter invited Elenya's father to bring his family to the Centrehead. He hoped he had made his willingness to forgive the feud between their families felt within his words. He also hoped his willingness would be backed up by the other members of his family, and that Elenya's family would do the same. Otherwise… It pained him to think of the heartache his Little One would suffer should any of them refuse to comply.

The warrior shook his head and rolled his eyes at himself. There was no doubt about it. He had fallen hard for the red haired beauty from Aleone's shores. It was time he quit fighting it and convince her of his feelings and that his every intention toward her was nothing but honorable. Hopefully what they found in the harbor would be a step in the right direction to doing exactly that. It had certainly taken some luck and the pulling of an awful lot of strings to make it happen on such short notice. Speaking of short time…

"Five more minutes, my lady," he called to her from his open bedchamber door. He ended up giving her ten, though he'd moved closer to her as time ticked by. Watching the depth of her contemplation, he understood the extra time was worth it when he caught a glimpse of the words she wrote with careful consideration that painted him and the situation in the best possible light. He smiled at the two different phrases he'd seen as he leaned down to kiss the side of her exposed neck. One was *exemplary hospitality bestowed upon her*. The other was *acceptable, though unconventional match within Zanak*. She hadn't bothered to hide the paper from him, nor had she squelched her body's response to his kiss, her shudder unmistakable. "Time's up," he whispered against her ear. "If we don't leave now we'll miss the captain. We may have to wait as it is unless we take a shortcut through the secret passages of Zanak in order to get there."

"Secret passages?" The excitement glowing in her green eyes made Tahruk smile. He held out a hand, which she took without hesitation.

"I'm looking forward to this afternoon's adventures with you, my lord."

"Which of our planned adventures would that be, my lady?"

Tahruk's quirked brow brought a deep stain to her

cheeks that made him laugh. Her remaining innocence warmed him as much as her obvious love of adventure. That was another area, beyond his bed, where they were an *acceptable match*.

Chapter 21

Elenya took to the roughhewn interior passages inside the walls of Zanak with the zeal of an exuberant child. It took her no time at all to grasp the concept of how they worked, how one was expected to move from one to another, and how to know where they would lead. Her sense of direction was uncanny, though not at all surprising considering her trek through the forest the night of the Dremis. No other woman he knew would have attempted to run, let alone into the dark woods. He'd thought her touched in the head at the time. Now he truly admired her for having done it, especially given the circumstances.

He watched her study the inscription on the wall, knew her reaction would be one of surprise when she realized the significance of this particular fork in the tunnel system.

"You have direct access to the Castle interior?" Her pursed lips and raised brows made him laugh. She continued. "One would have thought the castle secure from all entry beyond the front gates. I know you hail from the King's direct bloodline, yet I would think such privilege should fall to his heir apparent, not to the inhabitants of Zanak."

Tahruk shrugged and asked a question of his own. "You knew of me before we ever met, did you not?"

Elenya nodded, her green eyes wide with anticipation of the answer that had yet to come.

“And you thought what of me?”

“That you were pompous and arrogant, one who felt he deserved to take whatever he pleased.” She covered her mouth with her hand.

Tahruk roared with laughter. “I have no doubt you believed that. And perhaps your beliefs were true, though I am none of those without justification.” He waited a moment to see if she understood what he was saying.

Taking her face in his hands, he drew her near, rubbing a thumb across her drawn brows. Tension stiffened her body even though her dreamy expression told him she wasn’t afraid. The attraction between them was undeniable and he knew she felt it every bit as much as he did. His eyes roamed over her face memorizing the details, looking for comprehension. He ran a hand through the partially loose curls before ignited passion forced him to cover her mouth with his own in a kiss that left them both breathless.

She clung to him for support, their faces a fraction of an inch apart. “You are also mighty upon the battlefield—a force all your own, so I’ve been told,” she whispered.

Tahruk smiled, brushing her lips with his once again before answering. “Yes, Little One. I am. I hold a place of great honor. Before me, my father held that position, and his father before him. We are not only bound to the King by blood lineage, we have served our lord well throughout the years. He is a man who greatly rewards those who love him and those he loves.” He turned dark eyes to gaze over the inscribed plaque. “Castle tunnels and secret passages are not uncommon, though they were originally designed for security. Someday I’ll tell you how Andorak’s father and his family were spirited from the castle along these very passages only moments before King Venderlay and his men broke through the supposedly impenetrable North wall.”

"I know the lore surrounding the kingdom of Voringlok's failed attempt to take the throne of Dorengar, though the story only talks about the King's family. Zanak specifically was never mentioned."

"No doubt Aleone's history books have kept much of the truths about Zanak from you." Tahruk snorted.

The hurt expression on Elenya's face made him immediately sorry he'd made such a comment, whether it was true or not. She distanced herself from him and pretended a more in-depth study of the inscription. Tahruk pressed his lips together. He'd be damned if he was going to apologize, even if he did feel remorseful. This woman of enemy blood had changed him too much already. He was not about to begin dropping to his knee to beg for her forgiveness for every little thing.

"Come," he told her, taking her elbow to steer her through the passageway to the harbor and the ship preparing for her final night before sailing to Aleone.

Chapter 22

Elenya could smell the sea air as they neared the passage opening. Elation took hold, blotting out the disappointment of moments before when he'd commented on Aleone's shortcomings. Before that, she'd begun to believe they might find a way to live beyond the weight of their ancestors' mistake that continuously returned, threatening to lay heavy if she allowed it. Now all she could think about was the sight that lay somewhere before them.

"Yes, Little One. We're almost through the passage. Though you need to know the opening puts us very near a steep drop to the water's edge."

Elenya realized he was cautioning her not to get over exuberant and rush forward. She nodded. It made sense that the entrance was disguised lest Zanak become a target for every vagabond that wandered by. This whole crazy tunnel system made sense, actually, except for the access to the castle. True, it had been useful that time with Voringlok, though she still would have expected Andorak's oldest to have housed any escape route. There were pieces of this family's existence that puzzled her. Putting it all together fell to the back of her mind with the smell of the sea.

The next turn revealed a layer of thick brush, limbs and vines that appeared to grow down from what must be the hilltop that formed the ending of the elaborate passage system. Tahruk stopped before the jumbled mess, motioned her with a single finger to wait, which Elenya did in silence. The warrior stood and listened before carefully pulling aside a layer of the covering and peering outside. Elenya breathed deeply, welcoming the scent of the moist sea air into her lungs, though it brought with it a wave of homesickness. She touched the silk bag draped over her shoulder to hang at her waist and felt the letters to her family inside while murmuring a silent, hopeful prayer. She thought about the hastily scribbled note to Denya.

He is beautiful, just as we'd imagined, she'd written. *Hair as dark as the night, and eyes a deeper blue than any sky you might imagine. His countenance, while oft times cloudy, can be gentle and tender beyond imagine. I believe him to be a good man, overall, and hopefully willing to move us beyond the feud that has fueled our families for all these generations.*

His family, however, is truly divided and are a lot that will take time to understand. I haven't much time so will tell you more in a later writing. I am most hopeful that Father will see fit to bring you all to the Centrehead soon. It is quite beautiful here and my lord is taking me to an Aleone bound ship in the harbor as soon as I complete my notes. A harbor! I shall once again smell the air wafting from the sea! No doubt it shall make me miss you more than I already do, my sister.

Much love to you all. You are, as always, in my heart and I send kisses to all.

Elenya knew Denya would share her words with Taliana at least. They would sigh and giggle and verbally chastise her to one another for not providing more details. What silly girls they were.

Girls. She frowned, hit with a sudden, sobering thought. They would soon be young women. She wondered if her father had designs to send them to the Centrehead. If they were forced into the grouping of the Dremis maidens, being unmarked, would they be at the mercy of any man who chose them? The thought of any of them moving into a life as a Lady of the Courts caused Elenya to clutch her stomach and squeezed her eyes closed. That was one life she would not wish upon anyone, especially the ones she loved. She hated that the world where she lived considered such a position an honor. Their one hope would be a match with one of the lesser warriors. She looked at Tahruk's back, his head somewhere beyond the vines still. Could he, would he help her secure positions for her sisters? Her face flushed with anticipation as she began forming a plan.

Tahruk turned at that moment. He studied her flushed features, his own face washed with concern. "Are you okay, my lady?" he asked, moving quickly to her side.

Elenya nodded, swallowing hard before she answered. "I'm just excited. The anticipation has me all a flutter." It was a truthful answer, even if a bit misguiding.

The warrior stared at her a moment longer then nodded. "No one is about. We can easily scale the path and be on our way." He was already pulling at a rope that seemed twisted within the vines. He was explaining that it would be used to secure her about the waist to keep her safe should she lose her footing.

Elenya stopped him with a hand on his arm. She hadn't seen this path they must cross yet, but she felt sure all her scurrying about the land around Aleone with Shemek and her sisters had prepared her well to hold her own. Tahruk dropped the rope that had been fighting him and motioned for her to follow.

Relief settled in when she saw the path. It was wider than expected, though still edged a treacherous drop to the water beneath a jagged cliff. She and Shemek had wandered along paths much more dangerous at times. She'd often wondered what would have happened to them if her parents had found out. The thought made her giggle, and Tahruk turned a puzzled look in her direction.

"It's better than I expected, my lord. I am much relieved," was the explanation she gave, though she was a bit concerned about a patch of vines that covered the trail not far before them. She was mulling over her ability to cross it safely in skirts when Tahruk tightened his hold on her hand and pulled her through more hanging vines into what appeared to be little more than a dense section of the woods at the base of the hill. Elenya frowned, her sense of direction momentarily thrown off as he led her through this wooded passage, moving them farther away from the sea. She understood when they exited into the woods above the harbor. They would come in as if they'd traversed through the forest, leaving no one to speculate about a secret tunnel system.

"Brilliant." The words tumbled out unexpectedly.

"What?" Tahruk asked, his head snapping toward her.

Elenya smiled. "Nothing, my lord. Thank you for bringing me here."

He returned the smile before slightly squeezing her tiny hand still held firmly within his. Working it to where her fingers were loosely weaved into his, she leaned her head against his bicep, hugging his arm close with her other hand. The act gave her the same sense of security she felt when he held her. She sighed when he bent to kiss the top of her head.

Elenya smiled. If she wasn't careful, she could easily

fall in love with this man at her side even knowing he had the power to, and probably would, break her heart. Still, as they made their way to the ships in the harbor, she reveled in the feeling, very much living her dream, even if it was only for the moment.

The harbor was quiet as one might expect for mid afternoon. All cargo would have been loaded that morning, the crew dispatched at lunchtime with demands to return sober and prepared for a quiet night aboard the ship so they might set sail at first light. The familiarity of the setting heightened Elenya's excitement, as did the idea of perhaps seeing men from home that she'd know, since it was an Aleone ship.

"My lord," she whispered, still clutching herself close by his side. "I do not recognize any of these ships."

"No?"

She shook her head and Tahruk smiled.

"Perhaps because it's a new vessel for Aleone?" he offered.

Elenya's frown was heightened by her shrug. She hadn't considered that. She knew her marking had opened doors for Aleone, and she supposed her match to the King's finest might well have prompted her people to invest in luxuries beyond what they had before. Still, as best she could tell, these ships were much larger than anything owned by the ship masters of Aleone. She considered which one might have had the reserves to purchase such a fine vessel.

Her thoughts were interrupted by internal alarm bells going off when Tahruk stopped by the largest ship in the harbor, loosed himself away from her and began to climb the gangplank. Her hand still held in his had her following him upward.

"My lord!" she squealed rather loudly, stopping him when her physical resistance could not. "You cannot, you *must not* board a ship without the permission of the captain or the owner. Doing so will bring bad luck to the journey."

"Ah, Little One. Put your worries aside." He turned and attempted to continue his climb. This time, she pulled back with all her might, and although she was no match for the mighty warrior, he did stop at her urgings. She frowned at his chuckle.

"You may have no regard for the men who must make this voyage, but I shall not allow you to merely laugh away their safety, believing my concerns to be silly superstitions."

She had pulled her hand away from him and stood, fists on hips, glaring up at him from her position further down the plank. Tahruk's explosive laughter at the sight of her only fueled her anger. With a snarl, she turned on her heel, throwing her hands in the air as she began to stomp away, railing him as an insufferable beast not worthy of his title as the King's finest if he could not even show these men of the sea their proper respect.

Her exit failed. Tahruk had her caught against him by the waist, a hand over her venom-spewing mouth before she'd managed half a dozen steps from the ship. Only his barely contained laughter as he turned her to face him let her know she was not in the trouble she should expect for going off on him. Her brows drew down.

"Your worry is unfounded because I have permission, my lady," he whispered to her, his smile widening as if he held the world's largest secret. "*I* am the owner of that fine vessel. Or at least I am until it sails into Aleone harbor within three days' time."

Elenya stared at him, her eyes imploring his, attempting understanding. "What are you saying, my lord?" She finally relented and asked after pulling his hand from her mouth.

"Look at the name of the ship, Elenya."

She did as directed. *Petit Cadeau. Small Gift*. Still…

"This is my gift to your family, Elenya," he said, when she frowned and shook her head. "It's a small token for the gift they have given me."

Elenya stared at him for a moment more before her brows finally pressed upward. Her mouth fell open in most unladylike fashion, though she quickly closed it when Tahruk raised his own brows.

"You… you commissioned a ship for my family? A ship this fine? It must have cost you a fortune…"

He pressed a finger to her lips. "Shhh. There will be no talk of cost. And I did not commission the ship. I could have done so, though that would have taken much longer. When I learned this ship, having sailed on her maiden voyage less than three months prior, was to be sold, I realized she was perfect." *Not unlike you*, his sweeping assessment of her had Elenya blushing before leaning into the warrior, kissing the fingers of the hand she still held. She turned her face up to his, hopeful he would understand she desired his kiss.

Tahruk groaned and glanced back over his shoulder before complying with her wishes. Elenya realized only after they broke away that he was concerned about the men who had remained aboard the ships who now acted as audience to her wanton behavior. The blush that stained her cheeks when their whooping and hollering reached her ears would not soon leave. Tahruk chuckled when she pulled away and buried her face in his chest.

"Come, Little One," he whispered after kissing the top of her head. "Let's see if we can find the captain to take our letters to the shores of Aleone."

Elenya nodded, keeping her head down as he led her back toward the ship. "Thank you, my lord." Her words were so quiet she wasn't quite sure he'd heard her until she felt the slight squeeze of his hand again.

Yes, Elenya thought, *my heart truly is in danger*.

Chapter 23

Tahruk was delighted with Elenya's response to his gift to her family, especially when she slipped an arm about his waist and leaned into him on the walk back to the Zanak compound. He held her close to his side with an arm about her shoulders, reveling in the looks from the bands of seamen they passed along the more traveled, open path. Not all the men returning to their ships belonged to the crew of the *Petit Cadeau*, though those who were offered quick words of congratulations on the couple's union. Their open appreciation of his Chosen's beauty was not offensive in the least, in part because he shared their appreciation, and also because he knew they regarded him highly. Not one of them would have dared cross him, especially where his lady was concerned. He was also quite pleased with her response to the seamen. Her choice of words in her wishes for a successful journey to Aleone seemed wrought with perfection, bringing forth smiles of appreciation.

"You have a way about you, my lady," Tahruk told her when they were alone again in their journey.

Elenya laughed in surprise and shook her head. "No, my lord. I simply know the language of the sea," she answered after he explained his reasoning.

Tahruk smiled, enjoying the way her breath caught when he leaned down to kiss her temple. She may know the sea, though what he'd witnessed was much more. His lady was a diplomat of sorts. He'd seen it with the captain of the *Petit Cadeau*, and with her crew, as well as at the feet of Master Daruh, and again within the midst of his own family members. Elenya Sharanis was the kind of woman who could change the world if she wanted to. There was something about her that made people want to please her, do for her. Hell, even *he* had fallen under her spell. And that was certainly not his nature. He'd thought his feelings would lessen once the fires of the marking had been quenched, though having Elenya had not sated his desire. It had only made him want her more, and he had every intent of satisfying that longing when they returned to his chambers. It was a thought that had him moving her along at an ever quickening pace the closer they got to home.

As if she could read his mind, Elenya laughed as they moved faster. She broke from his side and took his hand. They were both breathless and laughing when they entered Zanak from the heavy door Tahruk had led her through that first day. Together they scurried to his chamber where Elenya twirled in a circle as the warrior closed and bolted the door. When he turned to her, she dropped her chin and look at him through lowered lashes.

"Vixen," he growled before catching her to him.

Elenya's head fell back, giving the warrior the freedom to devour her slim neck with greedy lips. Elenya moaned and then squealed when he scooped her up in his arms and whisked her to his bedchamber.

"It's daylight, my lord!" she squeaked when he unceremoniously tossed her on the bed and began removing his clothing.

"It was daylight by the time I finished with you this morning as well, was it not?" He hitched a brow, though his disrobing did not slow at all. Her wide opened eyes grew even bigger when he fell to her side, his hand immediately finding its way beneath her skirts, while his mouth covered hers with demanding hunger.

"Oh, my lord," she whispered against his lips, her voice breathy, broken with need. "I was so sure you should and then became fearful you might wait until the sun no longer colored the sky."

Tahruk pulled his face from hers to look into her eyes. "Waiting is not one of my virtues, I'm afraid," he told her.

"Nor mine," she whispered, snaking her hands around his neck to pull his head back to hers.

Tahruk chuckled against her lips, only too happy to hasten them toward the act that would momentarily quiet the fires that raged between them.

"Never has another woman so completely engulfed me, Little One," he told her as he held her after they'd made love.

Elenya lifted her head from his chest and stared at him for a moment. "Thank you for sharing that with me."

Tahruk rubbed a thumb across her cheek before running his hand through the red tresses he'd already grown to love so very much. Elenya smiled and then lay her head back down. She began tracing finger circles around the smooth planes of his chest before slowly moving her hand lower.

Tahruk groaned. "We haven't much time before the dinner hour, my Little One. Be careful what you start lest I find myself unable to stop."

Elenya stopped. "Must we venture out?" she

practically whined.

"Would you vex my father with our absence? My mother either, for that matter?" He laughed, reminding her of the note he'd received right before they left for the harbor requesting their attendance at the evening meal. His earlier demand that they be left undisturbed had gone unheeded. "I believe they'd like to see for themselves that you're okay."

Elenya sighed. "Very well, though I can't say I relish the whispers and covered mouth snickers that will accompany our presence."

With the swiftness of his warrior training, Tahruk rolled her to her back and settled atop her. "If they wish to whisper, let us at least show up with a glow about us that will leave no guessing as to why we're late."

The pressure of her young body against his let the warrior know he would get no disagreement from her.

Once again, before losing himself completely in the beauty that shared his blood, he thanked the Masters for their wisdom in his match.

Chapter 24

Tahruk knew he needed to tamp down some of the cheerfulness bubbling inside lest others see it when he and Elenya entered the dining chamber. It simply wouldn't do for him to be viewed as a love-sick dog. He failed to suppress a grin as Elenya chattered about unimportant subjects, feeling sure she didn't even realize she was doing so in her nervousness.

"My lady," he said in order to gain her attention just outside the hall, then covered her lips with his when she turned to look up at him without pausing in her ramblings.

"Must you tease me so, my lord?" She pushed him away and started to speak again then stopped. "Oh. Oh! I must sound like a brood of clucking hens." She covered her face with her hands making him laugh.

He took her hands in his and moved them aside where he could kiss her nose. "While I am enjoying your nattering, if you truly wish not to call attention to yourself, you may need to quell the chinwag before we enter."

Elenya dropped a mock curtsy, then laughed as she leaned up to whisper in his ear. "You are most gentlemanly in your demands of me, my lord, is it your custom to indulge a lady so?" He shivered when he felt her tongue against his lobe.

Grabbing her to him with an arm about her waist he returned the gesture, felt her tense, her breath catch. "Have you not yet learned I do exactly as I please?" He nipped at her earlobe then continued, "And if that includes indulging a lady, *my* lady, then I shall do so." He pulled back to gaze down into eyes that he was quite sure showed a woman who was as besotted as he. A noise from behind had him quickly stepping away from her. He straightened his back and turned to look at the servant who had dropped his load. A heavy frown settled on the warrior's face. "Come, Little One. Let's go in before they send someone looking for us."

He questioned his display of affection for Elenya in the hall. Had he not said he had no intent of allowing his family to see him behaving so? How would it look for the King's finest to be seen wearing his feelings where the world could see, especially when his immediate world consisted of a scrutinizing family, or more pointedly, his father and brother? He could just imagine the looks he was going to receive when they realized he had so quickly allowed himself to fall completely under the spell of the daughter of his enemy! Would his actions from that point be under greater scrutiny?

He supposed that meant he was not *always* willing to do exactly as he pleased, at least where his reputation as a hardened warrior was concerned. He would not compromise that, even for his lady, and especially when his lady was who she was. He hated this war he battled within and understood more Elenya's reservations in leaving his chamber to join the others. It seemed much easier when it was just the two of them.

Elenya frowned at Tahruk's sudden change in demeanor, though he didn't see it since her chin fell at the same time. Head down, she took his arm and allowed him to lead her into the hall, the cool atmosphere causing her frown to deepen. Instead of the festive chatter she was used to within the walls of Aleone's dining hall, they were greeted with a silence punctuated by tension. Alarm shot through her at the downturned faces of the hall's occupants. She looked at Tahruk, finding his expression every bit as foreboding, her tightened hold on his arm gaining a less than reassuring pat.

"Has someone died?" he asked after the silence had stretched too long.

Renaine pointed toward their chairs. "It seems there's trouble in Travensworth's kingdom." He looked at Nema who wore a grim mask. Neria's expression was not much better. He covered her hand with his before turning back to the now seated couple. "Andorak has sent word that we must be ready to move at a moment's notice."

"This is quite unexpected news. No one spoke of such at lunch nor was it mentioned by anyone when we visited the harbor this afternoon." Tahruk continued to question his father and brother about the matter, the women remaining silent. Except Elenya.

Leaning forward to gain full view of the elder Sharanis, she asked him, "Why should the matters of another kingdom concern our King, my lord?"

The hall fell completely silent. Even Tahruk didn't move beside her. Elenya felt the heat rushing to her cheeks knowing she most probably should have kept her dissention to herself. She kept her eyes on Renaine.

"It seems to me such actions only invite others to meddle in our affairs...."

"It seems to me," Renaine cut her off, "living in exile has impeded your manners. You also seem to know nothing about the interweaving of the Kingdoms and Drilles in order to forge lasting relationships so that we may come to the aid of one another to gain a more peaceful existence." Rehearsed words that did little to satisfy Elenya.

She started to retort then leaned back in her seat. "I see," She picked at an imaginary spot on the table. Her voice and smile were glazed with sweetness that didn't match her words. "We go to battle for peace. Makes *perfect* sense to me."

"Elenya!" Tahruk's whispered reproach had her pulling her hand out of his.

She returned her glare to the elder Sharanis. "My people spent almost a hundred years enjoying peace…"

"Your *people* had a trained guard that often fought alongside the King's men, your own father being the leader of them." Redahn's voice captured ears and eyes alike. "They weren't preparing in case of peace, now were they? And, begging your ignorance, but the King was prepared to defend you all as well, even though exile should have had him turning his back on Aleone completely. I know this only too well because I was injured in one such skirmish not far from the lines marking Aleone's territory. Your people enjoyed peace at the expense of others." He cleared his throat. "Your freedom cost me my ability to effectively wield a sword, *my lady.* As a warrior, I am essentially worthless."

The bitterness in Redahn's voice as well as the truth in his words turned Elenya's stomach. She watched him shrug off the nurturing touch of his mother, wishing his resentfulness could have been shoved away just as easily. She sighed. Just another reason for these people to hate hers.

"Whether you believe in war as a means to an end or not, my dear, sometimes it *is* necessary." Nema toyed with the stem of her wine goblet as she spoke. "Besides, we share blood with Corigan." She stole a quick look at Renaine. "Our lord's Chosen is the daughter of their prior king's sister. One of his sisters, at least. Above all others, it is our duty to step in and help protect their King, our kinsman."

Through Nema's speech, Elenya stared at Neria. "You are a princess, my lady?"

"Of lesser standing, yes." Neria nodded. "Our mother was King Mardek's youngest sister."

"Was?"

Nodding again, Neria blinked back tears.

"Elenya, can you not leave well enough alone?" Tahruk's chastisement came through clenched teeth.

It was obvious she had sorely tested her warrior as well as others around the table, yet she seemed unable to stop herself from giving voice to the thoughts forming in her head. "This King, his majesty Travensworth, he has no children, if memory serves. And he is the only son, which means his kingdom would fall to the eldest son of one of his father's siblings. And I'm guessing by the reaction of those within this room that none remain, making that title pass through…" She turned to Tahruk. "To you?"

His lips pressed firmly together, teeth clamped, he ground out, "It is believed so, yes."

Believed? There was something missing from this confusing puzzle. "You… do not know, my lord?"

When no answer came, Elenya leaned forward. Her elbows anchored on the table, she rested her chin against steepled fingers and looked directly at Renaine. Inwardly quaking, she didn't so much as flinch from his icy glare.

"There's talk of a son from an older daughter, though I don't see what concern any of this is to you," Renaine told her.

The laughter that burst from the young woman startled the group. "Begging your pardon, my lord. I believe it affects me greatly when the children I most assuredly will bear may one day be required to lead a kingdom. I can't believe I didn't know." She covered her head with her arms, continuing before he could answer. "What great responsibility rests upon the shoulders of the members of this family, on your oldest son and the woman marked with his blood! I should have been informed."

"Why do you go on about such things, woman? It changes nothing!" Renaine's fist against the table caused the silver and crystal, along with the occupants of the room, to jump. "Did you have any choice in becoming a part of this family any more than we had in whether we would accept you? And do you think the responsibilities that lay before us are something I have not considered every single day since the Dremis that brought my Chosen to me?" He looked at Nema then pushed his chair back and turned to stare at the blazing fireplace in the corner of the room.

"How we got here makes no difference," Neria said to no one in particular. "We're all descended from royal blood, the markings pulling us together for the sake of peace and stronger lines."

Her brows down, Elenya worked up a half-hearted smile before nodding to the lady of the house. For the first time she realized just how simple Neria was and that the lady had absolutely no idea the implications a kingship would mean to her son or to his children. Especially a kingdom wrought in turmoil.

The picture began to sharpen, every piece starting to fit. No wonder this family, the Zanak Drille, was afforded so many luxuries. She looked at Renaine. He didn't carry Andorak's name, which wasn't uncommon, but where did he fit in? She tried to remember what she'd heard, considering talk of Zanak was often squelched in Aleone. Zanak had been passed down to one of the King's sons, and the only way it made sense was for Renaine to have been the eldest son of the eldest son. The marking would have been no indication because the mates of all of a king's sons were often chosen by marking. She quickly calculated everything in her head. The age would be correct. Andorak was the oldest recorded living King. Of course it would have been the blood of his grandson most likely to become king, the son of the oldest, that would have been dispersed to a princess of another kingdom… What a grand plan. It was also no wonder the punishment of her people had been so severe.

Struck by another thought, she sucked in loudly enough that those around her turned to stare, not that it took much since she'd spoken out. Still, the thought that hit her was truly shocking. What if King Andorak was responsible for the young King of Corigan's death in order to secure a place for his own heir on the throne of that kingdom…

"Perhaps you would do well to return to chambers with your Chosen, my son? I believe she is not well."

"No," Elenya spoke before anyone could respond to the order issued as a question. "Forgive my outbursts, my lord. I shall remember my place here and remain quiet." Her eyes locked with Renaine's, who had turned back to the table. The older Sharanis reached for his wine goblet and swallowed down a good portion before nodding his consent. Elenya looked at Neria to his left. She stared off in an almost dream like trance. Beside her Redahn's frown left her wondering what he was thinking. No doubt something resentful. Nema gnawed at her bottom lip in stern concentration, though why she would have such concern over any of this was beyond Elenya's understanding. She reminded herself again to uncover Nema's true place within this family hierarchy.

Elenya could not bring herself to look at the warrior beside her. Tahruk had remained mostly quiet throughout the altercation and she could not bear to receive the look of disapproval she deserved from him. Closing her eyes, she bowed her head breathing deeply to quell the roiling of her insides. Why had she never mastered the ability to silence her tongue? She wouldn't blame her warrior if he was cursing the Masters for their irrational decision to put them together. No doubt her outburst this evening had killed anything that might have been forming between them.

The thought filled her with such sadness she could not contain the handful of tears that squeezed out to fall on her hands folded in her lap. She opened her eyes as the warmth of Tahruk's hand spread over hers. Slowly, she looked up at him, surprised to see him smiling at her, a look of admiration on his face. A small gesture, meant just for her, he winked and bumped her shoulder ever so lightly with his own before turning back to his father to ask more questions about the missing King and the dilemma it posed. The measure of relief that surged inside lightened Elenya's heart though the queasiness she'd felt continued its assault. Hopefully the food that was finally beginning to arrive would help. Heaven help her, she wanted nothing more than to stay and listen to everything these men had to discuss.

Elenya's flailing of the covers awakened both her and the man at her side.

"What is it?" Tahruk asked, sitting up as she did,

staring at her clutching the bed sheets tightly to her heaving chest.

"I dreamt men came and you had to leave. And because I had denied you the night of the Dremis I failed to conceive." She stared at him with eyes more troubled than his. "Forgive me my insolence."

He gave her no response beyond his lips covering hers before he pushed her back to the softness of the matting beneath them. He felt sure his duty had already been fulfilled, that his child lay in her womb—a son, a warrior mightier than even he could boast because of the strength of his blood that ran through her veins. Together, they would make fine children beyond the one she now carried, children who would grow up capable of ruling a kingdom, if necessary.

Still, he would attempt to quell her fears, making love to her every chance he had before the part of her dream where the men showed up, came true. He had no doubt, they would come and he would have to leave.

For the first time in his life he was not looking forward to that day.

Chapter 25

Some five days later the men came from the Royal Courts summoning the King's military forces. His sword draped in silk across her forearms, Elenya watched as Tahruk's armor was fastened. Her posture stiff, he knew she was fighting the same sense of foreboding she'd been filled with the past few days.

"This is who I am, Elenya," he'd told her one evening as she lay in his arms barely able to hold back her anger. The depths of her feelings had surprised him as much as her passion. "Whenever the King calls, I must go. This is what I have trained for my whole life. *This* is why *I* was born."

"Nothing is solved on the battlefields," she'd protested.

"You're wrong, Elenya. Fear is a great motivator. If we don't subdue the enemy, they'll continue to push until they overtake us and then we'll be at their mercy. We must protect all that is ours, especially in this case. We cannot fail in our attempts to find Travensworth and reinstate him onto his throne. You know full well this means much more to our family than simply helping a King regain his kingdom."

Tahruk thought of how their lives would change should this mission fail. Or, worse yet, if he should not return...

That was not an option.

"I will come back to you. I promise," he'd told her, kissing her, his hand covering her belly before beginning a more sensual assault of her body.

They'd talked of it no more though her fear of him not returning and leaving her childless remained heavy on her. Now, as she stood before him in the armory, one of many women of Zanak prepared to see their men off, he could do little to quell her misery. As he stepped forward, prepared for the first time to receive his sword from the woman chosen for him, he tipped her face up to his with a finger beneath her chin. Her shoulders squared, she smiled at him. Her eyes alone belied her confidence.

"We must go, my son." Renaine's voice intruded as the older warrior lifted his sword from Neria's arms. Neither Tahruk nor Elenya turned, the younger Sharanis leaning down to kiss his bride before claiming his own sword and slipping it into the sheath at his side.

"You have my promise," he whispered.

With one more look, he turned and followed the mass of warriors from the room.

From somewhere behind her, Nema commanded Elenya to come with her. "We need to hurry to get into position to see them when the procession begins. With the Elite riding out first before the King, they'll be toward the front."

Nema grabbed Elenya's arm and began pulling the stunned, younger woman along.

"He'll be fine, love. Your warrior is the best there's ever been. No harm will come to him, especially now that he has even more reason to return."

Elenya was almost sure she felt Nema's free hand graze her belly right before they pushed through the door, though the cloud that had ascended when Tahruk left kept her mind from forming the question she wanted to ask. Perhaps fear kept her from it as well. She uttered a silent prayer that her fears would be unfounded. First and foremost she wanted to believe his promise, to know this man whom she had feared and loathed not so long ago would return to her unharmed. Beyond that, she prayed his seed had indeed taken root inside her. Soon enough, she would know.

She caught her breath and held up her head with renewed hope. Catching one more glimpse of him was suddenly the only thing the girl with the honeyed-cinnamon crown of curls cared about. Nema chuckled, lifting her skirts and moving with a speed that belied her age as leader became follower, verbal directions taking them where they needed to be.

As the women crested the hill, they could see the assembly of armored men atop gallant warhorses working their way to the courtyard. The King and his entourage, traveling from the opposite direction, would meet them down by the copse of trees Nema pointed to.

"Go quickly," Nema told her.

Elenya's insides quivered as she ran down the hill to where she could plainly see the King with his closest confidant riding beside him. They were flanked by his flag bearer, two personal guards, and his only remaining son. The tiny group pulled up before the thicket at nearly the same time as Elenya. She stopped a few feet from them, stood unaware of the King's eyes on her as she watched the approaching military.

Elenya had watched the assemblage of the men of Aleone many times, her father leading them in later years, though never had the numbers come close to the mass that moved toward the waiting King. Briefly her mind flitted to her people back home, wondering if they were also gathering. She knew, especially since her delivery to the Centrehead, they would fight beside the King's men. Shemek. He hadn't crossed her thoughts for days.

Nema's eyes were on the King, watching him watching Elenya. Her disdain for him had not lessened in all the years. The thought that he'd have dissolved the ties between Dorengar and Corigan all those years ago had Renaine not fought for her to remain within his household sparked her ire anew.

"You are the Aleone woman?" Nema heard the King ask, watched Elenya turn toward him in momentary confusion before dropping into a low curtsy.

"Yes, my King," she answered softly before rising at his command.

"Your likeness to Princess Damalenya is strong. To whom were you matched?"

"She belongs to your lord Sharanis," Nema offered, coming up beside the young woman.

The King looked from Elenya to Nema. "To Tahruk? I'm surprised I wasn't told his Chosen had arrived, though I suppose with the unrest..." His astonishment gave way to a hearty chuckle. "Not a match I would have suspected for my great grandson." He studied the red haired beauty who had already turned back to search the approaching men. "I cannot say I am displeased with the Masters' choice in this match. Zanak has a reputation for the unusual, it seems." He looked back to Nema before the thunderous approach of horsed warriors pulled all attention in the direction of the majestic sight and away from the subject of matches.

Nema sucked in a deep, steadying breath. Even having

seen it so many times throughout her years, she still felt the same mixture of pride and revulsion she'd experienced the first time the King's forces had amassed. They might be mighty to behold, but their coming together meant lives would be lost, most assuredly on both sides. War was barbaric, even if necessary. This time it involved more of her people, which made it that much harder. She wondered whether these men of Dorengar would have been forced into battle, risking their lives, had she not been matched to Renaine for the purpose of uniting them with Corigan.

With the young King Travensworth missing, his kingdom under siege, it put those she loved in both kingdoms in harm's way and threatened to change the paths of their lives forever. It was unknown whether the King still lived, though whoever was in charge of his military forces plainly had plans to stay and may well march them upon Dorengar. Those willing to speculate believed King Venderlay to the North had taken control of Travensworth's kingdom, that his sending his daughter to marry the young King had been a ruse to work his way in. He was known as a power hungry monster who would go to any extent to get what he wanted. Nema shuddered remembering the one time she'd met the man. At only fifteen, already having taken on the characteristics of the beauty she would become, she'd found herself in a near compromising situation, not of her own accord, of course. Had it not been for her uncle, the current Travensworth's father, Venderlay would have had his way with her.

"She wears the sign of the marking, Venderlay," her uncle had said, his voice icy even as he wrapped a gentle hand around her arm to move her behind his formidable frame. "Would you jeopardize the uniting of my kingdom with Andorak's to satisfy your lusty needs with an unskilled girl when many beautiful and available women reside within the chambers of the Ladies of the Courts?" The elder King's voice had been as smooth and as sharp as cut glass. "I didn't think a wise man would make such a mistake," he'd said without giving the other man a chance to answer. "I demand you take your leave of my castle at once lest I be tempted to give you what the law allows for attempting to compromise a marked woman, since you know well that she lives under the law of another kingdom." With that he'd turned, tucked her arm in his and led her from the corridor back into the hall filled with guests enjoying holiday festivities.

He never asked how she'd come to find herself in such a position, though from that day forward, a corisan had been assigned to be with her at all times. She knew his words to Venderlay were not idle threats. He was as ruthless when necessary as he was filled with a compassion that was rivaled by none in his position. Always having treated Nema as if she was his own daughter, a bond had formed between them that had been unbreakable until his death some fifteen years back. That bond had made her inability to conceive and produce the heirs that would unite their kingdoms that much harder. The elder Travensworth, having experienced the woes of infertility for many years, had never seen her as a failure.

"You may not carry the children, but your blood, your sacrifices still united our kingdoms, my child," he'd told her when he'd come to bless the union of the man for whom she'd been marked and her younger sister, Neria. "Do not forget who you are and what you have done."

She'd been gone from the kingdom for some time before the birth of the King's son, the current king of Corigan. King Garrick Findlay Travensworth was closer in age to Neria and Renaine's sons. There was rumor of another, a son born to her uncle's sister after she'd denounced her royalty and kingdom and taken up with Durant, the leader of the vagabonds living in Corigan's woods. Their son was supposedly closer to Neria's age, though with the death of both her aunt and her mother, she supposed he'd faded away with the rest of the ruffians. He'd certainly never been a part of the family. She wasn't even sure if he was real.

For her, the mysteries of Corigan's people were quickly replaced by the joyful years of helping raise her own sister's children. She'd refused bitterness at her plight, choosing instead to gracefully accept her situation and make the best of it. She'd been the one who demanded to step down, relegating herself to a position as second with her sister claiming all rights as if she'd been the one marked with her warrior's blood.

In the early days hope had remained that she would still bear his child since he continued to visit her bed—which he had every right to do. Her need for fulfillment through her own children diminished with each babe born from her sister's body, and today, pride filled her as she watched the firstborn leading the warriors toward their King. The likeness of his father in his youth, Tahruk had indeed grown into a man deserving of honor. He was the epitome of elite with his superb looks and muscles trained and toned through hard work. All that was paired with superior fighting skills and reasoning that catapulted him to the top position.

Nema chuckled as she looked toward the young woman at her side, noting how completely enamored she was by the sight of the man whose blood she carried. She glanced at the King, wondering if the sight of Elenya reminded him of the Daughter of Damalenya that had captured his heart. If memory served correctly, she had been marked for another just as surely as he had a Chosen yet to come of age. Nema felt certain that repudiated desire had fueled his fierceness upon the battlefields and within the halls of the court for many years. He'd always led with a strength that made him nearly as mighty as the man who now commanded his military.

As the men drew in before the King all attention turned toward them. Tahruk raised a hand and the flag bearers to either side of him lifted their flags to stop the progress of the military grouping fifteen men wide and at least 300 rows in length. In unison, the armor of nearly 5,000 rattled as the mass of men covered the crests over their hearts with closed fists—a sign of loyalty to their King that caused the onlookers to erupt in a deafening chorus of cheers.

With a signal to his own flag bearer, the King's crested flag was raised. The crowd silenced, suddenly anxious for his words.

"We have reason to believe the enemy has come from the North, just as it has tried before. It appears most probable that Voringlok has laid siege to Corigan, turned our brother's own men against him, and now they ride against us. We know not whether King Travensworth lives, but by the grace of God almighty, this travesty will… not… stand!"

The roar of agreement from the horsed men as well as the people covering the hillside made Elenya wince. Nema wrapped an arm about her shoulders earning a slight smile from the young woman. She knew her heart rested with the warrior who would willingly give his life to defend his King and Dorengar, as well as those whose allegiance to the kingdom was known. That included his cousin, King

Travensworth, should he still live, and his kingdom of Corigan.

"The men of outlying Drilles and the inland kingdoms have amassed as we have and are now working their way to the rendezvous points where our numbers will nearly double. 10,000 trained men, all swearing their allegiance to the Centrehead." Again, the noise had to quell before he could continue. "The union of Aleone and the forces of our own mighty Zanak have further opened the channels of defense for us," Andorak continued when yet another outburst from the crowd finally quieted. Nema noted the color rising in Elenya's cheeks, especially when the King's outstretched hand turned all others to look in her direction. When her chin fell Nema nudged her, cocking her head in the direction of the warrior who returned her stare for the first time. There was no denying what passed between the young couple when their eyes locked. Nema wondered whether the King had noticed, though the valiant bow of his head when his first warrior looked back toward him told her he had.

"The ships of Aleone have already sailed, for which we are thankful…"

Elenya's head snapped toward the King. She sucked in a deep breath and Nema knew the full reality of this catastrophic event had finally hit the lass, though there was no time to reassure her in any way before orders were given. The men from the King's entourage wheeled about, forming two rows around him. Behind them were four rows of his elite warriors with Tahruk taking the center as their leader. On his orders, the mass began to file from the courtyard, but not before the mighty warrior caught the eye of his bride, his open palm covering the crest atop his heart. Nema watched as Elenya mirrored his movements, the young maid's smile faltering only slightly, her lips twitching with her attempt to hold back the tears that moistened the emerald depths of her eyes. She never looked away, even as the dust swirled around them and died down and people began to leave.

"Not yet, please." She pulled away when Nema tugged on her arm. Nema didn't try to make her go, understanding the desire to watch the men out of sight. As the crowds thinned, the older woman moved away and sat down on the hillside to wait, remembering how she'd felt the first time she'd watched Renaine and the other men ride away. His family had not been so accepting of her, had not welcomed her with open arms when she did not conceive in the first few months, acting as if the only thing of importance was producing children.

Was it not? Wasn't securing the bloodlines what the marking was all about? Though the idea of marking was designed to produce such an effect, she wondered just how often the matches result in what had quickly developed between herself and Renaine. She was pleased to see the same thing happening in these children of enemy Drilles.

"Nema?" Elenya broke into the older woman's thoughts.

Nema smiled. "Ready to go then?"

"From here, but may we walk? I'm not ready to return to the Drille just yet," she said, reaching for the hand Nema held out for help up.

With a sigh, Nema looked toward the cloud of dust far off in the distance already. She wondered at what point the King and his son would actually break off from the warriors and return to the castle. Andorak was far too old to ride with his military. His son had recently reached that age, and after an injury, he'd had to leave the battlefields, turning control over to Renaine, which he'd already been doing for the most part for quite some time. The thought twisted Nema's heart and she placed her hand over her chest.

An intense look of worry on Elenya's face caused Nema to stop and hug the girl before explaining.

"Some say watching them go is the hardest part, though for me it's waiting for them to return, and then the thoughts of how soon it will have to happen again." She smoothed her skirts and turned in the direction Elenya indicated she wanted to go.

They walked quietly for a while until Elenya broke the silence. "Tahruk told me last night the King's oldest son, Renaine's father, died on the battlefields many years ago. Since our King no longer commands his army, does that now fall to Shenai, and who takes over when they're all gone?" Elenya's interest, Nema knew, stemmed from her concern for her warrior and for her children yet to come.

"Renaine actually leads the army right now. Well, Tahruk does… It's complicated, but it works, especially with those two. I guess you could say Tahruk is the commander of the forces while all final decisions rests with Renaine as the oldest living of the King's bloodline on the battlefield, which places him in that position of honor."

"Honor!" Elenya snorted. "I am so tired of everything taking place for the sake of honor. Our families hand us off to unknown men for the sake of honor so that we may breed strong men who march off proudly, risking their lives to protect the kingdom in the name of honor."

"It has to be," Nema began, "Without honor, you have nothing, and without the marking…"

Elenya cut her off. "No. Without the marking, we gain choice. The honor remains with men that still train and protect. Only they come home to a real home, filled with children that all have the same opportunities whether they're marked or not. And a wife who has counted the days waiting there in anticipation for the man she loves. I am the product of a society without marking. And Shemek… my friend Shemek is a great warrior, as is my father and many other men of Aleone. If not, why would the King invite them to fight with his men? We have all that you have, and have maintained it for many years without the requirements of the marking."

All Nema could do was nod. She had no words to fight against the grandeur thoughts running through the young woman's head. She didn't disagree with them, but knew to fight something that had been happening for century upon century would be a battle of extreme magnitude beyond what any one person could do alone.

"Perhaps you might bend the ear of our King sometime…"

Side by side, the women walked in silence, their heads filled with many thoughts. Elenya was so lost in her own musings she didn't see Tahruk's brother until Nema called his name.

"Redahn!" Elenya jumped with Nema's shrill exclamation.

With a raised brow and a sneer, he looked Elenya up and down before pushing away from the blonde he'd cornered. The maiden scurried away without looking back, no doubt relieved at her good fortune.

"My brother has barely departed and already you've lowered yourself to visit the lowly merchant men in the harbor?" He licked his lips before reaching for an errant strand of Elenya's hair and wrapping it around his finger. "I could make a recommendation closer to home, *my lady*, if you're looking for someone to comfort you."

Elenya shied away as he leaned close, his breath hot on her cheek. The tug to her hair made her wince and Redahn laugh, garnering a cluck and a glare from Nema.

"Though we owe you no explanation, if you must know, your brother's Chosen has a desire to visit the docks and take in the familiar sights and smells." She took Elenya's arm and tried to push past the younger Sharanis.

"I'm sure she has need of many things." He halted their progress with a hand on the young woman's other arm. "Why she'd look for it here escapes reasoning, if you ask me."

Elenya bit at her lower lip, standing captive between the two.

"No, you wouldn't understand homesickness, would you?" Nema tutted at him.

Redahn paused and cocked his head. "No, I suppose I would not, though I do know what the shores of Aleone are like." He stared down at Elenya. "Never before have I seen fields so lush or rooms of tables laden with finer linens. And the fish along the coast provide a plentiful catch to fill the bellies of people supposed to be anguishing in exile."

Elenya ignored his rub. "Why would you have visited Aleone? One would think I would have at least heard stories of visitors from an enemy Drille being entertained within our walls."

"How many male visitors were you aware of who lodged inside the walls of your Drille? I can't imagine you were made privy to their company. No, they would have kept their precious jewel hidden from the outside world lest she become spoiled and worthless to them."

"Redahn! Behave as a man of honor should toward the woman marked with the blood of his brother."

"Honor? You wish me to behave in an honorable manner, Nema? What honor do I have left?" He shook his head, strands of his dark hair drifting onto his forehead. He freed Elenya to push them back. "My honor was taken when they pulled me from the battlefield instead of letting me die."

"You are every bit the man you were, Redahn, if you'd choose to be," Nema countered

"Ha! What good is a warrior who can't fight?"

"You have your mind, do you not? I have no doubt you'd be excellent with tactics and even better as an ambassador to other Drilles and kingdoms. You can be quite charismatic when you choose to do so." She raised a brow at his scoff.

Redahn shook his head. "I was born a warrior, bred to fight."

"Not all men within the King's guard fight. Look at your uncle, and even your father now…"

"Old men!"

"Old!" she scoffed. "They're both brilliant men, integral parts of our military forces."

Redahn was quiet for a moment, staring off at some unknown point. "I rivaled my brother alone as the King's best. His position would have belonged to me, eventually. Everyone knew it." He paused. "It's all I ever wanted…" Realizing his inner demons had shown themselves, he moved to flee.

"Leave it, Redahn. Do not let the disappointment and bitterness define your future," Nema called after him.

He stopped and turned back toward them. "You know what it feels like to bask in the shadow of one living within the position you desire, Nema. How can you not feel any bitterness knowing the man whose blood flows through your veins removed you to fulfill his duties through another? The shadow of second is a dark and lonely place." He lifted his chin, and with nose in the air he sniffed. "My brother should have taken care to assure his duty fulfilled as well lest he find that opportunity swept away." He laughed at the stricken look on Elenya's face, the spiteful noise fading slowly with his retreat.

"Lord help that boy," Nema whispered as she turned back to Elenya. "Elenya, love?"

"Oh, Nema. I don't feel well."

The only warning sign given before Elenya slumped against Nema was the color draining from her face. Lowering her as carefully as she could to the trodden path at her feet, Nema called for help which came in the form of Redahn's quick return. With little effort, he lifted Elenya, though not nearly as tenderly as Tahruk had the night she'd run. Nema remembered the majestic look of the warrior walking into Zanak with the girl nestled against his chest. She'd been a sight with her shredded dress and scrapes to her delicate flesh. And the tear stains on her perfect cheekbones—they'd touched Nema's heart. She'd sensed a kindred spirit with her and she had no doubt in her now that she loved this young woman every bit as much as she did the children of her sister and the man for whom she'd been marked.

Chapter 26

For the second time Elenya woke in a strange bed within the walls of Zanak.

"Where am I?" She tried to sit only to be hit with a wave of nausea that put her down again.

"Be still, love." Nema moved quickly to her side, settling softly on the bed. The coolness of her hand was soothing when she slid it over Elenya's forehead and cheek. "You don't feel warm," she said, speaking more to herself. "Though your stomach is tender?"

Elenya nodded only to wish she hadn't. Even the slightest movement made her fear her breakfast might reappear. "It seems some illness has overtaken me," she told Nema before closing her eyes again.

Nema's chuckle had her eyes popping open again. Elenya frowned. "Forgive me, love, though I thought you would have realized what has your stomach churning has nothing to do with the ills."

Elenya didn't understand. All she knew was that she felt awful. She asked for one of Nema's tonics to make her feel better.

"Of course I have them, though I dare not give anything to you."

"Why not?"

"Because the young master would have my head should any harm come to his child."

"I'm not a chi…" Realization bound her tongue. She touched her belly. "Do you think…"

Nema nodded.

"Oh, Nema! Truly?" Ignoring her digestive distress as much as she could, Elenya pushed herself up in the bed. Hope warred with fear as she tried to remember what she knew of women newly with child. What had she felt the last few days? A loss of balance a couple of times, and an upset stomach. She'd blamed that and her tiredness on sleepless nights she'd spent in her lover's arms.

"But Redahn said…"

"Redahn!" Nema swatted the air before her face. "Redahn knows what to say to get a rise. He's a master at ruffling feathers, that one is."

Elenya returned the older woman's smile, her lips setting into a content line. Closing her eyes, she settled against the tapestry covered wall at the head of the bed.

"Where am I? Surely not in my lord's chambers, though I am sure there are many rooms there that I have yet to explore."

She was surprised when Nema told her it was her bedchamber. The walls draped with dark silks and tapestries, the heavy furnishings, all seemed more masculine than she'd have envisioned for the colorful woman who seemed to have taken her into her heart from the time they met. She thought about Redahn's words.

"You were the Chosen among your people? Yet you live in this household as a servant?" Forehead crinkling with her thoughts, Elenya sought to understand.

"Not a servant by any means, though it's a complicated story. Perhaps best left for another day."

Elenya shook her head, gently so as not to upset her stomach which had settled again for the moment. "Please,

Nema. Tell me. I need to understand why the man for whom you were chosen would deny you the right to carry his children?" She struggled with her feelings, hovering between disgust and hatred toward someone she didn't even know.

"My warrior… he didn't remove me," Nema began, her words delivered haltingly. Elenya could tell she was thinking hard about what she would say. She coaxed her on by reaching out to take her hand. "I was the eldest daughter of the kingdom of Corigan."

"The kingdom they ride to defend? Lorded over by Travensworth?" Confusion continued to cloud her green eyes. "I remember the talk at dinner about how the bloodlines had crossed kingdoms in Neria and Renaine's case. But… Are you saying they were not the ones matched to unite Corigan?"

Nema nodded. "It was back when Garrick's father was King. A wonderful man..." She shook her head and smiled. "Yet another story for some other day." They both laughed. "Yes, my marking was to unite the kingdoms, did unite them, just as your marking dissolved Aleone's exile. Only, I was unable to produce an heir to secure the bloodlines between the kingdoms. I loved King Travensworth as a father, and wanted nothing more than to provide that alliance for him, so I suggested my sister become the mistress of Renaine's household."

"Lady Neria is your sister?" Suddenly more pieces fell into place.

Nema nodded again. "Neria's needs have always been simple. She's never harbored designs that life would bring love beyond that provided by her family. Her dreams were centered more around societal prominence, leaving her more than willing to take on the role as the head mistress of the man who might well be King of Dorengar someday." Of course she'd been willing. The situation was perfect for her, Nema thought, remembering how beautiful Renaine had been back then, already the growly bear that he often portrayed. But his position had afforded those within his household status and security well above many. It had been an easy step for Neria from one princess role to another.

She knew it was an odd relationship, especially considering how it had continued. Few knew the depth of the relationship between Nema and Renaine and how quickly it had grown, beginning with the tearful taking of her innocence by a fierce warrior turned gentle lover. She smiled, pleased that his nights home were usually spent with her—a privilege accepted in their society by his position as lord and hers as his second. Though her living in his home, sharing the running of the household and the raising of his children with his pseudo-Chosen made for a unique situation, it was possible only because of the bond of the sisters and their very different desires for what life had to offer.

"That cursed marking," Elenya protested. "You have all given up so much to make this work, Nema. It's not fair."

"Life is seldom fair, love." She shrugged. "Everything worked out for the best." Patting Elenya's hand, she continued, "And the best thing for you right now would be rest." Nema's chuckle accompanied Elenya's bold attempt to voice her need to return to the quarters she shared with Tahruk. "Stay here for now. I would sleep better knowing you're nearby."

Another half-hearted protest had Elenya breathing deeply to stave off another wave of nausea. Nodding, she slipped back down onto the pillows already fighting to keep her eyes open.

"If you need anything, just yell," Nema whispered.

"Thank you, Nema." The final word was spoken on a breathy whisper.

Nema was sure the young maid was asleep before she was out the door. She'd check on her later and have some soup brought up from the kitchen. She hoped her hunch was correct and the lass was carrying Tahruk's child. Their baby would not be Renaine and Neria's first grandchild, but he or she would be the most celebrated, the one whose blood would be drawn or whose body would be injected to carry on the tradition of the marking. Silly, antiquated ritual that it was, she was glad for it. Had it not brought her and Renaine together and Elenya into their lives in pairings that would have otherwise never been imagined?

With one last look at the young woman nestled into the coverlet on the bed she often shared with Renaine, Nema left the room wondering what to do with herself. It wasn't often she found herself confined to her quarters, not that she minded staying nearby in case Elenya needed her. Perhaps she'd do a little sewing. If there was a baby on the way, she would enjoy presenting a gift she'd made herself. She sat down and pulled out the box that contained all she needed, selecting a soft, buttery yellow, one of the finer materials she had, straight from the merchant ships of Aleone.

Chapter 27

Nema must have heard Elenya rousing, the older woman showing up even before the younger woman had fully pushed herself up in the bed.

"What time is it?" It appeared the sun had already set, though Nema wasn't dressed in her night clothes.

"We're about three hours past dinner. How are you feeling? Are you hungry?" Her cool hand felt good on Elenya's forehead.

Elenya sighed, letting her head fall back against the headboard. She supposed she should try to eat something.

Nema chuckled. "Nothing sounds good yet?" The older woman pushed back a reddish curl that had fallen across her charge's face when she'd shaken her head. "Perhaps you could try a weak broth. Cook has kept some warm for you these hours. I don't want to see you grow weak or dehydrated."

Elenya's half-hearted nod caused Nema to smile. "Though not much, please. I don't ever want to feel as bad as I did earlier. I am near thankful my lord was not here to witness my weakness." Her eyes moistened at the thought.

"No doubt you could not have imagined missing him the night of the Dremis when you first realized you'd been paired with the warrior from Zanak." Nema chuckled.

"No doubt." It seemed like such a long time ago. How quickly he had become very much a part of her to the point she already could not imagine life without him by her side. She wasn't sure Shemek had been correct in his statement that the warrior would fall madly in love with her, but there was no doubt about her feelings toward the man. As unique as their relationship was, it would become more so since the official bonding ceremony had been cancelled by the unrest. Elenya knew it didn't matter. He had already completely bound her heart.

She sighed again before pushing back down into the covers to await the soup Nema had gone to fetch, her thoughts deep within the chasm her warrior's absence left within her. A hand on her belly, she pushed away the doubt planted by Redahn and prayed Nema was right that she now carried Tahruk's child.

Chapter 28

The passing of time brought a welcomed end to Elenya's suffering. The nausea lessened and her confidence that she was pregnant grew with the days. Only the derisive looks from Redahn when their paths crossed caused pangs of doubt still. She had taken to spending the majority of her time within Nema's quarters, where she'd remained by mutual, unspoken consent, or in the woman's presence when outside the confines of her chosen sanctuary. She hated the wariness she felt, longed to return to that adventurous girl who had instigated secret missions back home, though she would not trade those days for the ones to come. She caressed her belly hardly able to contain her desire to rush time forward to a time when she would feel her child move, providing her with a reassuring confirmation.

Each afternoon found Elenya retiring to her bed for a short time before joining Nema for a walk to the Great Hall within the Centrehead. She was desperate for word, carried back by the messengers and the wounded each day, of the battle and the warriors who remained on the fields. Elenya's thoughts jumped between the baby and learning how Tahruk and Shemek were doing as well as trying to find out how her family fared in Aleone. Even Renaine garnered her consideration, perhaps more so because she knew how Nema felt about the man than because of any great feelings for him on her part. Other than finally blessing the union between herself and his son, he'd done little to endear himself to her.

Still, he was the father of her beloved and the grandfather of her child, and she knew his skills in logistics and maneuvers were vital to the battle. Even though he was not nearly as young as the majority of the warriors, he was still considered a formidable opponent on the battlefields as well. His loss would be greatly felt among many.

Two and a half months had passed since the warriors of Dorengar had gone to the aid of their brother kingdom. Word had it they'd moved along the Western coast, northward toward Voringlok, with a smaller brigade heading inland to refurbish the men from outlying Drilles, including Aleone horsemen, who fought their way across the country. Aleone's ships were said to have sailed around the lands to renew the supplies of the brigade on the opposing coast. She knew her father, along with Shemek and his brothers, would be among the men from Aleone. So many cares heaped themselves upon her slender shoulders—shoulders that ached for the feel of her husband's hands, his lips…

She shook her head trying to push away the thoughts that served only to fill her with an aching want. Nema reached for her hand as the small group walked in silence, each hopeful the news of the day would be positive.

Close to the edge of the courtyard leading into the Great Hall, a disturbance had the two women stepping back behind the safety barrier erected by the presence of the male corisans who traveled with them whenever they ventured outside the walls of Zanak.

"Cerissa!" Elenya hissed as the blonde woman who'd

had such little regard for her before the Dremis, the same woman who'd attempted to find favor with her husband even before he had fulfilled his duties to her, pushed free of the group at the courtyard's edge.

"Ah!" The smile that lit the celestial features as she stared down at Elenya denoted she was pleased their paths had crossed once again. There was something about the coolness of her look, especially as the woman's blue eyes settled on Elenya's mid-section before flicking back to her face, that had Elenya bracing for whatever was to come.

"Are you well?" The curtness of her question and the silky tone of Cerissa's voice caused Elenya to shiver.

She chose not to answer, turning instead to continue her journey toward the Great Hall.

"I fear word is not good for you today." Her words reaped the expected result and the group stopped. "They're saying the warrior has gone missing along with your father and a group of the Elites."

"What?" Elenya stumbled in her too quick attempt to turn back toward the messenger of news she refused to believe. She was surprised to find Redahn's strong arms her saving grace from a trip to the earth beneath her. Her mind swimming, she turned her head from side-to-side looking for a means of escaping this onslaught.

"Settle, woman," Redahn's voice came as a soft, deep whisper near her ear. "Be still so I might find out what the vixen knows about my family. If you act rashly and fall, no doubt I will be obliged to carry you home. You seem to enjoy that. It's such a pity your little game was wasted on my brother the night you bolted away from him into the dark." The upturning of a single corner of his lips, so much like those of the man she loved, told Elenya her actions would not have gone unpunished should it have been

Redahn's blood that coursed through her veins instead. When she tried to move away he pulled her back tightly against his side. "Now, behave like a good little sister and accept the services offered by your brother in marriage."

She dared not look at him again, opting instead to stand silent and still by his side. Her attempt at taking in the information being imparted to Nema by the blonde temptress was greatly impeded by the fingers that caressed the uncovered flesh of her upper arm. She shivered at the unwelcomed gesture that made her long desperately for her husband's touch. She closed her eyes, wishing it was him by her side.

Cerissa's voice was lathed with indifference as she told what she'd heard of the missing guard. Eighty of the King's finest, handpicked from various Drilles, had been commanded to ride to where they believed Travensworth was being held. The mission that should have taken only a few turns of the moon had played out for over a fortnight without their return. Even though proof had not presented, the worst was feared. Renaine, now commanding the remaining men, had sent out parties to find them to no avail. All eighty men seemed to have vanished.

It was all too much for the young woman who found herself in the arms of her lover's brother after all. With ease he lifted her swooning body while Nema fussed over her.

"Let me take her home, Nema. You go to see what more you may find."

Elenya shook her head and began wiggling out of Redahn's hold. "Please, my lord, no. I wish to continue on. It was simply the heat of the moment. I'll be fine." Feet back on the ground, she placed a hand on Redahn's chest, her other hand coming to rest over her stomach. Redahn's mocking snort at her protective gesture earned him a deserved glare before she stepped away, choosing to ignore completely the less than subtle speculative once over from the blonde maiden. Lips pressed into a thin line, her nose crinkling slightly beneath the squint she trained on the small group, Elenya turned on her heel and began to walk away from them.

"I am fine!" she snarled without looking back. She could care less whether they followed or not. She simply needed to know more before any hope she harbored was completely quashed.

Chapter 29

Elenya jumped at Nema's light touch when she came up beside her, though she continued on undeterred even as the group moved closer. No one spoke until they had maneuvered their way through the throng of people awaiting news of their loved ones. Elenya stopped only when she stood directly before the table holding the crested emblems of the fallen.

"You won't find what you're looking for there, my lady. I've been keeping watch."

She jerked her head in Cerissa's direction despising the fact that the woman always seemed to be meddling in her life. How many times had she found her the guest of Zanak or sitting near her at some event? And now she stood much too close to Redahn. Elenya wondered what her lover would think of the vixen who had tried to seduce him already beginning to work her dark magic on his younger brother. She looked from one to the other before offering a stilted shrug and turning back to the table just before a figure walking toward the area caught her attention. Master Daruh. He was looking right at her, his lips set in a grim line that pitched her stomach into a sea of nausea. Even before he bid her to come, she forced herself to move toward him.

"Master Daruh," she whispered before bobbing a small curtsy when they came face-to-face. Her eyes searched his as her head came back up. Her trembling lips a fitting companion to the questions within the green depths. He nodded, took her arm, and began to lead her away, motioning for the rest of her group to wait. Elenya's heartbeat hitched up a notch. That it could beat faster than it had been surprised her. Again she placed a hand on her still flattened midriff.

"Please, my lord. Tell me…"

Daruh looked at her hand, though said nothing about it. "Your presence has been requested by one among the wounded. He called for you through his delirium and asked again not long ago, but it is not the man for whom you were Chosen." A slight crease marred the expanse between his brows.

Elenya nodded, his answer filling her with an odd mixture of relief, concern, and uncertainty. Her mind whirled with so many thoughts and questions. She prayed whoever she found on the end of her short journey with Master Daruh had not suffered greatly. Though at the top of her concerns loomed her fears for Tahruk. "Is there no news of the missing men?"

Daruh shook his head, a compassionate smile forming on his lips. "Please, do not fear, my lady. We know little, though sometimes that is the best news."

Elenya nodded again, halting at his command at the entrance to the Great Hall turned infirmary.

"I apologize in advance." He paused, looking back to make sure those who had accompanied her to the Centrehead had maintained their distance. "There are visions within that a lady should scarce have to look upon." He breathed deeply, let it out slowly, then scrubbed his wearied face with his hand. "Your… *friend...* he begged your presence. Has called for you throughout the night…"

Shemek? It had to be. "Please, my lord. Take me in,"

she interrupted.

Daruh nodded then handed her a cloth before turning to open the door.

Even before she could see the fallen warriors in the dim light, the smells assaulted her, making Elenya glad for the cloth Daruh had given her. She placed it over her nose before moving further inside. The sounds alone filled her with unease. Muffled moans, whispered prayers, the labored breathing of the sick and wounded… Someone behind a curtain cried out, no doubt in pain as his wounds were cared for. She was unprepared to see so many.

"This way, my lady." Daruh ushered her toward a door in the far corner of the room. "The men whose injuries are not as severe have been moved into the smaller meeting rooms."

Daruh's words brought a measure of relief to her reeling senses. Battle was a fact of life. Aleone's army trained for war and skirmishes, preparing their men as did all the Drilles. They'd even had to defend the shores of Aleone a time or two during her short life. And factions of their guard were often called away to fight alongside the King's men.

Still, she had been unprepared for visions that brought home such reality. She had never been allowed to see the wounded, and those who had fallen in battle were buried on the fields, only their crested emblems returned to their mourning families. She glanced back, her eyes roaming over the sea of men, many slowly dying because of the extent of their wounds.

"War is so pointless," she whispered, blinking back welling tears.

Daruh shook his head. "No, my lady. War is necessary

to defend that which belongs to us. That others believe they have the right to take what we hold dear, without regard, is what is truly irrational."

Elenya contemplated his words. She studied the lines of wisdom etched in his weary face then offered him a smile which he could see only in her eyes because of her covered mouth.

"I believe this young man that awaits you would do well being graced with your sunshine. Though be forewarned. These men do not feel so poorly as to not take notice of the presence of a beautiful lady. You will not be allowed to stay long and I shall remain close by."

"Yes, my lord. Thank you." Elenya's answer was accompanied by her hand dropping to her heart. She sighed, thankful the smells within this part of the hall were not so strong. She was glad to leave the images of death and sickness behind.

They passed by a handful of closed doors before Daruh stopped in front of a room whose door stood slightly cracked. Elenya could hear the voices of the men inside as they talked amongst themselves, though a silence fell over them when Daruh pushed open the door and Elenya stepped in.

"Bring us a bit of entertainment, Master?" one of the men hooted. Amidst their laughter, she caught sight of someone rising.

"Hold your tongue, hooligan. Can't you tell a true lady when you see one?"

Shemek! Seeing him drowned out the retort from the other warrior, though Elenya's smile faded as her friend hobbled toward her, his grin twisted by obvious pain.

"Ya." He stopped in front of her, glancing at Daruh

before taking her hand in his and pressing a kiss to her knuckles. "What a sight for sore eyes you are."

She tried to smile, though his disheveled look, the thick bandages wrapped around his bare torso and across an arm that he kept pressed firmly to his side, chased the gesture away. "I wish I could say the same about you."

His bark of laughter finally brought the upward curving of her lips. "That's not what I meant and you know it. It's just… you look a mess."

"I see you still speak openly, my friend. At least that has not changed."

Instinctively her hand went to her stomach causing Shemek to look down then back at her face.

"All of Aleone has been concerned since we learned of your match, Ya. You're… you're well then?"

"Yes," she responded too quickly.

He searched her eyes, probing her soul for truth. "Ya?" he whispered, leaning in to pursue his questioning. "He hasn't hurt you, has he?"

"No. No. Not at all. He is a fair man, Shemek. He is." Her voice softened as did her features when she spoke of Tahruk. "It's just… it's difficult being away from home, away from my family. And with all the turmoil and not knowing when we will be reunited…"

"And your concern, Ya? Does it lie with your family or with *him*? No doubt you know of the missing men?"

Elenya stiffened, stepping back slightly. "I've been informed. Just." She frowned, confused by his tone. "Though I've been told not to be overly concerned."

His eyes bore into her. "How can you truly care for him, Ya? This… this *man* from the family that sent Aleone into exile in the first place? He's your enemy, a trained killer. I know, Ya. I fought beside him on the fields," he hissed.

Elenya shook her head, the vigor causing her curls to sway unsteadily. "No, Shemek. He's a warrior, trained to kill or be killed. Just like you."

"No warrior should find glee in taking another man's life, and yet I witnessed his smile as he thrust his sword through another man and the whoops of enjoyment when his battle-ax came down on his victim's neck."

"Do not mistake zeal for pleasure, my young friend."

Both Elenya and Shemek turned to an older man dressed much as Shemek with a bared torso revealing scars of battles past as well as the dressing of a newer one.

"You should be proud of your warrior, my lady. The man is magnificent, fighting with both purpose and conviction. He has the strength of many men and the singleness of mind to persevere. The King should be grateful he is among the men who rode out with the smaller group. If they do not perish, it will be in no small way due to that man alone." He squinted his eyes and pointed at Shemek. "Why, if not for him, you would not be here, lad."

"This is not your discussion, old man," Shemek barked at the older warrior. It was rather obvious this information imparted to Elenya was not something Shemek wanted shared with her.

"He saved your life, Shemek? And yet you would speak ill of him? Why?" Her eyes implored him, trying to understand.

"I can't believe this! You're in love with him, aren't you?" She shushed his raised voice when Daruh looked at them. "He wants one thing from you, Elenya, and that only because he is forced, unable to control his needs because of the marking. Once you have produced his family's heir he will turn from you because you are his enemy."

She pulled away, anger and sadness churning her

insides. "Master Daruh, I must go now. I do not feel so well."

"Just like that, you're leaving? Are you choosing, Ya? Putting this man you do not know above our friendship? Did you not feel anything…"

"Be silent, Shemek! Your lips speak foolishness." She hissed a whispered warning as Daruh approached. Forcing herself to relax fists clinched at her side, she placed her hands on Shemek's shoulders and leaned up to kiss his cheek. "The choice was made for me even before I was born. You said so yourself—my destiny is one of sacrifice." Her quiet words were for him alone. "Be well, Shemek." And with her parting pat to his shoulder, she turned and stepped out into the hall.

She could feel Shemek watching her walking away.

"You weren't supposed to give him your heart, Ya. He'll only break it, you know," he yelled at her as she neared the end of the hallway. "Those kind of men always do if you let yourself fall for them. You'll see. If he returns at all."

Daruh stopped, motioning for one of the nurses to go to Shemek. Turning back to Elenya, he apologized. "Please, my lady, pay him no mind. The pain and the drugs often make the wounded say things they shouldn't."

She nodded and looked back, noticing another wounded warrior around the same age whispering to her old friend as he urged him back into their room. Beginning to move, she went through the outer hall without even bothering to cover her nose from the stench. Her one thought was to get out and away from her old friend.

Friend. She wondered if she could even consider him that anymore.

Blinded by the bright light as she burst through the door, she nearly toppled, saved once again by the strong arms of Tahruk's brother. She looked up at him as he steadied her and was surprised to see concern flit across his face before his mask of derision slipped firmly back in place.

"You'd best be careful, my lady, or I may begin to think my arms are a place you wouldn't mind being."

"I'm sure your brother would enjoy hearing your theory of where his Chosen would like to be. Unless you also intend to try to convince me he's not returning," she countered in a less than friendly tone, then took her hurt out with a slap to his chest as she moved away.

Redahn looked from her to the Great Hall before turning and falling in at her side. "Were you told otherwise inside? Why did Daruh take you in? What was said?"

"Nothing," she snapped. "And his reasons are none of your concern."

"All things pertaining to my brother are my concern." He grabbed her arm, halting her progress toward the small group waiting for her under a nearby shade tree. Turning her to face him, he forced her to look up at him and studied her green eyes. Satisfied, he released his hold and they continued toward the others. "I'm not afraid for my brother, and you shouldn't be either. He has a knack for all things working out for him in life."

Elenya thought about his words. She contemplated her warrior's brother, realizing he'd given her a glimpse into his true nature, as had Shemek. She tried to come to terms with how she felt about her old friend and the unseemly way he had acted. And also with what he'd said about Tahruk. Where did the truth lie? No doubt reality fell somewhere in between.

"I find comfort in your words, my lord. Thank you for that. It was quite… brotherly," Elenya told him just before they reached the group.

"Brotherly!" Redahn's hooting laugh caused more than just their small group to look in their direction. "Do not misjudge me, my lady. I assure you the thoughts I have of you are anything but brotherly. Though, if comfort is what you desire, I'm certain something can be arranged between the two of us…"

"Thank you, no." She rolled her eyes and stepped back from his reach just before Nema grabbed her hand. She glared at Redahn over her shoulder, resisting the urge to stick her tongue out at him before turning back to Nema and touching her stress-worn cheek. "Don't worry, Nema. They know little, though sometimes no news is best," she repeated Daruh's words before giving the older hand a comforting squeeze.

What had Nema said? The waiting was the hardest part, and then once they return, you wait and wonder when it will happen again. She thought about that as they turned for home, wishing this part of the waiting period was already over, wishing she'd had more time with her warrior before he'd gone so that she might be assured of her position in his heart. She silently cursed Shemek for acting as he had and filling her head with doubts and concerns.

Chapter 30

Three Month's Later...

Waiting became an even more unwelcomed visitor as the leaves turned, signaling the advancement of time. Elenya's worries increased along with her midsection, though some relief had come with the first movements of the baby. She now spent her days watching Nema prepare the garden for cooler weather while she sat at the very table where Master Daruh and Renaine had first spoken of the conflicts that had taken her lover away. To occupy her mind, she'd added page upon page to her journal, writing about everything from her arrival at the Centrehead to how she felt when she realized she'd been paired with Tahruk as well as her devastation when the turmoil took him away so quickly. She'd recorded everything about her pregnancy in hopes that she could someday share it with Tahruk, making him feel more a part of this special time. It was a calming tonic to an otherwise relentless string of waiting.

With a satisfied smile, she closed the book and leaned back in the chair to watch Nema move among the flowers and vines. Elenya sighed, so thankful that Nema was there. She'd have been surprised at how quickly she'd come to love her, every bit as much as her own mother, if it had been anyone but Nema. Without her, she was quite certain she would have gone mad while they waited. Some days the melancholy was near unbearable and there were nights when her dreams were plagued with fear Tahruk would not return, or that something would happen to their baby. She dreamed of never seeing her family again, or of that awful encounter with Shemek. And when she would cry out, Nema was always there to comfort her, whether it be with stories of assurance or to sit by her bed until she fell back to sleep.

Elenya watched her, knowing she had to have concerns of her own, and yet she remained solid, taking care of everything, her confidence in their return never wavering. She was a true pillar of strength within this family, taking on the duties as household mistress when Neria seemed remiss to do so. Had fate not seen fit to keep children from her, Nema would have the title to go along with all that she did. Elenya placed a hand on her belly, refusing to think of the what ifs.

Neria reached for Elenya's hand and smiled. She'd assured her so many times that all would be well, that Tahruk would return and their child would thrive. She always seemed so nonplussed and certain. Elenya gave her hand a light squeeze and looked back at Nema, her mind drifting to the odd relationship between the sisters. As much as she loved her own sisters, she doubted she could have so gracefully handled sharing Tahruk with any of them. That thought always led to visions of Cerissa and an unwanted dose of jealousy. There seemed to be no jealousy between these women, each accepting her position as an honor bound duty. They both seemed content with where life had landed them.

Elenya caressed the moving bundle beneath her dress and wondered if anyone besides the baby had heard her growling stomach. She chuckled when the servants beginning to arrive with the trays of cold meats, cheeses, fruits, and breads for lunch, almost as if the sound had been a dinner bell.

"I think I'd like to walk down to the harbor this afternoon," she told the two women as they ate. Neria agreed that it would be a wonderful idea. Nema was a bit more hesitant.

"I know you miss the sea, but please do be careful down there. Make sure you have at least two corisans with you. And don't stay long. It's a farther distance. It wouldn't do for you to wear yourself out."

Had it been anyone but Nema, Elenya would have graced her with one of her placating smiles and a hidden eye roll. Pursing her lips, she looked away.

"You do not appreciate my concern?" Nema asked with a quiet chuckle.

Elenya's face reddened before she laughed. She shook her head. "Actually, your concerns made me think about my childhood, how growing up there were so many restrictions. It seemed the job of everyone to protect the Chosen, when all I wanted to do was run free and wild." She laughed a little, and tipping her head down lest she meet with disapproval, told them how Shemek would sneak her and her sisters out through her window to explore their world. She regaled them with stories that had all of them laughing.

Neria patted her hand at one point and told her every young girl should have the freedom to explore. "Nema and I had our share of questionable outings growing up." She and Elenya both laughed when Nema frowned and shushed her.

"Our mother was the youngest sister of the King of Corigan. There was also an older sister…"

"Neria! Do not bore the poor girl with stories of our lineage." Nema sat back and crossed her arms. It was obvious by her deep frown she didn't really want her sister sharing their ill deeds.

"Oh no. I'd love to hear." Elenya couldn't help herself. She laughed again when Nema shook her head. Folding her hands in her lap, she sat back as Neria leaned closer and began sharing their secrets.

"Well," Neria leaned closer and continued, "This older sister... some thought her a bit touched in the head. She was always wandering off, getting herself into one mess after another. But those are mostly stories for another day. This one involves Nema and me." Neria glanced at her oldest sister then winked at Elenya.

Elenya smiled and shook her head, her brows drawing down. "But… the King's daughter, she wasn't marked, then? Being the oldest and all…"

"Oh no, dear. Corigan doesn't practice the ritual of marking. Nema was the first one, and that was at the request of King Andorak to unite the kingdoms. Now mind you, royalty is still not free to marry whomever they desire. Many say that's why Princess Lauris ran away in the first place. She'd been promised to one of King Venderlay's brothers. The current King Venderlay, Lord Gaius, is not the eldest son of his family, you know." She stopped and looked around to see if extra ears were listening. "There were three sons before him who all died mysteriously," she whispered then nodded slowly when Elenya jumped back with a start. "He is power hungry, that one is."

Elenya felt an added weight settle on her already burdened heart. She placed one hand over it and the other on her protruding belly. The baby squirmed before quieting again. With this ruthless lunatic as their enemy, and knowing Tahruk could well be in line for the throne, Elenya wondered if Venderlay could possibly let her husband live.

The thought that her baby might never see its father had plagued her since she knew for certain she was carrying his child. If she could turn back the hands of time, she would not have wasted those first days, instead allowing herself the pleasures of lying in his arms that first night of the Dremis—a magical night that almost assured conception.

She looked at Nema. It hadn't assured a baby for her, though Neria and Neria's children had no problems conceiving, it seemed. Could it be possible their father was not one and the same? Or maybe she had a different mother. That would make more sense even if not quite as exciting. Elenya chastised herself for liking the more romantic notion about a clandestine affair between a lonely queen and someone besides the King, a man who allowed her to produce a daughter who conceived much easier than did her older two children.

With a mental shake, she pulled her mind back to Neria's story about Lauris running away and wedding a forest vagabond who supposedly saved her from a band of thieves. How they had a son and lived in a small settlement across a great chasm toward the edge of Corigan. The story said Princess Lauris yearned for her easier life back at the castle until one day she could take it no more and threw herself off the side of a chasm that kept her from going home.

"…and to this day," she was saying, "her ghost is said to still inhabit the settlement. The people abandoned the place shortly after she died." Neria's voice lowered yet again. "I believe there was more to her death than anyone knows." She glanced again at Nema, who seemed completely lost in her own thoughts. "She used to sneak away and visit our mother, Princess Emylene."

She nodded when Elenya's brows shot up.

"How did she get away when they were supposedly unable to cross the chasm?"

Neria shrugged. "That's what we set about to find out one day. We'd heard stories from our mother our whole lives, how she would sneak out to meet her sister. How Lauris would come to her from a secret passage that blended into the hillside, much like our tunnel system blends into the cliffs of the sea."

Now it was Elenya's turn to nod. "Did you find it? The opening, I mean?"

Neria laughed. "Oh no, dear. We never even made it anywhere near the settlement before our voyage was found out and cut short. We managed a ruse to flee our corisans, and elicited the help and protection of some young warriors in training. I scarce care to think of what punishments befell all of them."

Elenya laughed with her before asking, "So do you believe you would have found it? And what if you'd come across Princess Lauris' ghost?"

Nema's quick rise from her seat halted the answer on Neria's lips. "That's it!" The older woman mumbled to herself, obviously lost somewhere other than where she was.

"Nema, dear? What is it?" Neria asked.

"What?" Nema looked at her sister as if she was surprised to see her. "Neria. Don't you see? That's it. That's where they are. King Travensworth, Elenya's father, Tahruk, the others. They're at the settlement. They have to be. It's the only place that makes sense!"

Nema's excitement caused the other women to sit taller. Neria slowly began to nod her head. "You might be right, Nema."

"Before he left, Renaine told me that he'd received

word that the forest vagabonds had attacked the carriages of Garrick's bride-to-be on her way to the castle. They were in search of the jewels and gold she carried to present to the King. Only the King was with them, unbeknownst to anyone other than his second in command. Regardless of who is involved and how, the King and now our men are a part of whatever is going on. Venderlay has already sworn he has no involvement. Whether he is to be believed remains to be seen, but we know someone has taken over Travensworth's kingdom. Whether our cousin is in hiding or captured, I believe the answer lies within the confines of the settlement." Nema turned without explanation and began to leave the garden area.

"Where are you going?" Neria asked her fleeing back.

"To send someone to find Redahn so he may meet me at the Centrehead. I need to speak of this to Master Daruh to see what he thinks of my hunch," she called back before disappearing into the dimness of the stone hallway.

Elenya turned to Neria who stared at the empty opening her sister had gone through. "What do you think, my lady?" she asked.

"I suppose she could be correct, though I'm not sure any of them would have known the way. Because of the hauntings, the vagrants stay away from the place. It's been all but forgotten all these years."

Elenya nodded though she was thinking that might make it perfect, especially for a hiding King, and now for a King and a small brigade of warriors. But why would they be hiding? Even if Venderlay's troops had taken siege of the castle, one would think Tahruk and the other men would still attempt to get word to Renaine to let him know they were okay and apprise him of the reasoning they were in hiding. They really should let someone know.

She felt a momentary jab of anger at the thought of them prolonging the battle, not to mention the men who still fought and died on the fields every day. There was so much about war she didn't understand.

"I think I'll join Nema," she told Neria as she rose from the garden table. "I'd like to see what Master Daruh thinks of her hunch." She leaned down to kiss her mother-in-law's upturned cheek before exiting by the same doorway Nema had used. Not surprising, two large male corisans and Larina, her favorite companion from among the Ladies who acted in whatever capacity Elenya needed, were all waiting for her.

"Lady Nema said you wished to visit the harbor," Lady Larina told her as she fell in at Elenya's side.

Elenya shook her head. "I've changed my mind." Even though she was anxious to smell the sea air, to remove her shoes and stand in the edge of the lapping waves, to feel the spray misting her skin, she had another mission. She told Larina of her new plans. "Besides," she added with a bit of a snort, "Lady Nema is looking for Redahn and it seems when I leave the walls of Zanak, he is never too far behind. No doubt my presence will lure him to her side."

She wasn't sure, but Elenya thought she caught an exchange of shadowed glances between the members of her little entourage. She frowned and pushed her thoughts to all that had been said in the garden, wondering if Nema could possibly be correct. If she was, what would that mean? Would they send troops to rally with the men already there? What of Tahruk, her father, Renaine… Had the elite guard been held up, or had they been captured? If they had been captured, everyone was sure their captors would be gloating over their victory already. They weren't talking about just anyone. This was Dorengar's Elite. No, they were hiding out, waiting, biding their time. But why?

"Are you unwell, my lady?" Larina asked when Elenya released a loud sigh. "It's not the baby, is it? Your lord would have my head if something happened to either you or his child."

Her choice of words reminded Elenya of Nema. She laughed and shook her head. "We're both fine, Larina. And I thought we agreed there was no need for the *my lady* added every time you speak to me."

Larina nodded. The dark curls piled neatly atop her dainty head barely moved with the motion, reminding Elenya of just how proper her companion was. She'd been trained as an unmarked lady from birth only to remain unmatched when the time of the Dremis came, regaling her to a life as a Lady of the Courts. She was not a bad looking woman, though all her training had left her… stiff, standoffish. Elenya knew from having been around her for the past few weeks and also on the trip from Aleone, that she was a sweet, mild tempered young woman with a desire for true romance simmering just under the surface. She would have been perfect for Shemek.

Shemek. Sharing her stories with Nema and Neria had eased some of the hurt from their meeting at the Centrehead Hall. She thought of his words the night before she left Aleone, how he'd handed her the rose with its single thorn, and told her to be strong in fulfilling her destiny. He'd also assured her the warrior whose blood she carried would fall in love with her. Was it not reasonable to believe that she might also fall for him?

Shemek knew her. He could see her feelings for Tahruk in the depths of her green eyes, knew she was carrying his child when he saw her hands splayed across her then still flat belly. He should have been happy for her.

Instead, he'd erupted in anger, making her doubt that her warrior cared. Making her doubt that Shemek cared either.

She wondered where he was. He hadn't tried to get in touch with her even after he was released from the infirmary, though she knew he remained within the Centrehead. There was no way yet to go home and he would be unfit to return to the battlefields until his wounds were properly healed and his full strength had been restored. Perhaps she would ask Master Daruh if she got a private moment with him when they reached the town center.

Larina slid back, walking just in front of the other corisans when Redahn sidled up beside Elenya. "I heard you were headed to the harbor, *my lady*. You seem to have lost your direction."

Elenya twisted to look at Larina, her brows raised in an *I told you so* glance. "Plans change, Redahn. My apologies if your informants failed to deliver the new order."

Redahn laughed. "Oh, I knew of your decision. You know, it's too bad you won't relent and allow me to put that smart tongue of yours to better use." He sidestepped the slap Elenya aimed at his arm.

"Of all the improprieties!" She glared at him for a moment, then crossed her arms over her chest and huffed when he merely shrugged.

"Come now. Can you tell me you don't enjoy sparring with me? I believe you use it to make yourself feel alive, just as I use… other things." He looked back and winked at Larina.

Elenya rolled her eyes though his comment did make her think. She supposed in some ways he was right. It wasn't like there was any way she could deny that Redahn definitely reminded her of Tahruk in intellect as well as looks, even if she didn't feel the pull toward him that she did for his brother. With her warrior, their verbal exchanges were mentally stimulating, and unlike with Redahn, usually ended with physical fulfillment as well. She felt the heat rise up her body, creeping ever higher until it stained her cheeks, she was sure.

"If I didn't know better, I would think you're giving my suggestion added thought, *sister*. Now that would be improper, would it not?"

Elenya's mouth gaped only a second before she clamped it tightly shut, unable to find the words.

"Don't play innocent with me, *my lady.* Your disappearing waistline tells me you are far past that. Though it does appear my words have rendered you unable to fight me. Does that bespeak of your desire for me?" Redahn whispered too close to her ear. She pushed him away and quickened her pace. "Relax, Elenya! I have only the best interest of the heir of Zanak at heart. I'm only thinking of your comfort," he called after her in feigned thoughtfulness. "Surely you know my attentions are always in the right place."

She turned back to see that he had draped an arm around Larina's shoulders. "Leave her be, Redahn. The lady has been brought into the house as my companion, not to find herself subjected to your sordid affections."

"Sordid?" he said under his breath and tightened his hold on the now blushing Larina. He leaned in to breathe deeply of the dark curls on her head. His fluttering eyelids and the sultry smile aimed at Elenya when he finally looked back at her led her to believe he was remembering a time when perhaps her lady assistant had not objected to his attentions. Redahn laughed. "Perhaps my brother's not the man I thought him to be if you still believe what goes on between a man and a woman a *sordid affair*." He raised his brows. "I received no complaints when *this* lady was in *my* bed. There was no attempted escape into a darkened night."

Elenya covered her ears and shook her head. "Enough of this! I refuse to listen to talk of your escapades, and I will never share with you what I have with your brother." Her narrowed eyes raked across the small group before coming to rest back on Redahn. "You believe your conquests lay only in the bedroom now that you're no longer a mighty warrior on the battlefield, Redahn." Elenya ignored the warning flash of his dark eyes. "And when you're not engaging some woman within your chambers, you use your tongue and your intellect to spew venom and inject your pain on everyone else. You and every other man in this kingdom who created these stupid rules think your station affords you the right to use women at your discretion. Whether we are *chosen* or sent to the Centrehead by our families for the *honor* of serving in the beds of the fighting men of the courts, we're marked for your pleasure with no rights of our own." She threw her hands up and huffed in disgust before turning to continue toward town.

"No one stands up and says *this is not fair!*" she called back over her shoulder. "I don't understand why some of you men aren't willing to stand against this treatment of women. Do you not care? What about love? And what of marked women whose warriors fall on the battlefields before they're paired? They're left to a life of loneliness without the ability to ever know a man's touch or to carry their own child. Are we supposed to believe ourselves *flattered* by these injustices?" Again, she shook her head. "These women. They're your mothers. And your sisters. And someday they will be your daughters and your granddaughters. You joke about *my* wagging tongue, Redahn. How about you using *your* tongue for good, instead. Why don't you use your place in society, your position as the great grandson of the King to speak out against this madness and stop this abhorrent behavior against women?"

Redahn, who had long since released his hold on Lady Larina, stepped up and grabbed Elenya's arm. "My brother would have done well to have taught you to quell your tongue among the other lessons he should have given you. Your talk might well land the both of you in trouble, you know. Besides, I never bring a lady into my own bed. It isn't right."

She raised her brows at his final comment, ignoring the cool warning in his tone as well. "You're a fine one to talk, Redahn. What do you know of right? And don't you dare lecture me on what I should and shouldn't say, or tell me what your brother has done wrong. You're not half the man he is."

"And you know my brother so well! You believe because you shared his bed, because his child lies in your womb that you *know* him? You were with him such a short time, Elenya. How many days? What can you possibly know about him?" He shook his head. "We are brothers. Did you forget that?"

She stared at him, their faces mere inches apart. "I share his blood. *His blood*! We are one well beyond our bodies, Redahn. We have been since I was three years old. Did you forget *that*?"

Pulling away, Elenya marched off as quickly as she could. Scurrying to cross the threshold of The Masters' home where she could join Nema and Daruh, she missed the downturn of Redahn's mouth. If she could have read his thoughts, she would have known he believed she would do well to be careful about spreading her ideas and sentiment around. There were those who would not welcome the changes suggested in her disgust of the current way of life and they would stop at nothing to quiet her before her discontent spread unrest to others, especially now that she was carrying a child that might one day be King.

Shrugging at the three corisans who waited behind them in uncomfortable silence, Redahn stepped into the house of the Masters to catch up to Elenya before she reached the room where the others were meeting. He pushed their exchange to the back of his mind, turning his thoughts to seeing whether Nema's hunch was just that, or if there might be merit to her feminine ramblings and what part he would play. Redahn was always looking for an angle that would allow him to show himself worthy, one that would remove him from the shadow of an uncertain future. Just once, he wanted to prove he was every bit the man he knew he could have been had he not been wounded in the battle to protect the exiled people of Aleone.

Chapter 31

Elenya froze at the door to the room where Nema and Daruh and a few others were meeting. Several of them, including Nema, leaned across one of the very large, hand drawn maps kept in the house of the Masters for the purpose of keeping track of the Marked and their warriors. She could hear them discussing the abandoned settlement, knew they were looking for the chasm that divided it from the remainder of Travensworth's Kingdom, though her eyes were riveted to one individual. Shemek.

"Are we to wait at the threshold after scurrying to get here?" Redahn's low voice rumbled in her ear. When she remained motionless, he leaned forward, craning his neck to look at her face. A derisive chuckle rose from his chest, just loud enough for the two of them to hear. "Perhaps you are more fearful of your past than an uncertain future?"

His words had their intended effect. Her eyes snapped to lock with his momentarily, her brows drew down, lips pressed together as she elbowed him back and entered the room. Without looking again at Shemek, she crossed the floor to stand beside Nema, pleased when Daruh stopped his perusal of the map to welcome her with a kiss to the cheek. He pulled her forward, providing a better vantage point to see what they were doing.

"Redahn." The Master motioned toward a particular section of the map. "What do you think? Lady Nema believes King Travensworth and Andorak's men could be here." He pointed at a specific section of land across a water laced canyon a good half days ride from Corigan's Dunover Castle. It's an area that hasn't been well platted, though your aunt remembers stories her mother told about a specific bend in the river. It has to be here." Again, he pointed and tapped the same area of the map.

Elenya watched his expressions closely as Redahn leaned over the table, his eyes darting about on the map, a frown creasing his forehead. "Why?" he asked before straightening and looking to a spot behind them. Elenya knew without turning that he was looking at Shemek. He stared at the other man several seconds longer before turning his attention to Elenya. Eyebrows raised, he addressed the group while continuing to stare at her to the point she felt uneasy and broke eye contact to turn back to the map draped table. "The question we need answered is if they've not been captured, then why would a King hide instead of returning to his castle? And why would our King's best warriors hold up in an abandoned settlement instead of returning the missing King, ending the battle, and coming home where they belong? They have to be in the hands of the enemy." His glare pierced through Elenya when he spoke his last word and she shifted uneasily, waiting for someone to voice the thoughts in her head. Surely one of these men was thinking the same thing she was.

No one within the group spoke up to answer his question.

"Perhaps they're surrounded and can't get out." Elenya stiffened at the sound of Shemek's voice, cringed when she sensed he was moving toward her, though he continued until he stood on the other side of Redahn. Leaning down, he began to study the map. "If the settlement is where you believe it to be, they have two options to leave. One is here." He pointed to the great chasm that seemed to come inward from the sea and run many miles along the edge of Travensworth's kingdom. "If they were unable to cross the canyon, they would have to turn back toward the sea and work their way South." He traced the route with his finger. "If this route was cut off… It's very narrow and wouldn't take much…"

"What about the sea itself? Could they not venture into the water to escape?" Daruh interjected. His voice raised in pitch with his obvious interest in their theories.

Shemek shook his head. "I've heard much about those shores. They're rocky and treacherous. That's part of why the forest dwellers chose this place. They viewed the very things that may be keeping the warriors and the King in as ways to keep others out. They were all points of safety."

The group lapsed into silence, each lost in thought as they studied the map.

"I believe they're unsure as to who the true enemy is and need this time in hiding to ferret out the truth." All eyes were suddenly on Elenya. She looked first at Redahn, then Shemek and Daruh before continuing. "Trapped? These are the King's finest men. They would rather die fighting than to hide away somewhere without a good reason."

"Good point," Redahn answered. "But why not send word and rally more troops to aid in their mission to find out then?"

"Why not, indeed? That's the real question that begs an answer. If your brother or my father, or even King Travensworth himself questions who is behind this… What if it's us and we don't know about it yet?" She ignored the gasps from those around her and continued, "So, how do we go about finding out the truth?"

Elenya had been unable to restrain giving voice to her misgivings about their own King and whether he might attempt to instate his bloodline on Corigan's throne, even though she probably should have. There was also Verderlay, as well as the forest dwellers. Elenya locked eyes with Redahn while she thought, then turned to Nema. "What of the hillside passage Lady Neria mentioned when she talked of your mother and her sister meeting? Once they got to the bottom of the chasm on one side, how did they cross over the water and get up the other side? Is it such that someone knowing that passage could slip in undetected?"

Nema let out a weary sigh and shrugged her shoulders. "I don't know. Our mother only mentioned her sister emerging from the hillside. I don't believe she ever ventured across."

Redahn straightened, drawing all eyes to him. Caressing his chin, he stared off, his eyes moving as if he studied something unseen. "A group of the King's finest, along with Elenya's father as logistics expert, were dispatched to find Travensworth. Our best spies would be with the missing guard." He stopped and turned to stare at Shemek. "Is there someone in particular among the men you've been with lately who would be able to sneak through enemy lines to scout this out for us?"

Shemek frowned, his eyes darting to Elenya. They both knew the other was thinking there was no one better than him. Who else?

After naming a few men, Shemek shook his head. "I am Aleone's top informant. I'm the best at slipping through enemy lines and finding a way in or out… I'm the one who should go." He looked again at Elenya before turning to Redahn, the look in his eyes a mixture of certainty and sorrow.

Redahn studied the younger man with a steady, prodding gaze then turned abruptly to Daruh. "Good. We leave at daybreak then. I'll assemble a small group to travel with us."

A unified "what" went up from the group as Redahn turned to leave the room. Elenya stepped into his path.

"Of all the ridiculous ideas! What could you possibly be thinking?" Her raised voice and rigid posture earned her nothing but a lazily raised brow and lifted corner of Redahn's mouth on one side. "*He* has not yet been released to duty after his injuries." She thrust a finger in Shemek's general direction. "And *you*! Are you not unable to fight after your own injuries healed improperly? And yet you would risk your life as well as that of others?" With a huff, she pushed away tufts of hair that had been annoying her since her hasty walk into town. "Exactly what are you trying to prove?" Hands on pregnancy rounded hips, she stood nearly toe to toe with the battle proven warrior, her shoulders back, head held high with no thought for the audience that watched her behaving quite improperly for a lady.

"Ya."

Shemek's hand on her shoulder was forcefully shrugged off. Her frown deepened, even though her eyes never left Redahn's.

Narrowing his eyes at her, Redahn shook his head. "I owe you no explanation, as you well know," he told her in a low, even voice. "And I do not pretend to understand your anger. One would think you would want me gone as well as attempting to bring your lover home." He paused before continuing, his tone not wavering. "I have no intent to spend the rest of my days away from the battlefield. If this is a way I may serve, then so be it. I would rather die in a show of my allegiance to my kingdom than to watch those who fought for me perish while I sit idly by when I could have helped."

They stared at each other for several tension filled moments before Elenya quietly asked, "If you *all* perish, what becomes of Corigan?"

Redahn's features softened somewhat with the misting of her eyes. He looked down at her hands that now covered the roundness protruding from her midsection. With a shrug, he answered, "My concern is not with my cousin's kingdom, my lady. Rather, I wish to do my part to protect my family—my brother and father, on the battlefield." A mischievous smile began to pull at his lips. "Saving both shall be a mere bonus for me."

Elenya couldn't help the somewhat sad smile that spread itself across her face. "It takes the whole of the military forces for success, Redahn. There are other ways you can help."

Redahn's face was an unreadable mask. He shrugged again, and with his hands on her shoulders, he gently moved Elenya to the side. Without looking back, he called to Shemek, "We leave at sunrise."

Only, before he could leave the room, Daruh's voice brought him to an abrupt stop. "I'm afraid I can't let you do that, Lord Redahn."

Wheeling around, Redahn blasted the Master with an icy glare, his brows lifting in an unnatural, mocking arch. "Excuse me, *Master* Daruh. I don't believe I understood what you just said. Are you now commanding the military as well?"

Daruh, a peaceful man, though not overly small in stature himself, dragged in a hesitant breath and held it for several seconds before slowly exhaling. "You will be unable to accompany the men tomorrow, my lord. Another will have to lead them."

A loud barking laugh tore from Redahn's throat. He took two steps back toward Daruh, stopping only when Elenya's forearm fell across his chest. The look on his face when he glared down at her made her shiver, though she stood her ground. He looked back at the old Master. "And by what authority do you believe you will stop me, Daruh?" Redahn asked, his tone mocking and biting.

"Under the authority I have given him, Redahn." The group turned in unison to see Mordin Andorak, the King of Dorengar, walk through the door with his son, Shenai. After a moment of frozen shock, the men, save for Redahn, went down on one knee, heads bowed, while Nema curtsied as low as she possibly could. Andorak stopped Elenya's downward motion with a hand beneath her elbow. "Rise," he told them all, his steel gray-blue eyes never leaving those of his great grandson. "I have given orders that you are not to venture beyond the Centrehead."

Redahn's mouth dropped open, then closed again as he studied his great grandfather, the question burning behind his dark eyes needing no words.

The King shook his head. "I knew there would come a day when the threat of your inabilities due to old injuries would no longer hold you here. But *here* is exactly where you need to be, especially now." He glanced at Elenya's burgeoning middle, a look that made Redahn's forehead crease grow deeper. "What was it you told the girl? Your concern was in protecting your family?" He leaned closer to the younger man and whispered, "You've done a fine job of protecting her up to now. My expectation is for you to continue, especially during this time of unrest." His own brows now raised, Andorak continued by motioning for Redahn and Shenai to follow him.

The old King stopped in the doorway, looking back at Elenya. "Come see me soon, child. I've heard passing murmurs about your thoughts on the practice of the marking. I'd like to hear what you have to say firsthand," he told her.

Elenya worked to keep her mouth from falling open and her brows out of her hairline. She nodded at him for fear her voice would betray her should she try to answer. Folding her arms across her abdomen, Elenya wished she could follow, knowing it would be in bad form. She'd already exhibited enough of that. Instead, she looked at Nema who nodded, then dipped into a small curtsy before turning to leave the confines of The Masters' home.

Chapter 32

Elenya's every step felt hindered by her increasing bulk and by the thoughts that weighed her down. Redahn was right. She wouldn't have minded his absence. Now she had to wonder what was being said between him and the King. And then there was Shemek… Her thoughts jumped around while her emotions flared. She'd been so angry with Shemek after his outburst in the infirmary, so angry she hadn't tried to seek him out even though she'd secretly wanted him to come to her, to explain. She still cared about him, about them. Seeing him at The Masters' house, behaving more like the man she knew, confirmed that. Their ties were strong. They'd been friends for far too long. Had he not been the first man to ever kiss her?

She paused, her lids closing to veil the heavy emotion that threatened tears and overwhelming confusion.

"Ya?"

As if she'd conjured him, Elenya's old friend was by her side. His scent, his presence, the soft touch to her elbow by a known hand… it was her undoing.

"I'm sorry," he whispered, pulling her in and circling her with his arms, holding her as she sobbed against his chest. "I have to go. You know I do," he told her when her tears subsided and she pulled back to look up at him.

Moving away, Elenya shook her head, a sad sigh escaping her. "Oh, Shemek. Your world is so simple still. If only *that* was all." She sniffled and turned to leave only to stop again. "Don't you see? Whatever happens to my warrior and his family… it all affects my future, my baby's future." Elenya thought she saw a momentary flash of that man she'd witnessed within the walls of the infirmary, though his face quickly softened again. No doubt it was hard for him to see her carrying another man's child, even though it was something they'd both always known she would do.

She stepped forward and touched Shemek's cheek with a gentle palm. "And then there's you, my friend." She moved her hand down to trace the pattern over his heart where her tears had wetted his shirt. "You've been badly hurt. Are you sure you're ready to fight again? I don't know what I'd do if I didn't know you were somewhere sharing this world with me." She looked up into his eyes seeing her own emotions mirrored back.

"Your world is so simple still, Ya." He echoed her words back to her and laughed at her wide-eyed response. "Lord Redahn is right, you know. It is much preferred by all warriors to die serving than to sit in idleness and watch life pass them by. Besides," he whispered leaning in to kiss her forehead, "I don't believe any of us ride out with the intent to die, but rather with the hope of helping others to live. We'll be okay. All of us." He tapped her nose and pushed her away. "I believe your corisans have received quite a show today. Pray they are loyal and your honor is not called into question."

Elenya nodded. If he only knew all they'd seen. She laughed, feeling suddenly giddy in the presence of this man who had all but confessed his love for her under the stars of Aleone. She kissed his cheek, and as she turned, noticed for the first time the presence of the other young warrior who had been hospitalized with him in the back room of the Gathering Hall. She looked to where he stood staring at her, then back at Shemek before tipping her head and turning to leave. "God be with you and the other men," she called back. "The lives of many I hold dear, including yours, rest in your hands."

Shemek watched Elenya, marveling that she had grown even more beautiful during her days within the walls of Zanak. Careful to choose a surefooted path, she made her way to where the trio of corisans waited for her. He saw her smile at Lady Larina and nod her head at both men. He could see by their responses that they were all endeared to her. He wasn't surprised. "I can't imagine anyone not loving her," he said under his breath.

She turned to look back at him one last time before she disappeared into the forest and he waved.

"She's a beautiful woman," the other recovering warrior said once she'd gone.

Shemek nodded. "Perhaps too much so." He added a shrug, which Garin mimicked.

"You still wish she could have been yours?" he asked.

Shemek turned toward his new companion and squinted, looking at the man but seeing into his past. Again he shrugged. "I'll always love her. But that's a creek I'll never cross. Come on Garin. Let's get ready. The morning will be here before we know it." He motioned for the other warrior to follow.

"Your Drille would have done well to teach your lady friend how to hold her tongue. She also seems ill equipped to distinguish between true friends and enemies."

Startled by the voice behind him, Shemek still laughed. He turned to the man who had appeared, undetected, not two steps away.

"She's a smart woman, Lord Redahn." The two men stared at one another. "And aren't you a stealthy one?" With a quirked brow, he added, "Perhaps someday you may have the chance to surpass even me."

Ever the arrogant one, Redahn answered him with a rippling snort. He leaned in and tapped the young warrior in the spot darkened by Elenya's tears. "I know things, my young *friend.* You will do well to keep that in mind." Redahn looked at Shemek, then settled his gaze on Garin before turning to walk away. "Come along, gentlemen. I believe we have much to discuss before you leave."

Chapter 33

Close to a month and a half later…

Tension mounted within the walls of Zanak making every day of waiting for news more unbearable than the last. Elenya felt especially apprehensive as the time of the baby's birth grew closer. She was anxious to have Tahruk back by her side and was hopeful the fighting would end so her mother and sisters might visit her. She missed her family even more as the days of her confinement stretched on. Nothing seemed to occupy her besides the counting of those insufferable days, though she supposed she could take pleasure in the fact that her testiness had succeeded in keeping even Redahn away.

That's what she was thinking about when an excited runner burst through the garden entry exactly forty-eight days after the small group of fifteen men had ridden out to determine what was going on with Corigan's King and the missing men of Dorengar.

"They are returned!" he huffed out, bending at the waist, his hands on his knees as he sucked air after his fast-paced run from the Centrehead.

Nema asked him if they were able to locate the missing men and what they had learned, all the while the boy shook his head, his too long locks sticking to the moisture on his cheeks.

"No, my lady. *Our men.* They are back. The men of Dorengar have returned, or are returning, rather. They were on the outskirts of the Centrehead when I was dispatched."

Elenya sat forward in her seat. "Dorengar?" she whispered almost afraid to believe.

Without waiting for more information, Nema began barking orders to assure everything was ready for the men's return. After lining out the servants, she turned to Elenya who had remained seated, nerves causing the butterflies in her belly to begin a high speed flutter. "I'm going to meet them. I think you should stay here." She motioned for Elenya to sit back down when she started to rise. "I'll send him to you, love, though I'm sure it would take a whole band of warriors to keep him away any longer than he has to be."

"Are you sure they're among the returning men?" Elenya asked.

Nema chuckled. "Of course, otherwise the runner would have been dispatched with different news." She bent to kiss Elenya's cheek before holding out a hand to her sister. "Come, Neria. Let's go bring them home."

Elenya remained in Zanak's main garden unable to concentrate on anything but waiting, the time slipping by at an unbearably slow pace. She knew the men had to follow certain protocol, including a visit to brief the King, before the warriors were dismissed. Still, Tahruk's delay in coming to her grieved her. She was sure her father had hastened to her mother's side at a much faster pace.

Shemek's words echoed in her head, her heart breaking

with each moment that went by, and she crushed the rose she'd been de-thorning to add to the pile of blossoms that already had all but one thorn removed from each. Bereft, she leaned forward, her head down against crossed arms on the table with the tears she'd attempted to hold back breaking through. She wasn't sure if it was her sniffling that shook her midriff or the pressure of her bent body that upset the life within her and set the baby to kicking.

"Shh, my Little One." Her thoughts to her baby were whispered in her ear causing her to jerk her head up and turn to face a slightly thinner, longer haired, yet otherwise unchanged Tahruk. Disbelief colored her features as her eyes roamed over him to confirm her initial assessment. Crouched beside her chair, one arm on the table, the other around the back of her seat, he smiled at her.

"Oh. My lord," Elenya whispered, finding her voice at last, even if her vocabulary was lacking. "Oh." She cupped his face between her palms, reveling in the feel of him beneath her fingertips. She touched his arms, his chest. She just needed to feel him, to assure herself he was really there.

Tahruk laughed, though quickly sobered at her next words.

"I thought you had chosen not to come back to me." Her hands fell to what little lap she had left when he stood abruptly. Confusion and concern replaced the relief of the moments before.

"I had to speak to the King, and… my father suffered an injured arm in their final skirmish. I had to assure he was settled."

"But, he's okay?" Elenya was almost afraid to ask.

Tahruk nodded. "Nema and my mother are both cosseting him as we speak. It's just all been…"

His eyes held such heaviness from all he'd gone

through the past few months. When he turned away without finishing, Elenya moved from her seat and went to stand behind him, slipping her arms around his waist and leaning her head against his back. He turned in her arms and encircled her with his own, his chin resting against the top of her head.

"Oleander." He breathed in deeply. "That scent wafting through the settlement was all that kept me going some days," he told her. She knew by the husky sound of his voice it wasn't so much the flowers' essence, but their scent on her that had sustained him.

Elenya leaned back to look at him, the action causing her belly to press against him more firmly. The baby's kick exacted a surprised hoot from the warrior who pushed her back some.

His eyes wide, he dropped to his knees, both hands splayed over the round mound that moved beneath his touch. They both laughed. "How soon?" he asked after several awed moments of simply taking it all in.

"Very soon. The midwife said yesterday she expected four weeks or so," she answered as he rose and pulled her back to him.

"Son or daughter?"

Elenya laughed again, thrilled at his excitement. "Oh, heavens! Who can know such a thing until the child is born? Though if I had to say, I would say you had a son simply because of the strength of the imp's kicks. He is a feisty one!"

Placing his hands on both sides of her face, Tahruk held her firmly yet gently as he gazed into her eyes. "Being away from you was the hardest thing I have ever done," he whispered before closing the distance between them, his lips brushing hers softly at first then becoming more demanding. Clinging to his waist, she leaned into him as best she could.

"I missed you so," she breathed against his neck when he finally broke the kiss, his arms tightening to keep her close.

"Did you miss me as well?"

"Redahn!" The word sounded very much like a swear.

Redahn tutted at her and shook his head. "I suppose it wouldn't do to have you giving me the same welcome you gave to him, even though it's been me who has kept you from getting yourself into trouble all these months."

Elenya tensed, her forehead crinkling in irritation until he pushed away from the garden entry. She relaxed slightly, thinking he meant to leave. Instead he crossed to the table where she'd been seated when Tahruk arrived.

"I will not miss your lack of attention in the least now that your brother has returned home, Lord Redahn," she quipped, crossing her arms awkwardly over her belly when Tahruk nudged her toward the table. Reluctantly, she took a seat near her brother-in-law, where she glared at him in open disdain.

"I see my time away did nothing to bring the two of you closer." Tahruk's chuckle caused her concerns to fade away. Her husband was home! She sighed and smiled in Tahruk's direction, earning her a snort from Redahn that she ignored.

"I hear thanks are in order for watching out for her, Brother," Tahruk said while absently removing two glasses from the tray brought in by a serving girl. He jerked back after placing one before Elenya, surprised by the glare she leveled on him.

"It was *you* who set him on my tail, then? Next time please forego doing me any favors, thank you." Her nose crinkled and her lower lip jutted out.

"Not me!" Tahruk threw up his hands in a defensive stance. "You may blame our great grandfather for your troubles, my lady."

"King Andorak? Seriously? Why in the world would he do such a thing?" Elenya asked, shaking her head in disbelief.

A look passed between the brothers that she didn't understand, though the arrival of yet another servant pushed all thought of it from her mind. He shifted impatiently waiting for one of the brothers to acknowledge him so that he might deliver the note he held in his hand. After more brotherly bantering, Tahruk finally reached for the note and unfolded the parchment. A secretive smile covered his face as he read. The occasional glance at Elenya told her the note must have something to do with her. She frowned, waiting for him to finish.

"Tell them I said yes," he told the servant after he refolded the paper and slid it down the table farther away from Elenya.

"Well?" she asked, her brows lifted impatiently.

"I do believe you grow more testy by the day, Elenya. Perhaps now that my brother is home you'll relearn what it takes to relax," Redahn declared with an air of indifference that caused her to stick her tongue out at him.

Again Redahn tutted at her. "I thought we'd talked about better uses for that tongue." He wiggled his eyebrows at her, earning him an eye roll and a growl.

The corners of Tahruk's mouth twitched as he ran a hand down her arm causing her to shiver. "Perhaps she's tired, Brother. I seem to recall our sisters claiming discomfort as the time of their babies came closer." He leaned close enough Elenya could feel the warmth of his breath on her ear and cheek. “Perhaps we could return to our chambers to rest before our special guests arrive. Would you like that, my lady?” he asked her quietly before nuzzling her neck.

Elenya’s body tensed as a familiar tingle engulfed her, making her forget all about the contents of the note or the guests he mentioned. She turned to look at him with the realization of just how quickly breathing became difficult in his presence. “Yes,” she answered on a whisper, already sliding to the edge of the chair so she could rise. Tahruk stood and offered assistance with a hand beneath her elbow. He pulled her close to his side as soon as she gained her balance.

Redahn snorted and reached for the abandoned note only to have Tahruk grab it before he could get a hold on it. “All in good time, Brother. All in good time.” Tahruk laughed turning back to Elenya.

“You’d better consult with your elders to make sure the *rest* you have in mind is okay for a *lady* in her condition,” Redahn called after them.

“Is it not okay?” Elenya could be heard asking as they walked out of the garden.

“It’ll be okay,” Tahruk assured her.

Redahn’s laughter echoed through the halls after them.

“I’ll need to go by Nema’s chambers to collect some of my possessions, my lord. We can ask her then,” Elenya told him, fighting to concentrate with the feel of his fingers stroking her neck and shoulder. “I can do that later.” She gasped when he began to trace the line of her collarbone.

“I’ve already taken the liberty of moving your possessions back to our chambers,” he whispered when he leaned in to kiss the delicate flesh behind her ear. “Nema reluctantly released you to my care in exchange for my father. She'll have him close by in case he needs anything, though I believe his wounds are more superficial. But, do tell me, Little One. Why did you move in the first place?"

She turned to him just outside the door to their chambers. "I collapsed by the harbor the day you left and awakened in Nema's chambers. She suggested I stay, and I wasn't opposed."

Tahruk had already folded her in his arms and was removing the pins from her hair, brushing his fingers through the length of her thick, reddish tresses. "Were you unwell then?" he paused to ask.

Elenya smiled, her jutting belly bumping into him. "Not exactly. It seems your child merely wanted to make his or her presence known."

They both laughed before he kissed her quickly and pushed them through the main door of their chambers.

"Besides, the thought of being alone in this place, without you, was more than I could bear," she told him, caressing his face. "Without you, they were just empty rooms that reminded me of the emptiness in my heart that is only filled by you."

Tahruk wasted no time in crushing her to him, his mouth covering hers while his hands molded her to him as much as possible. Without thought to whether it truly was okay, he easily scooped her up in his arms and carried her to the bedchamber where their child had been conceived, a place that would always be a reminder of the love that had hastened to bloom between the two unlikely lovers.

Chapter 34

Elenya swiped at the hand that attempted to wake her, unappreciative of the gentle shaking of her body. She was dreaming her warrior had returned, that they had made the most beautiful love, and she didn't relish the idea of waking to an empty bed and aching heart. The warm lips that pressed against her bared shoulder and the gentle hand that swept down her body had her awake instantly, however. She sat up too quickly, then clutched at her side as a cramping pain ripped through her, forcing her back onto the mattress. She breathed through it, though the horror stricken warrior—a man who had seen much worse on the battlefields without ever flinching—hovered over her until the pain subsided and she was able to assure him she was okay.

"I have much to learn about women and babies, I'm afraid," he told her. Elenya nodded and attempted to pull the covers back over her only to have him pull them away. "We have to hurry, Little One. Special guests are coming to dinner and we are already late."

She remembered the note and realized the requests from these guests to join them must have been inside. "Who's coming?" she asked, rising quickly and beginning to twist her hair up.

Tahruk smiled and she blushed when she realized he was watching her move, unhindered by clothing, about the room. "I enjoy this more confident side of you, my lady," he told her moving to stand behind her, his arms wrapped around her caressing her bulging midriff. "You are too beautiful for timidity."

"My lord," she whispered. "If you keep this up, I will be unable to attend dinner. Then what will your special guests think?"

Laughing, he spun her around. "They will be disappointed, no doubt." He tapped her on the nose before turning away. "As will you."

Elenya frowned at his back. "Will you not at least give me a hint?"

Tahruk shook his head. "Get dressed, quickly, and you will know!"

Elenya sighed and then shrugged her shoulders before turning her attention to doing exactly as Tahruk bid. Redahn had been right. Spending time in her warrior's arms had relaxed her too much to even muster the strength to spar with him. She smiled as she slipped through the door of the room that housed her belongings. She'd almost forgotten how beautifully her warrior had decorated her rooms, even before he knew her. Her smile broadened. Perhaps he had known her. After all, they shared a bond of shared blood that was unbreakable. She truly had been his since she was three years old.

Pulling up short, her smile fell. For the first time, the full realization of how the marking was supposed to work hit her. It was meant for more than just creating a breeding frenzy when the marked women came of age. It was supposed to forge an unbreakable bond, creating a true union as the two became one through the sharing of blood as well as body. Perhaps it wasn't the marking that was wrong, necessarily. Maybe it was more the way the couples were brought together. It was something she'd have to think more about.

Chapter 35

Elenya cursed the hormonal mood swings that seemed to be growing worse every day. She was thankful to be all smiles again when she finally noticed Tahruk leaning against the door jamb watching her. She suppressed a shiver, standing tall as his appreciative gaze traveled down her body, not unlike his hands had earlier. Even in their made up stories of the handsome warrior, never had Elenya imagined loving a man could be as beautiful and fulfilling as what she'd experienced with Tahruk. She laughed as she went to him and slipped her arms up and around his neck, pulling his face toward hers.

"You are so much more than the man I dreamed of for so many years," she whispered before brushing his lips with hers. She pulled back, confused, when she felt his mouth turn down.

"You had feelings for another?" He quirked a dark brow.

Elenya laughed. "No, my lord." Thoughts of Shemek tried to push in but she refused them. "Only of the man I imagined I had been marked for."

"Good," he told her, cradling her face in his hands. "I do not like the idea of your heart beating for anyone but me." He kissed her gently then took her hand. "Come, Little One. Our guests await. I'm surprised my mother hasn't already sent someone to fetch us."

Elenya nodded. "As am I." She laughed. The months of the men's absence had allowed her the chance to get to know her husband's mother much better. In that way, she was glad for the time. It didn't seem quite as unbearable as it had actually been now that her warrior was home. She hugged his arm, occasionally kissing the firm bicep beneath his shirt as he pulled her out the door and they walked toward the dining hall.

When the voices floating from inside hit her ears, she nearly forgot the man at her side. She stopped, a look of confusion filling eyes suddenly clouded with tears.

"You're not wrong," Tahruk whispered to her. He smiled watching her pull in a shaky breath. "Go on in. He's anxious to see you."

Elenya nodded and hesitated just a moment before moving toward the door. She glanced down at her body then back at Tahruk.

He chuckled and added, "I think he's rather expecting, or at least hopeful, for a noticeable change in your form."

"Thank you," Elenya whispered before allowing herself to be pushed into the dining hall where the large group was already seated at the table.

It only took a moment for the hall's occupants to register the couple's presence and all the men stood, though Elenya only saw one. Her shallow breaths must have concerned Tahruk because he was suddenly holding her tightly to his side. "Papa," she whispered, the tears coursing unhindered down her cheeks, especially as she watched him working to move away from his seat at the table. She swallowed hard, still unable to move as he hobbled from Neria's normal spot. The moment he had cleared the other side of the table, Elenya broke free and ran to him, cautiously throwing herself into his opened arms.

She continued to whisper his name, their arms locked about one another there in the middle of the dining hall. She could feel him kissing the top of her head. His hand stroked down her back, soothing her much as he had when she was a child.

"Let me look at you, my daughter." He pushed her back, smiling down at her through misted blue-green eyes, and dropped a hand to rest with affection on her rounded belly. "All is well?" he whispered.

"Of course, Papa. Now that those I love are safe, everything is wonderful." She glanced over her shoulder at Tahruk, who stood a respectable distance back. Elenya held out a hand toward him. "I take it you have already met my husband," she stated, feeling a bit giddy at the words. Both men nodded and clasped outstretched arms before Tahruk took Elenya's offered hand.

"Your warrior is quite a wonder on the battlefield," Madrik Avenille told her as they moved back to the table.

"So I have been told." She suppressed a frown when she looked at Shemek standing behind the chair next to hers waiting for her to be seated. "You shall have to tell me all about these mighty battles at a more appropriate time, Papa." She wished it had been him beside her so she could take hold of his hand as she wanted to. Always proper, her father had been seated at Renaine's right hand, Neria next to him, and the rest of the table as it usually was. That put Shemek, a special guest, though not as revered as the eldest son, next to her and directly across from Redahn who raised his brows, his eyes moving from Shemek to his brother before settling back on her. How she wanted to wipe the sardonic grin from his face!

"Though talk of battle is best left far away from delicate ears, I must say everyone displayed magnificently during this particular trial."

Everyone, including Elenya, looked at Renaine when he spoke. She'd almost forgotten he'd sustained injuries as well.

"I was most troubled to hear of your injuries, my lord," she covered, though he quickly waved away her concern. Inwardly, Elenya smiled. Renaine was too much of a growly bear to ever let others know the full impact his injuries had made on him. "I'm pleased to see you looking quite well, though if you will indulge me this talk just this once, I would like to know what happened to my father." She watched the look that passed between Madrik Avenille and the warrior at her right hand. She raised her brows when no one answered.

"The short story is we ran into a renegade band of men from Dunover castle after we broke from the main brigade to try to find out what had become of Travensworth." Tahruk explained in brief, clipped sentences of the smaller band fighting their way to the settlement where Corigan's King was held up, leaving out details that would have been considered too much for the company of women, regardless of whether they were at a dinner table or not.

"Your lord helped care for my leg, Elenya," Madrik told her. "Had it not been for him and King Travensworth's *friend,* I'm sure I would have lost my leg to the infection. Thankfully the woman knew the land and the treasures it held, along with their healing effects." He locked eyes with Tahruk. "I am forever and eternally grateful to you for much." He glanced at Elenya then back at the younger warrior.

Tahruk gave a short nod and a quiet answer. "As am I," he told Elenya's father, reaching for Elenya's hand.

Elenya's pride swelled. First Tahruk had saved

Shemek, or so the older warrior at the infirmary had said. Then he'd nursed her father back to health. He really was a hero.

She looked around at the table's occupants. Nema seemed more at ease than she had in a very long time, as did Neria who had begun to graciously engage her father in conversation. Redahn and Shemek talked of upcoming training sessions while Tahruk and his father discussed Corigan. For the moment, the members of the Sharanis family were all back in their element.

Even the baby seemed more settled, perhaps due in part to the warm hand that had released hers and now rested against her belly beneath the table. She smiled at her warrior, her small hand covering his as she leaned her head against his arm. Even the discomfort of being wedged between the only two men who had ever caused her heart to stir fled at her refusal to let it dampen her sense of belonging. She would not let it lighten the mood that would inevitably carry her through a night in the arms of the man who completed her—spirit, soul, and body.

Chapter 36

Elenya's night was all she expected, though her spirits plummeted the following morning when she realized just how little time she would have with her father before he went home. She didn't begrudge him wanting to get back, especially with the holidays approaching and colder weather causing the seas to swell at unexpected times. Still, her heart was already heavy again with missing him, the feeling growing when she learned the *Petit Cadeau* was preparing to leave harbor the next day to return the Aleone warriors to familiar shores, and he planned to be on it.

"Will Shemek go with you?" she asked, almost hopeful her father would nod his head. Shemek had been quite instrumental in aiding in the acquisition of the information that freed the men to return home in the final leg of the battle which meant he would be welcomed at Zanak anytime. Though she'd handled his presence at the family dinner quite well, having him around too much would prove taxing, especially as the time for the baby's birth came closer. She sighed.

Madrik patted his daughter's hand, then held it. "I'm afraid Shemek plans to return to Aleone," he told her, misunderstanding her sigh. "I know you must feel alone here at times, especially with *this* family…"

She shook her head. "No, Papa. It's not the family at all. They've been wonderful, especially having to take in the daughter of a Drille that wronged them so many years ago." She silenced his protest with a waved hand and laughed. "You know it's true, Papa!" He relaxed and she went on. "I miss Mama and my sisters though. Is there… Do you think they might come to see me?"

Silence stretched between them causing Elenya's stomach to churn. Madrik laughed when he sensed her anguish. "We were discussing our trip for your private binding ceremony when the unrest broke out. I'm sorry you had to forego both that and the grand gala at the end of the Dremis. It's said to be a spectacular event, being presented before the King and all. Though I suppose marrying his finest, who happens to be his great grandson, will afford you many an opportunity to be in his presence."

Elenya waved away his concerns and shrugged at the other part of his statement. "I don't mind missing the ceremonies so much. They're but two of many within a lifetime."

Madrik nodded. "So true, but with you always harboring such romantic notions, I was concerned you'd be let down." He laughed at her look of surprise. "Did you think I wasn't listening when you and your sisters played with your dolls before the fire in my study?"

Now it was Elenya's turn to laugh. "You appeared so absorbed in your work." She sat back, gazing off into the past for a moment. "That old rug you brought from Burnos was the best place to play. With all its patterns and colors, it was rather like a mapped out township for our dolls. It was wonderful."

"And yet your mother refused to allow it into any other part of her home." Madrik chuckled.

Elenya smiled. "Our matches, They're most often so unconventional, aren't they?"

Madrik agreed. "But necessary at times for the greater good of the people."

They lapsed into silence for a few moments before Madrik added, "Your new family has extended an invitation for us to join you here permanently."

Elenya nodded and sat forward, her heart beating madly.

"We had such a small amount of time to ponder the offer before I had to leave. There's no telling what your mother has been thinking about and scheming while I've been gone." They both laughed, their thoughts on Senya, the perpetual planner. I feel quite certain she'd have much rather been here with you than waiting without word back in Aleone. I can guarantee she will demand to *see* you and the baby, at the very least."

"Oh, Papa. I hope she'll come, and I hope you'll consider my lord's offer." She threw her arms around him.

"I have. I will. Though I must also consider our Drille and who will lead their forces." Madrik wiped a single tear from his daughter's cheek when she pulled back.

"I'm okay, Papa." She smiled through quivering lips and looked away, garnering a gentle shoulder bump from her dad before she continued. "This ritual of the markings… it's difficult on the chosen women. It's not like you with Mama where you got to meet her beforehand, to take some time to get to know her before you were thrust together. I don't understand why the markings continue to take place. Aleone maintained the bloodlines without it." Elenya turned back toward him, her eyes asking questions she knew he couldn't answer.

"It wasn't that simple with your mother and me either. We did meet beforehand and I was allowed to court her, in a way. But even then, our union had already been chosen."

He smiled. "Thankfully, it worked out. Probably because your mother is very much like you—she has a way about her that makes people fall in love with her." Leaning closer, he whispered, "Besides, without the marking, I have my doubts you'd have found your way into the house of Zanak. You would certainly have missed your warrior, yes?"

Elenya could feel her insides fluttering. Her father was right. Had she not been marked, she would have most likely married Shemek. She shivered realizing her heart truly did belong to the man whose child moved within her.

Nudging her arm again with his, Madrik chuckled. "I have to admit, I was concerned when we first learned of your match. We all were. But he's a fine man, Elenya. Better than most, I believe. And you believe so as well." He nodded and raised a brow, making her blush and look away. He laughed again. "I may be a man, but I still know these things. I see the way you look at him."

Elenya's laughter turned her cheeks an even brighter shade of red. She fanned herself and shook her head. "Oh, Papa. He is fine. Far better than I ever imagined." She paused, her smile flattening somewhat. "It's just… To be taken so far away from home, removed from those you love, then put through The Dremis with those men… That's terrifying for a young woman, and especially when one believes her match must be a mistake. There has to be a better way and I have told the King as much." She covered her swollen abdomen with protective hands and whispered, "I pray this child is a boy." She closed her eyes, her lips trembling again.

Madrik slipped an arm around her shoulders and pulled her close. He kissed the top of her head and for a moment she was his little girl again. "It's good you have married as you did. If anyone might effect change, it might well be you." Her father laughed and tapped her nose. "Yes, child of mine. I know all those thoughts that swirl in your head, but you have to remember, you're not going to do away with everything at once, and even trying would be a death wish." He waited for his words to sink in, watched Elenya's eyes round, her lips purse. "Choose what you would like to see changed first. Concentrate on that one thing, and once you achieve that goal, then and only then do you move on to the next."

Elenya smiled at him. "You're a wise man, Papa."

Madrik returned his daughter's smile and shook his head. "Years of training. It's what we do in battle. And it's exactly how I've always dealt with your mother." They laughed before he began to push himself up from the garden bench. "I must work this leg of mine. Will you walk with me a bit?"

Elenya had already risen and was attempting to help him up. "We'll make quite the sight—the crippled man and the round lady." They both laughed again.

"Next time you see me, I vow I shall not have to use this cane, nor will I walk with a limp."

"And I shall not be so round!" she announced as they walked out of the garden arm in arm.

Chapter 37

Tahruk carefully handed Elenya up into the carriage the next morning, waiting to see whether she would sit next to her father or him. He wouldn't lie—he'd have preferred no hesitation before she lowered herself into the seat where he would ride. He was working hard at being understanding, especially when she sat staring down at the toes of her shoes peeking out beneath her dress hem. He'd noticed since his return she seemed continually on edge, hopefully due to the pregnancy and not her natural state. It made him realize just how little he knew about the woman he'd left.

While he'd watched her sleeping during the wee hours of the morning, he'd thought about those first days. They'd been hard, and even he had to admit the way the Dremis maidens and the warriors were thrown together created a less than perfect starting point. One also had to factor in who he and Elenya were. He had to suppress a chuckle remembering the way she'd run that first night. That was the first time he could ever recall experiencing anger and attraction at the same time. And he'd definitely felt them both, not only then, but many times after in the presence of this woman marked with his blood.

She looked up at him as they rode and returned his smile with slightly quivering lips. Her attempt at trying to be so strong pulled at Tahruk's heartstrings. He slipped an arm around her shoulders and pull her closer to him—

probably not the best thing to do, he realized when he felt the moisture on his shirt. Unsure how to help her, he looked across at her father who merely smiled and nodded causing Tahruk to tighten his hold on her and continue doing what he had been doing. She would be okay. He knew that. So did her father. He'd helped raise a wonderfully strong daughter.

Tahruk and Madrik shared small talk as the carriage made its way to the harbor making Tahruk think back again to their conversations during those days while he'd sat by the ailing man's bedside in the abandoned settlement outside Corigan. They'd discussed many things—life as they knew it and the changes before them, Tahruk's match to the man's daughter, whether the wrongs of the past could be forgotten.... He'd learned Madrik was not native to Aleone, that his father-in-law's grandfather was the head of the Burnos Drille—a line from the prior king's younger brother, Kahlan. Elenya's father—Madrik Kahlan Avenille, had been matched to the head of Aleone's daughter, Senya, so that he might be groomed to lead Aleone's military forces. He'd done well, making his family proud and surpassing all expectations by producing the child who would release their people from the bounds of exile.

Most of their conversations found their way back to that subject they both very much enjoyed—Elenya. At first, Tahruk was surprised to find himself interested in the stories Madrik told of his Chosen as a young girl. Such stories would have bored him if they'd been talking about anyone else. But he'd enjoyed the stories. He'd learned, with no surprise, that she'd been overly inquisitive about everything and had given the special instructors sent by the Centrehead the dubious task of keeping her in books. She learned quickly, had a penchant for reading and writing, as well as exploration. More than once they'd found her missing and had combed the area surrounding Aleone only to have her turn up later with her sisters and a few of the Drille's youthful population. When they finally realized her friend Shemek was the artful one behind her escapades, they'd put his skills to good use and commissioned him as an infiltration expert within Aleone's forces where he'd proven to be an exceptional warrior.

Tahruk hadn't enjoyed hearing about Elenya and Shemek together. Even knowing the young warrior had been the one to sneak into the abandoned settlement as well as infiltrating the ranks of the soldiers who'd seized Dunover Castle, and was instrumental in finding out who was behind the foul play within Corigan's borders, didn't keep the jealousy over all he'd shared with Elenya at bay. He hadn't liked it at all when they'd finished each other's sentences at dinner or smiled in anticipation of something the other was about to say. It had served to remind him that his Chosen knew the other man in that way that comes only from being around someone for years and years. Jealousy was not a feeling Tahruk was accustomed to experiencing any more than this need to protect his Chosen, both physically and mentally.

His head shot up when the carriage pulled to a stop just short of the docks. Elenya righted herself and fished a small handkerchief from the tiny bag attached to her wrist. Peering out the window, Tahruk could see the *Petit Cadeau* bobbing in its moored position. He waited just long enough for Elenya to dab the tears from her face before he slipped from the carriage, made sure everything was set for her father's trip, and returned to help them out. He stood back, allowing them a moment that seemed somewhat anticlimactic even though he knew both of them were burdened with emotions. The lack of excitement was probably better for the baby.

The baby. He felt that rush he'd been getting since they'd first brought news to him in the fields that she was, in fact, expecting his child. Then again when he saw her, belly rounded, features aglow… there were no words to explain the joy that flooded his senses. And now, she was even more beautiful standing there beside her father, her eyes and nose slightly reddened from the tears, than she had been the first time he saw her. Tahruk could hardly believe that was possible, but she was.

He would have also said it was impossible for his heart to break because hers was. But, as she watched her father hobble up the plank to the deck of the ship and he returned her to the carriage, she collapsed, her head in his lap while she sobbed. He felt her gut-wrenching heartache as much as if someone had plunged a knife into his chest. Again unsure how to respond, he rubbed her back with one hand, the other stroking the top of her head until her tears finally stopped. He looked out, surprised to see the entrance to Zanak.

"I'm sorry, my lord," she whispered sitting up abruptly when they slowed and brushing frantically at her tear streaked cheeks. "You must think me a complete mess."

Tahruk's raised brows and pursed lips were probably all the answer she needed. He stared, watching her pat down her dress in an attempt to smooth out the wrinkles.

"I assure you I am not given to fits." She practically barked.

"Ohk… okay." Quite honestly, she looked a bit like she'd gone mad with her breathing still labored from the crying and the way she worked over the reticule in her lap, intently picking at the tiny beaded flowers.

A frown pulled at her brows and her lips when she glanced up at him. “You do not believe me.”

Tears again! He could see them welling in her eyes. “I do. I absolutely do!” he told her holding his hands up in front of him in a defensive posture.

She laid the bag on the seat and moved closer to him. Taking his hands in hers, he was sure she was attempting to impart some information to him through a stare that made his insides quiver like no opponent on the battlefield ever had.

She sighed, her shoulders drooping. “You believe it’s because I don’t want to be with you, don’t you?” She paused. “That’s not true. That’s absolutely *not* true.” A single tear slid down her cheek. “I just… Seeing him leave, and not knowing when I will see them again… And you’ve been gone… And then there’s this…” She looked down at her moving abdomen.

Tahruk wondered why his training had not included a lesson on keeping up with the thought processes of a woman speaking in only partial sentences. He felt certain he should have been completing them in his head just as her old friend Shemek would have. A pang of jealousy stabbed through him that he had to fight away.

“I’m sure you’ll be seeing them again very soon. I might even take you to see them once the baby is big enough, if they haven’t come yet.”

“Take me?” She whispered the same question that had popped into his mind the moment his statement hit his ears. She looked so hopeful all he could do was shrug and agree. He was quite certain he looked the part of a jester sitting next to her smiling and nodding his head. Her reaction, however, made the moment of embarrassment completely disappear.

When she lunged as best as she could with the added bulk about her middle and threw herself into his arms, his moment of embarrassment evaporated. She hugged him tightly, then smothered his face with kisses. Only when she finally covered his lips with hers did she slow down, pulling back and looking at him with heavy lidded eyes that lowered to his mouth before her tongue darted out to moisten her own lips. After their eventful beginning, she'd never been hesitant in accepting his advances. But for her to take the lead…

Tahruk waited. He knew she wanted him to make the next move. He *wanted* to make that move and close the distance between them. The tension inside the coach had him barely able to breathe with her heart racing against his, her breaths coming shallow. *Please*, he thought as the seconds ticked by.

A groan ripped from his chest when she finally covered his mouth with hers, her tongue tracing the line of his lips much as it had her own just moments before. Tahruk slipped an arm beneath her legs and settled her more securely on his lap, making it hard for him to remember to let her lead, especially when she pressed herself more tightly against him, her tongue demanding entrance where she began a tentative exploration of the inside of his mouth. He tightened his hold, his arms still easily encircling her, his fingers itching to undo the tiny buttons that ran the length of her back.

As Elenya ran a hand up into his hair, raking through the thickness, Tahruk was forced to break away. "My lady, if we do not stop, I will be unable to hold back," he groaned. Her nose crinkled, bottom lip jutted out just before her eyes widened and her hands moved to cheeks that had begun to burn a bright red. Her obvious distress had Tahruk babbling his next words. "Noh… not that I want to, uhm, s… stop, but I, uh, I'm not so sure you want to crawl out of this coach after… after being ravished in the center of Zanak's undoubtedly busy courtyard."

Elenya stared at him for a minute then groaned, her forehead dropping to Tahruk's shoulder. "What was I thinking?" He could barely hear her muffled voice, prayed tears would not come next.

Tahruk hugged her tightly. "Love doesn't think, Little One. It reacts."

She lifted her head and stared at him. There were no tears falling, though he could see the pools in her eyes. "Do you love me, my lord?" she whispered.

He hadn't anticipated her words, hadn't really thought when he'd said it. Love. What was love? It was an endearment he'd always used with his family, telling his mother or Nema, even his sisters, he loved them. There was a bond between him and his father, and even Redahn that could be described as love. He felt an admiration for Elenya's father that went beyond simple respect. He even felt more for Elenya than he had for any other woman he'd ever been with. But love…

He felt a certain bumping against his hand and looked down at the bundle between them. He laughed, rubbing the top of the rounded bulge. "Yes, I love you," he answered her at last.

"Because of the baby?" she asked turning her head ever so slightly to avoid his eyes.

Tahruk studied her face for a moment before answering. He shook his head. "No, my lady. The baby is the reason you were sent to me. And I am beyond proud that you carry my child. I think I knew before I left though, and certainly felt it while I was gone…" He paused, taking the time to caress her cheek and wipe away a stray tear, pleased he was not nearly so alarmed by the moisture droplet this time. Turning her face back toward his, he gently brushed her lips with his. "Somehow, you have crept into my heart, Little One."

She smiled—a tentative gesture. "I am stealthy like Shemek."

Tahruk smiled as well, though the mention of Shemek brought unwelcomed feelings, the mood cooling instantly inside the carriage. Still, he whispered an endearment in her ear that made her cheeks grow red as she suppressed a giggle. Moving her off his lap, he winked and opened the carriage door, then turned back to help her out.

"My bag!" She spun around, swaying on unsteady legs.

"I'll get it," Tahruk assured her, moving past her and back into the carriage. "I don't see it," he called seconds later.

Elenya frowned. "Perhaps it slipped behind the cushion?" She tried to peek back inside, though the brightness of the daylight in the courtyard contrasting with the coach's darkened interior made it difficult to see.

"Ya? Are you okay?" The familiar voice that sounded at her back made Elenya and Tahruk both stiffen.

"Shemek!" Elenya's swift turn had her grabbing his hand to steady herself and Shemek slipping an arm around her.

"Careful there. You certainly don't want to fall now." He chuckled, moving her a step or two from the carriage door, just out of Tahruk's view. "Are you well? It seemed to be taking you a long time to exit the coach. I was concerned since you went to see your father off..."

"Yes, we did." She paused and cocked her head. "Weren't you to go too?

If Shemek noted a less than welcoming tone or her skirting of his concern about their less than hasty departure from the coach, he didn't let on. He just shrugged. "I was given an offer I couldn't refuse." He leaned his head closer and whispered to her, "It hasn't been announced yet, but I've been given a position in the Elite forces. Infiltration Specialist for the King himself."

"Really?" Elenya felt his elation, her voice rising as she began to congratulate him. Shemek shushed her with a finger to the lips. "Congratulations," she whispered when he pulled his hand away and nodded. She hugged him. "Oh, Shemek, that's great!"

Or was it? She noted the frown on Tahruk's face when he exited the coach with the missing bag looking even smaller now in his clenched fist.

"It had slipped down at the far end of the seat," he told her returning the bag, cool eyes assessing the closeness of his Chosen and Shemek.

"Thank you for finding it, my lord," she answered, her voice wavering. After studying him for a moment, she turned back to Shemek. "It was nice to see you again, Shemek. I'm sure we'll bump into one another now that you're staying. My lord and I have business back in our chamber…"

Both men started to speak at once interrupting Elenya. Shemek laughed and motioned for a sour faced Tahruk to go ahead.

"I just remembered something I need to take care of. I won't be long." His final sentence was spoken as a stiff-mouthed warning that had Elenya's back straightening and her chin jutting up before she frowned and turned back to

Shemek.

"Walk with me then, since I've been dismissed?" she asked her old friend. "You can tell me whatever you were going to say before you were interrupted." She cast a pouty glance back at her warrior, noting the dark glint in his eyes, before slipping a hand through Shemek's offered arm and turning in the direction of the family gardens, not their rooms. She may have had a misguided moment of boldness, but even she wasn't fool enough to take another man to their chambers. Especially when she wasn't quite sure she was fully comfortable with that man anymore.

Come on! This wasn't just any other man. This was Shemek—her dear friend for life.

So why didn't it feel like it used to before she left Aleone?

Once they reached the gardens, Elenya seemed unable to find a comfortable position. She tried to force herself to sit still while she visited with Shemek at the table where she'd spent so many of her waiting hours at Zanak. They skipped around subjects, talked of the battle, how Shemek had been wounded and then even his hand in helping to figure out how to bring it to an end. He admitted that King Travensworth and Andorak's warriors already had a pretty good idea who was behind the travesties, but that he had been instrumental in ferreting out the depths of the man's powers and who could and could not be trusted so as to reinstate Corigan's King back to his throne. Elenya enjoyed hearing about all he'd done. Or at least she tried to, but as the conversation turned to Shemek's commission to become a part of Andorak's Elite warriors and that the Sharanis family had offered him lodging in their guest quarters, Elenya's discomfort grew to an unbearable level.

"I need to be going now," she told him abruptly. "I really should rest before the lunch hour. Be warned. Lady Neria's a stickler for being on time." She laughed, trying to cover what she knew had to be odd behavior.

Shemek nodded, his face settling into a mask of confusion before he rose quickly to assist her with her struggle to push the chair back and rise to her feet. She stepped away from him as soon as she was up, but softened just a bit when he handed her the rose he'd picked earlier. She noticed all but a single thorn had been stripped away.

"It must be hard for you. I don't know if I ever imagined you looking this way."

Elenya felt the heat rise up her neck into her cheeks. She could think of nothing to say so remained quiet, staring at the rose.

"I enjoyed the visit, Ya. Perhaps I can see you again." He laughed. "No doubt I will since I'll be staying here until I'm needed or we go for extended training drills."

Elenya hoped her smile didn't look as fake as it felt. She knew it didn't reach her eyes. "Of course. Good day, Shemek."

Hurrying from the gardens, she didn't see the figure turning the corner from the other direction and would have ran straight into Redahn had he not stepped aside and caught her with an outstretched arm. The momentum swung them both around, her back colliding with his chest.

"What's the hurry, little white-faced girl? You look like you've seen a ghost. Perhaps you have a wardrobe full of skeletons from your past?"

Pushing his arm off, Elenya stepped away and turned to glare at him. "Marked women do not have the luxury of skeletons, Redahn. Surely you know what would happen if we did." She smacked his chest with the rose which caused it to drop from her hand before she turned to leave. "You are so annoying! All of you," she called back to a chuckling Redahn.

"You really shouldn't do that to her, you know. Especially in her condition," Shemek said as he bent to retrieve the discarded flower.

Redahn shook his head, his mouth turned upward on one side in a lopsided grin. "Neither should you. The girl's confused enough as it is. Between her concerns over her feelings for my brother, her disdain for the marking, and fretting about her family being so far away, especially now that she's having a baby… She certainly doesn't need an old boyfriend thrown into the mix." He snatched the rose away from Shemek, raising a brow as he tapped the single thorn with his finger and stared at the other man, hitching a brow when Shemek didn't outright refute the claim.

"You heard her, my lord. Marked women have no skeletons."

"Maybe not, but they can still wish they did. That's close enough."

Redahn thumped Shemek on the chest, much lighter than Elenya had him, and both men laughed.

"Come, my young friend, I'll show you how to get to the guest chambers from here. You're actually in the family wing and I'm not so sure you'd be welcomed here without a family member. At least not yet. If you work things right, you'll have full run of Zanak in no time. You've already endeared yourself to my father, which is akin to a small coup. My mother will be no problem at all, though Nema…

she's liable to see right through you. And my brother. Ha! There's no hope for you there, I'm afraid." Redahn threw his head back and laughed, then continued talking without bothering to keep his voice down even though some of what he was saying should have been reserved for the two in conversation only, not for others who might be listening nearby. Even the walls of Zanak were said to have ears.

Chapter 38

The day was closing in on the noon hour and Tahruk still had not returned to their chambers. Elenya paced around the sun room wringing the small kerchief she'd been using to fan herself. She'd felt overly warm since she'd returned from the gardens. Why had she gone with Shemek instead of demanding Tahruk escort her to their chambers? Surely once inside she could have convinced him with a few more kisses that he needed to stay with her. She felt so confused.

Sitting down with a soft thud on the overstuffed settee, the emotions of the day, the past three days, weighed heavy on her. She leaned back, fanning herself with her kerchief. *Why* could she not cool down? The baby's slight movements unsettled her stomach as did the ache in her back and lower abdomen. She squirmed trying to get comfortable, deciding to prop her feet on the sofa even though it would look quite unladylike if someone was to come in and see her that way. She was beyond caring at that moment, her dislike of mankind, especially men, was at an all-time crest.

There, she thought, spreading her skirts about her legs to maintain some modicum of decency before reaching up to rub her temples. Her head had begun to throb. She closed her eyes and leaned back, her neck no longer interested in supporting a too heavy head.

That's when she felt it, the moment of extreme pressure and then the moisture that made her think she was either bleeding or had lost control.

"No, no, no," she whispered, suddenly paralyzed and unsure of what she should do. The midwife to the Courts who had come to check on her a few times had said four more weeks at least. She'd told her a bit of what she might expect and had assured her everything would be okay, that she was nearby. Elenya had been nervous but everyone just kept reminding her women had been having babies since the beginning of time. It was a natural process, right?

She shook her head, fairly certain this wasn't how it was supposed to happen. Fear gripped her as her stomach clinched tightly around the baby only to let up and do it again much too quickly. The moisture had begun to soak her skirts and seep into the cushions beneath her. "Think, Elenya, think," she told herself. Instinct whispered that she needed to go for help.

The contractions picked up their pace, coming in progressively harder waves, making movement near impossible. She worked with a slow, continual determination until her feet were firmly planted back on the ground and pushed herself into a standing position. It was a battle in itself, though she finally managed. "Good," she encouraged herself, hating the way her wet skirts felt clinging to her. "It's no different than when you'd get all wet with the sea spray," she chastised her body. This was not the time to get all squeamish, not when her baby's life might well lay in the balance.

With slow, deliberate movements, she made her way to the door. Hand on the handle, she looked down. Okay, she was up, walking, and the pains had subsided just a bit. Surely she could change before going for help.

Breathing in and out with loud, deliberate breaths, she pushed away from the door and waddled toward her rooms. The bell pull caught her eye while she held tight to the door jamb through another bought of increasingly harder pains. *I thought you were tougher than this, Ya.* She heard Shemek's disapproval from years ago when she'd refused to get up after tripping and bloodying her knee during one of their secret excursions. She shook her head remembering how he'd confessed later he'd been terrified she was seriously hurt and he'd be found out for helping her carry out her crazy schemes all those times. She was barely thirteen at the time, him not much older. She doubted he'd have been in too much trouble. What she wouldn't do to have him there to chastise her now.

Her vision swam and blurred, then refocused long enough for her to locate the bell pull. "It's okay, baby." She patted her stomach and reached for the rope, unsure if her hand actually made contact before she went down.

Chapter 39

When Tahruk stalked into the smaller dining hall off yet another garden, he'd fully expected to see his Chosen talking close-headed with her old friend. His face, contorted in anger that quickly turned to confusion when his brother and Shemek looked up at him from what appeared to be a concentrated conversation they'd been having for a while.

"Where the hell is my *wife*?" he demanded, glaring down at them, his curled fists on his hips.

"Tahruk! Settle," his mother demanded, a hand fluttering to the neckline of her dress.

Nema, who had walked in behind him, stepped around the rigid warrior. Her dark blue eyes darting around the table's occupants. "Where's Elenya?" Her words set a concentrated murmur humming around the small crowd. She set her gaze on an indifferent Redahn while Tahruk continued to stare down the object of his jealousy.

"She knows better than to be late. *You* were the last to see her." He thrust a finger in Shemek's direction. "Now where is she?"

Shaking his head, Shemek threw his hands up and scrunched his shoulders. "Technically, he was the last to see her, as far as I know." He said pointing to Redahn. "Honestly, though, I thought she was on her way back to your chambers to see you. She seemed rather… agitated during our talk. I assumed it was over whatever had transpired between the two of you on the carriage ride back from dropping her father…"

"Agitated how?" Nema interrupted, placing a hand on Tahruk's arm.

Again Shemek shrugged. "You know, just… fidgeting and moving around a lot. I don't know. She seemed to lose the conversation as if she had other things on her mind. She wasn't like the Ya I knew at all…"

Both Nema and Tahruk glowered, their foreheads creasing, causing the younger man to let his words trail off. "I don't like this," Nema whispered even as Tahruk was already on his way out of the hall.

"If this is some sort of game, I shall throttle her the moment that baby is born," Tahruk's angry words vibrated back into the room.

"Stay here. There's nothing the two of you can do." Nema's hands on their shoulders reseated a rising Shemek and Redahn. Concern was mirrored on the faces surrounding the meal-laden table.

"Nema…"

Nema was already nodding her head even before Neria could get the words out. "I'm going,"

"If he hurts her…"

Nema turned to look at the young guest before exiting through the same door Tahruk had taken.

"He won't hurt her." Her voice grew fainter with her hastened steps. "You understand nothing about the marking and the sharing of blood. He loves her more than he's ever loved anything. And probably more than he ever will."

Chapter 40

Tahruk broke into a sprint from the dining hall entry, stopping only long enough to let himself through the door to their chambers. The atmosphere within the passageway had grown thicker the closer he got. It was a feeling he'd experienced time and again as his military forces had moved into battle. The prize, this time, was more precious than any he'd ever defended.

He didn't bother calling her name as he gained entry. He didn't have to. The trail of blood droplets led him to her laying in a heap just inside the door to her dressing room. She moaned when he crouched down and reached out to touch her. Guarded relief flooded the seasoned warrior when she mumbled incoherently as he worked to get his arms beneath her.

Elenya's eyes fluttered, the vision of an angel filling her sight. She smiled. How very much like her warrior he looked. She wanted to reach up to touch his face but her arm refused to move, the weight of her hand holding it down.

"I have never seen such beauty in a man before," she told the being, her lashes drifting back to rest against her pale cheeks. Her voice sounded airy, far away, and she frowned. "I will go with you, angel," she told the being when his arms slid beneath her and she felt herself rising into the air. “Please… my baby. Let my baby stay behind. Let him grow up to be a great and powerful man.”

“Oh, dear Lord!” Nema screeched when the warrior nearly plowed her down in the hallway and she took in Elenya’s blood-drenched skirts.

“Get help, Nema. We need the midwife.”

Nodding, Nema pushed past him into Elenya’s dressing room and gave the bell pull two hard tugs. “She’ll be okay,” Tahruk heard her yelling as he disappeared into the bedchamber, her steps sounding in the direction of the main chamber door. He wondered if she had a basis for her statement other than wanting it to be so.

Careful of Elenya’s lolling head and dangling arm, Tahruk laid her on the bed, oblivious to the blood that now spotted his front. Her eyes fluttered again, she moaned, and he soothed with a gentle shushing sound.

“Ah… my warrior.” Her words were slow, labored, her eyes closed. She attempted to look at him and smile. “I… I’m afraid I… ruined… the yellow settee.” She groaned and arched her back. Tahruk watched the mound at her middle grow more rounded and firm. She grimaced, gritting her teeth as her body fought against the pain. He noticed the red stain on her skirt growing.

Never before had he felt so helpless as he did sitting there beside her, unsure of what he could do for her. He wondered if there was anything anyone could do, then chastised himself for the thought.

Voices and scurrying outside the bedchamber had him on his feet, blocking the door. His mother took in the blood on his front and screamed.

“Get her out of here!” He spoke through gritted teeth, looking at his father while pointing at his mother who was threatening to fall into a fit of hysteria. Nema re-entered the room and grabbed hold of Neria's arm, pushing her toward Renaine. He held the sobbing woman to him, the worry in his eyes the only thing breaking his emotionless mask.

I know, Nema expression conveyed when their eyes locked, then she tried to quietly explain what appeared to be happening. She looked at the main chamber door and noticed Shemek, his face drained of color.

"Young man," she said as she walked over to him. "You need to go." Shemek looked at her, his stare vacant, as if he wasn't seeing any of them. Nema nudged him and he pressed back enough that Renaine could steer Neria past him.

"Is she…" His eyes found Nema's before she turned back to Tahruk's empty bedchamber door.

"She'll be all right!" Nema almost yelled at him. Biting her lip, she dropped her head and took several deep breaths before looking up and patting him on the chest. "Go and wait by the gates for Redahn to return with the midwife. Then get them here posthaste," she told him in a more controlled tone.

Shemek looked past her to the bedchamber. He hesitated several seconds before nodding and turning to leave. Nema could hear him tell a servant just outside the door to come at once if there was any change in the Lady's condition. She didn't wait to see what the servant said. She really didn't care as long as they got help to Elenya.

Closing the chamber door, Nema nodded to the three servants waiting to clean up the mess then pointed to the hallway leading to Elenya's dressing room and drew an air circle around the room they were in. As she turned to go, she paused, noting for the first time the stains on the floor coming from the sunroom direction. Without adding to her orders, she looked at the head maid who bobbed in understanding. Her kind eyes were glossy with tears for the young mistress' plight. Elenya hadn't been with the family all that long and still she had endeared herself to every one of them, relatives and servants alike.

With a sigh, Nema turned around. The path to Tahruk's bedchamber seemed lengthy and yet not long enough. Her footsteps were heavy, filled with dread. If she'd been able to remove this burden from this young couple, she would have given up all she had to do so. Gladly.

Tahruk didn't look back when Nema entered the room. He was on his knees beside the bed, his forehead resting against the hand that he held in his. Nema felt her own tears threatening when she looked at Elenya—her face ashen, lips pulled thin though slightly apart as she struggled for shallow breaths.

"We should get her out of those wet skirts, my lord," she said in a low voice. Tahruk didn't move, even when she placed a hand on his shoulder. About that time, Elenya made several guttural sounds, her body contorting as it had earlier. Nema watched in horror.

"She just keeps doing that. And then there's more blood." Tahruk's voice was muffled by his still downturned face. "She's losing too much blood, Nema, and they're not coming." He rose abruptly and turned to her, his eyes wild with worry. "What in bloody hell is taking them so long?"

"It takes time," Nema answered, reaching out to try to sooth him, but he pushed her hand away.

"Why isn't the midwife stationed here? She knew Elenya's time was near. Hell and damnation! Why did I leave her alone?" The battle-hardened man sucked big gulps of air and quickly blew them out to help him regain control, his shoulders rising with each one before he dropped back to Elenya's side.

Nema started to tell him the midwife wasn't close by because it was too soon. She also wanted to reassure him it wasn't his fault, that he'd done all he could have done. But did she believe that? It was true that neither one of them was equipped to aid a woman in childbirth, but if someone had been with Elenya that person could have gotten help much faster. They could have already had the midwife there to keep a closer eye on the mother-to-be. Nema could have insisted the young woman remain in the chamber adjoining hers...

So many coulds and only one reality.

Nema jumped when the main door of Tahruk's chambers slammed open with a loud cracking sound. Seconds later Redahn and the Court physician burst through the bedchamber door.

"Oh, dear God!" Redahn pulled up short causing Doctor Jorian to bump into his back. Both men stared at the bloodied heap on the bed, her body beginning another round of contorting contractions. Snapping out of it, the physician moved to the bedside behind Tahruk and watched closely.

"May I?" He was politely asking Tahruk to move, though the warrior seemed reluctant to give up his position. "I need to check her, my lord." The doctor turned a pleading eye to Nema.

"Tahruk, love, you need to move back and let the physician in so he can begin to help her," she whispered, leaning closer to him. Still, he didn't budge. Standing, Nema turned to Redahn who had remained motionless, gawking at the disturbing scene.

"Boys!" Her voice, firm but still quieter than it could have been, got their attention much as it had when they were young. They both looked at her. "Leave. Now!" she commanded.

Redahn blinked a few times then shook his head as if clearing away cobwebs. "Brother, come," he said, moving forward when Tahruk still didn't obey. His hands on Tahruk's shoulders were flung off in a violent shrug that did little to deter the younger brother. "You have to move."

"I'm not leaving her!" Tahruk's voice came out in a choked growl.

"Then she's leaving you."

Doctor Jorian's words hung in the room, though even they did not move the warrior by Elenya's bedside.

"Son. You have to give the physician room to work." Renaine's presence surprised them all. He grasped his son by the upper arms and lifted him to his feet. The dark eyes, so nearly the same, locked—one set crazed with worry, the other conveying sorrow for the situation.

There was nothing weak about the tears that careened down the face of the battle-hardened young warrior. He collapsed against his father in grief, the older man's shoulder muffling the great sobs that shook them both. Motioning for Redahn to help him, the two men moved the heartbroken man from his wife's bedside.

"Merciful Mother of all that is sacred!" The barn owl screech from the doorway had them all turning that direction. Hands covering her mouth, the usually pleasant eyes of the midwife devoured the three men standing together to one side of the room. "The birthing chamber is no place for men folk." Starting into the room, she stumbled back a few steps when she saw the state of Elenya's body lying on the bed. "Oh dear Lord," she whispered. "What a pity. She was so young and beautiful. I never would have guessed after checking her last week."

Both the physician and Nema glared at the woman who

seemed to have left her brains outside the room. No doubt her position would be at stake once they were finished with Elenya. It was a wonder the grief-stricken warrior hadn't take her head off right then, though his breaking heart seemed to have quenched any fire within him.

At the door, struggling to regain his voice enough to speak, Tahruk looked at the physician and then Nema. "Please…" The devastated look caused Nema to falter in her steps toward the bed. "Please… do what you have to. Just… help her," he pleaded in broken sentences.

The physician, already moving to a table near the garden door where he'd set out some of his instruments and supplies, nodded. "We'll do all we can," he told the men as they exited and he turned his full attention to the battle at hand. "Nema, we need the standards. Water, linens, string…" He began naming off the typical items used in the birthing process.

"I have them here." The midwife seemed to have regained her composure, an air of professionalism returning to her actions as she and Nema began to work together to remove Elenya's soiled skirts.

"Oh!" Nema jumped back. "The baby's turned wrong." She pointed to the movements visible on Elenya's uncovered abdomen. The midwife began to feel the hardened mass and nodded.

Doctor Jorian moved toward the bed. "As many births as you two have attended, I would have thought that obvious." His tone wasn't harsh, just matter-of-fact as he eased a syringe into Elenya's arm. The doctor stood back for a moment until they could see her visibly relaxing. "We'll have to turn the baby. I fear the placenta has detached as well. If the tear is only partial, our turning the child may result in more bleeding. But, without it, I'm fearful we will lose them both." He talked while beginning to manipulate the form within his patient's swollen abdomen. "We're fortunate the infant is still quite small."

"As is the lady," Nema added dolefully. Jorian nodded his head.

"Yes," he agreed. "But she's young and healthy. We have to think positive and keep our heads about us. Her life, and the life of this child are in our hands."

Nema moved to the head of the bed. She stroked the sweat tangled tresses back from Elenya's face. "Be strong," she whispered leaning down to kiss a colorless cheek. Sniffling back threatening tears, she rose and watched the physician pull a clean cloth up to cover Elenya's exposed lower half. She had to smile remembering Elenya's horror at the midwife's confirmation that others would actually *see* her when she gave birth. Had Tahruk not been so charming and Elenya not nearly as crazy about him, she might have wondered exactly how he ever got close enough to this modest creature to put her into this position.

Ah, Tahruk… No doubt he would blame himself if anything happened to either of these two lives that he loved so deeply after knowing them for such a short time.

Almost as if reading her thoughts, the physician looked up at Nema and nodded. "Sit beside her while I go talk to the father. I believe I have been successful in turning the baby." He offered only a slight smile at Nema's relief. "We still have the birth before us, but I believe half our battle has been won."

Nema nodded. Half was better than none.

Tahruk sat in the same chair he'd lounged in to watch

Elenya's bath the first day she'd entered his world. Leaning forward, his head in his hands, he questioned how they could have ended up with this trial before them. The physician's words had been both encouraging and disheartening at the same time. He'd told them the blood seemed worse than it actually was because of the maternal fluids mixed with it. They had managed to successfully turn the infant, which from his best guess had probably turned earlier that day when she was in the garden. He'd shrugged when asked why.

That was the good news. The main issue now was a successful birth without internal damage. Tahruk didn't fully understand it all. Childbirth around Zanak was something that just happened, and without the men being involved. When he asked if he could see her again, the physician politely discouraged it.

"We need her as calm and relaxed as possible. If she hears you or senses your presence…"

Tahruk's nod had confirmed his understanding, even though his heart screamed that he needed to be by her side.

With a firm squeeze to the young warrior's shoulder, Doctor Jorian left, again assuring him he would do all he could to save both mother and child.

The silent room where the three men sat hummed with nervous tension. Tahruk now stared at the empty space where the yellow settee had been. When they'd entered the room and he'd seen the servant girl on her knees beside it scrubbing frantically at the stains, he'd almost lost it. He'd attempted to turn back, though his father and brother had held him firmly. Renaine had instructed the girl to get someone to remove the piece of furniture and the spotted rug as well.

He'd just sat back down when a disturbance in the main entry had him returning to his feet. Only Redahn managing to step before him kept the frantic warrior from lunging into a startled Shemek.

"What's *he* doing here?" he growled, barely contained by his brother's back and his father's strong arms.

"They've been friends since childhood, Tahruk. Surely you can understand him wanting to know how she's faring." Daruh stepped forward.

"Do you think I care what he wants? Perhaps if he'd been so interested in her well-being he'd have realized she was in distress when she left him in the gardens!"

"Perhaps if *you'd* not been so ready to dismiss her, she would have been with you instead of alone!"

The two men stared at each other until Daruh moved Shemek back, concerned by the depth of crazed despair in Tahruk's glare. He frowned, then looked past the two brothers to Renaine.

"The physician is doing all he can, though the situation remains dire." Renaine paused. His brows drawing down, he looked toward the bedchamber door. "No doubt she doesn't need to hear all of this."

"If she's hearing anything at all." Shemek's added statement had Tahruk again straining against his brother and father.

Neria swept into the room, pulling their attention from the tense moment, though the wringing of her hands did little to lessen the chaotic atmosphere. One hand fluttered to her mouth when she again took in the blood on her son's front. "Oh, dear God!"

"I thought you were resting!" The stern rebuke in Renaine's voice drew her stare from the sight.

"The sedative didn't work well. I'm just so worried…"

Redahn cleared his throat. “Shemek, will you please assist me in escorting my mother away from here. I need something to drink and would appreciate the company.” Redahn’s request cut his mother off and surprised them all, though someone needed to act. “Master Daruh? Would you like to join us?”

The older man considered the choice for a moment then shook his head. “I would like to remain here for now.” He looked at Renaine, not Tahruk, for permission.

Back in the garden room, Tahruk was surprised to see the afternoon sun streaming in through the now opened doors. What seemed like an eternity had not been all that long at all. The smell of oleander wafted in from the plants that grew just beyond the doors. Tahruk closed his eyes and breathed deeply.

“My whole life has been centered around learning to defeat the enemy. I played battle games with my brother and then with the other boys my age. We grew up believing victory was all that mattered.” He rose and went to lean against the door jamb. “We were told Aleone was our enemy as well, that we should despise these people who took one of our own all those years ago. I never understood how love could have made them do what they did… until now.”

Renaine started to say something, but Tahruk’s raised hand silenced him. His son continued, “The true enemy is that cursed marking that steals one’s ability to choose should love knock from a door other than the one someone else has chosen. We’re pawns in a game. And for what?” He laughed, a bitter sound that conveyed no humor. “Elenya once described being a part of the Dremis as belonging to a pack of dogs in heat waiting for the hounds to descend. If I have a daughter, is that how I want her to feel? And if my firstborn should be a son… would I want him to behave as I did?" He turned to stare at Daruh, then looked at the floor, a sad smile covering his face. "I remember her at your feet, Daruh, how frightened she was. And with good cause. When I realized I had been matched with Aleone I wanted to make her pay for the sins of her people." He looked at both men then turned back to stare outside "I actually considered sending her away. After I'd used her, of course. I suppose that was actually one of the kinder thoughts I had. At least that way she'd have been free to be with another, but I viewed it as just punishment at the time, short-lived as that was." He shook his head. "But I fell in love with her, just like everyone else does. Only, I had an advantage, because I was already a part of her." Tahruk breathed deeply and expelled it slowly before moving back to his chair.

"The very thing you now curse brought you together. It cannot be all bad," Daruh responded in the silence.

The young warrior snorted. "But for what? For her to lose her life and me my heart?" He stood abruptly. "This agony is unbearable. I need to know what's going on."

Both Renaine and Daruh were on their feet attempting to reach the door before the younger man. His determination outmatched them, though he stopped abruptly, his way blocked by Nema.

Tahruk tried to read the look on her face, though all he could see there was the tired wariness. At last she smiled.

"You have a son, my lord."

Tahruk backed up, falling hard into the seat of his chair. Elbows on his knees, he leaned forward breathing into his steepled hands. He pressed his eyes tightly together. "And Elenya?" He held his breath waiting for her answer.

Nema kneeled before him, taking his hands in hers and waiting for him to look at her. “As soon as she’s cleaned up, you’ll be able to see her.”

Tears prickled his dried out eyes, his quivering lips unable to form a smile to match the one on the lips that bore him the good news. Instead, he dropped to his knees and pulled Nema into a fierce hug that had her gasping for air.

“You need to understand she’s sleeping still. Doctor Jorian felt it best.”

Tahruk nodded at Nema’s explanation.

She continued, “I won’t lie. She’s had a rough time and probably wouldn’t have made it had Redahn not thought to go for the physician. I don’t know that old Nellie would have known what to do.”

Tahruk was barely listening by that point. He closed his eyes, thankful he’d been given another chance.

Chapter 41

His heart beat wildly within his chest as Tahruk crept into the bedchamber. Elenya lay much as she had when he'd last seen her, only there was no blood and her face seemed peaceful, even though it was still void of color. She was covered to the shoulders in a down coverlet of the softest butter cream yellow that did little to enhance her pallor. Normally, she looked striking against that coverlet—another indication of the gravity of the situation

Tahruk looked first to Nema then to Doctor Jorian who tipped his head in approval for the young warrior to go to her. He slipped into the chair Nema had scooted closer to the bedside and reached beneath the coverlet for her hand. Elenya moaned softly as his fingers closed around hers causing him to cast a worried look at the physician.

"She's not in any distress. I've given her a mixture of poppy seed, basil, and willow bark to help her sleep and ease the pain. But the mind is powerful, and she's been through a lot. Your support now will help her more than anything."

Tahruk nodded. He was thinking about Redahn when he was injured, how hope had pulled him through before the discouragement came when his arm didn't appear to be healing properly. More recently, there'd been Elenya's father. Talk of his daughter and family had seemed to bolster him, keeping him from letting go when the infection raged through his body. Too bad this new physician the Courts had found had not been around for either of them. Thank goodness he had been her for Elenya…

"Would you like to hold your son?" Nema's voice cut through his thoughts and he turned to where she stood beside him cradling a bundle of blankets.

His son! Of course, he wanted to see his son. He looked at the baby then back down where his hand clasped Elenya's, his brows furrowing. Nema's chuckle at his obvious dilemma made him laugh too—the first in many hours. With a light squeeze, he released Elenya's hand and raised his arms to receive the bundle.

How weightless the baby felt, even wrapped in multiple blankets. He had worked a hand free and gnawed contentedly on a fist while seeming to study the man who held him. Tahruk marveled at the clarity of his baby blue eyes that glowed with just the hint of emerald green. Fine, dark hair—a Sharanis trademark in newborns—covered his tiny head. He was a definite combination of his parents.

Tahruk looked from the baby to Elenya then carefully scooted to the edge of the chair before lowering himself to his knees beside the bed. "Little One, you were right. You have a son—a beautiful, perfect little boy." He laid the bundle near her head and caressed her cheek. She seemed to turn her face toward the baby and draw in a deep breath. Tahruk, holding her hand again, leaned in and did the same thing. He chuckled. "It appears Nema has bathed him in Oleander, Little One. The fragrance mixed with his scent, he smells like you." Elenya mumbled something that had Tahruk raising his head. He looked around for the physician.

"A good sign she can hear you, I'd say. Give her time. Let her rest. She'll awaken at her own pace. Until then," He turned to address Nema, "I'd like to stay on to keep watch through the night. It's just good practice," he added when Tahruk's gaze turned troubled. "She may need something more to keep her comfortable. There's just no way to tell until she wakes and tells us herself."

"Will you be okay here, love, while I get the good doctor settled in?" Nema asked, slipping into the chair Tahruk had vacated and leaning forward to slip her arm around his shoulder.

He patted her hand and turned to kiss her cheek. "We'll be fine. Will you also let my mother know all is well?"

"I'll convey that message." Renaine's voice sounded from the doorway. Both Tahruk and Nema turned to look at him.

"We have a son." Tahruk beamed at him.

"So I heard." Renaine moved toward the bed at Tahruk's beckoning. He leaned over his son to look at the newest member of the Sharanis family. "Have you chosen a name?"

Tahruk nodded. "Rennicus Kahlan, after your father and Elenya's."

Renaine nodded, his mouth curving upward in a pleased smile. "They go well together." After staring at the now sleeping baby for a few more seconds, he stepped back and offered Nema a hand. Arm in arm, they escorted the physician out of the room, leaving the new family to share their first moment alone.

After a few seconds, Tahruk rose and carefully repositioned the baby on the other side of Elenya before he washed up and changed his clothing. His stomach growled and he ignored it. He'd missed lunch and dinner, but he didn't care. There'd be time enough for eating. But for now, he felt exhaustion creeping in. A few moments of rest beside his wife and baby were all he could think about, except for his extreme thankfulness to the good Lord above for saving both of them and giving him the opportunity to do so. Had he known she would have had to endure all that she had in giving birth to their son, he wondered if he would have stayed away from her? He doubted he could have considering the pull of the marking. He looked at their son and smiled before drifting off with visions of Elenya fussing over the baby dancing through his thoughts. That was all he needed. She would say it was worth it, no matter the cost.

Chapter 42

Tahruk dreamed he was being watched and quickly clawed his way back from a wary slumber. He'd slept as he did when engaged in battle—sliding just deep enough into the realm of inertia that he could rejuvenate without sleeping so soundly he became vulnerable. He opened his eyes, taking but a moment to reorient himself before looking up at Elenya. Her green eyes on him were the most beautiful sight he'd ever seen, flooding him with such great joy he had to blink several times to hold back tears.

"Hi," he whispered, reaching up to brush his thumb over her upturned lips before pushing back a stray curl from her cheek.

She caught his hand to her cheek then turned her face to kiss his palm. "It was your face I saw. You were my angel," she told him, having to stop to clear her gravelly throat. "You saved me."

Tahruk shook his head and wiped away a line of moisture from beneath her lower lashes. "No, Little One. You were the hero, and your will to survive kept you here and saved our son."

"Our son…" She grimaced as she turned her body toward Tahruk and the tiny bundle that lay between them.

Tahruk could read the concern on her face as she tried to push herself up on an elbow for a better look at the baby. The infant who must have sensed a change began to stir. Elenya's eyes grew big as a he registered a complaint in the form of a squeal. She glanced at Tahruk though her eyes sprung right back to her baby.

"Months of having him growing inside of me and now I'm scared to death of him," she whispered. "I... I don't even know what I'm supposed to do."

Tahruk chuckled. "I'm sure you'll do just fine, and if I know her, I'm sure Nema is nearby. His cries will bring her quickly."

Elenya's face contorted. "I don't want him to cry!"

His father's hoot of laughter startled the baby, and his mother's desires went ungranted. As expected, Nema bustled through the door, took control, and calmed everyone. The enormous amount of admiration Tahruk already felt for the woman grew even greater as he watched her tending the baby and teaching the mother. He felt a momentary pang of sorrow that she hadn't been able to mother her own children, though she'd always seemed content to mother the children born from her sister's womb. His father was, indeed, a fortunate man to have gained the hearts of not one but two women who loved him. Tahruk looked at Elenya, offering her an encouraging nod. Even if she had not produced a child for him, with him, he knew he could never love another like he loved her, though he was thankful that was not something he had to even consider.

After helping her up, he moved to sit next to where she was propped against the headboard attempting to feed their son for the first time. He stroked the downy head of the contented infant and kissed Elenya's temple before she leaned against him using his strong arm for support. He smiled at Nema who beamed her approval at what he was certain was the picture of the perfect family. *His family*. He breathed deeply, his chest swelling with contented pride, almost wishing he could freeze this moment in time.

Chapter 43

Elenya was confined to bed rest far longer than her patience could endure. Only the steady stream of visitors and the time alone getting to know her son made her confinement bearable. Tahruk had returned to the training fields, though he was home with her every evening and quite often in the late afternoon. He tried to keep her spirits up, regaling her with stories of the jousting matches or happenings about the Centrehead. Sometimes they were stories she'd already heard from another guest, but she encouraged him to tell her anyway, enjoying the interaction. She desperately missed the physical closeness they'd shared and longed for the day when he could, once again, take her in his arms for more than just a cursory cuddle.

Slowly, she began to venture from her bed to the sun room and then to their private garden for short periods. Around Rennie's fifth month, Doctor Jorian released her fully, though he encouraged her to take it easy. His expectation was that it could take up to a year for her to feel like herself again and she shouldn't push it nor allow others to expect more from her than she was willing to give. As she relaxed in the chaise in a far corner of the family garden while Rennie napped in his basket at her side, she remembered how embarrassed she'd been to ask if that meant relations with her husband. Doctor Jorian had been so kind and professional, patting her hand while he explained to her that she was free to do whatever *she* felt comfortable doing. He'd also instructed her to let him know immediately should she become pregnant again—said in the same professional manner he used to address all things.

Elenya had held her excitement in until he exited the room, then she'd thrown herself back, kicking her feet on the bed while she rolled back and forth like an excited child. Tonight, she'd thought, closing her eyes to capture the feel of remembered caresses for a moment before rising to prepare for the dinner hour and her husband's return from the training fields.

She was sure her desire had been palpable during the meal, and her interest laid open on the table, so to speak, once they returned to their chambers and she'd put the sleepy baby down for the night. But Tahruk had thwarted her plans, her advances met with a cool reception that left her crying softly into the pillow, her back turned to him. Embarrassed and hurt, she hadn't tried again, instead putting all her hopes into him coming to her.

It had been over a month—time that had not been her friend. He'd seemed to distance himself from her, coming home later or venturing out again shortly after dinner, to the point now where he'd left on a four day training mission that would lead up to this season's Dremis. Thoughts of her Dremis assaulted her mind, visions of Cerissa mocked her. She'd heard the woman had yet to accept another and it was rumored that she was holding out hope still that she would belong to one of the elite warriors. Elenya dropped her chin to her chest, blinking rapidly to hold back tears. Had her warrior succumbed to the charms of the blonde goddess? Would she be the one he'd go to under the pull of the Dremis moon?

"What's your problem?"

She looked up swiftly, instinctively moving a hand to press lightly against Rennie's back. The loud gruffness of his uncle's voice hadn't disturbed the baby in the least, unlike the effect it had on her.

"What do you want, Redahn?" she asked, bristling. "I thought you'd gone with the other men?" The words turned her stomach to churning. If Redahn had returned, where was her husband? If he didn't come to her tonight, of all nights, she would know. She looked up to see where the sun lay in the sky and wondered how she'd manage to make it through the rest of the day and evening.

"For a woman married to the King's finest warrior, having produced for him a beautiful child—a son no less—you have the appearance of a youngster whose birthday celebration has been cancelled. Apparently, you have suffered disappointment and you have no idea what to do with yourself. Perhaps I could offer my services."

"Redahn! Even if you were the last man in the Kingdom, I would reject your assistance. You are a lurch of the highest level." Her voice caused little Rennie to jump, though she was able to settle him with a few gentle pats.

Redahn's chuckle turned to an all-out laugh when she cut her eyes in his direction. "You should let your concerns lie, Elenya. Imagine life's hand on your back and allow yourself to settle, much as your comforting touch has settled your child."

Elenya looked away, not bothering to watch Redahn make his way from the garden, though she sensed when he was gone. She sighed loudly then practiced the deep breathing Nema had taught her to help her remain calm when tending her baby. She thought of the note she'd placed in the bottle thrown overboard on her trip from

Aleone. She'd selfishly asked for a life filled with love from a man she adored. Her penned words had also revealed a desire to bear his children. She smiled, looking at her baby. She'd given one perfect child to the man she adored.

Closing her eyes, she prayed the love she believed that man had for her had not grown cold.

Chapter 44

Nema met Elenya and Rennie coming out of the garden.

"There you are!" She kissed Elenya's cheek then peeked at the still sleeping bundle. "He's a sound sleeper, isn't he?"

Elenya nodded. "Yes, especially now that there are no more night feedings to be had."

Nema nodded and looked the young mother over. "And you are comfortable? Redahn seemed to think you distressed."

Elenya rolled her eyes. "Redahn's company is enough to distress a soul."

Nema laughed, though quickly sobered. "Are you headed back to your chambers?" When Elenya nodded, she indicated she would walk with them. "How is everything between you and Tahruk?"

Tension seeped into every inch of Elenya's body, her posture became rigid, her face a mask of taut concern. Did Nema know something? If he'd been seen with another, Nema would have been informed…

"Don't fret, love. He was quite moved by the events surrounding Rennie's birth. That fear will not soon leave him, nor will the thought that his love for you might easily produce another child." She stopped Elenya with a gentle hand to her arm. "Do you understand what I'm saying?"

Looking first at her baby then down the long, empty corridor, Elenya thought about Nema's words. Could that be it then? A bubble of hope expanded within her chest, dipping down to unleash butterflies in her stomach. Without thinking, she placed her hand over her flattened abdomen. "Oh, Nema. I hope you're right. I couldn't bear to think he no longer wants me or that I've been replaced so quickly by another."

Nema's soft laughter echoed in the hallway. "Oh, my dear, no." She shook her head and took hold of Rennie's basket handle. "There will never be another for Tahruk. He simply needs to be reminded of something he told me once as he left for the battlefields and I handed his sword to him. When I kissed his cheek and told him to be careful, he shook his head, telling me caution and fear are for those who don't understand how precious life is, that to truly live one must be willing to risk all. It's time for him to live again where your love is concerned. He simply needs something to remind him, that's all. Tonight, you have both the Dremis moon and old Nema on your side. Come, let's discuss what you need to do," she called back as she began to carry the baby toward the wing occupied by the couple and their son.

An hour later the two women and the baby emerged again from the chamber door. Elenya juggled a basket filled with Rennie's belongings needed for his first overnight stay away from her.

"Are you sure you want to do this, Nema? Babies can be such a handful."

Nema pushed her concerns away with a wave of her hand in the air. "Nonsense. He's not the first young lad I've tended, are you Master Rennie? No!" Rennie smiled up at the older woman, his little body wiggling in the basket making them both laugh. "Besides, it's not like we're that far away. If we need you, I will send someone. And his nurse will be close by as well." She laughed when Elenya bit her lower lip and sighed. "He'll be just fine while you take care of equally important matters."

"I know, I know! Oh, Nema. I want this and I trust you completely. It's just so much harder than I expected to put him in someone else's care."

"And where would you fine ladies and gentleman be off to in such a hurry?"

Elenya pulled up short, nearly tipping the laden basket she carried in order to avoid running into Shemek and his constant shadow—his warrior friend from the hospital—as they stepped into her path.

"Careful there," Shemek continued, seeming to have forgotten his question. Elenya swung the basket away when he reached out to help her.

"I've got it, though you startled me, Shemek. What are you doing here?"

"We haven't been away so long that you've already forgotten I'm an invited guest here, have you?" His teasing smile took Elenya back to a time when her dreams centered around a *what if* that would never be. How she had loved him then, always hopeful but never believing she might one day have even stronger feelings for someone else.

"Of course I haven't," she answered, her brows drawing down as she struggled with the meshing of her past and present. "I just assumed the lot of you wouldn't be back for a while longer."

Shemek shook his head. "We were released early. The Dremis gathering begins tonight, you know. The King wants his men turned out in their finest."

"Too bad their manners don't match their attire." Elenya bit her lip and turned her head, silently cursing her loose tongue. How she wished she could take back the words that made both Nema and Shemek chuckle, even if Shemek's friend remained straight faced.

Rennie chose that moment to let them know he was tired of standing idle, his commanding squeal giving Elenya a good reason to bid the two men good day.

"Please, let me carry that for you. I don't mind at all, and it appears we're going in the same direction."

Elenya hesitated, unsure how she could refuse without being blatantly rude. Shemek was obviously trying to regain the casual comfort they'd always experienced together. Elenya nodded and relinquished her load, rubbing the imprint of the wicker basket from her forearm.

"Shemek?" A question niggled as they made their way to Nema's chambers. "Why were the two of you so far back in the family quarters?" She noticed Nema raising her brows at the question, though Shemek seemed nonplused. He shrugged.

"It seems no matter how long I've been here I still get turned around from time to time. I guess the tiredness from training coupled with the excitement of the Dremis has my internal compass completely wound the wrong way. Garin here said it was this way. Last time I listen to him."

The small group laughed though he quickly looked away after his eyes briefly connected with Elenya's. *Shemek*, she thought, *what are you up to and why are you lying*? She had no doubts in her mind that Shemek had the layout of Zanak down after his first day there, if not sooner. She shuddered as imaginary cold fingers danced down her spine.

"Shall I wait to escort you back to your chambers,

Elenya? I noticed you have no corisan with you this afternoon."

Elenya frowned. "I shouldn't need one within the walls of my own home, not now that we're no longer battling."

"Which I hope doesn't happen again for a good, long time," Nema added, not really paying attention to anything beyond maneuvering through her chamber door.

Once her son and Nema were through, Elenya blocked the doorway, holding out her arms. "I can get that from here. Thank you, Shemek." Her dismissal was blatant, finalized by her closing the door behind her. She leaned against the smooth wood surface trying to settle the butterflies in her stomach, wishing that day at the infirmary had never happened. He had seemed more himself, for the most part, when they'd met after he'd been released. It made no sense, had to be her imagination. This was Shemek! Her best friend from childhood.

Shaking her head to clear her thoughts, Elenya pushed away from the door to follow Nema and Rennie into the room Nema had occupied during Elenya's stay with her. She stopped just inside the threshold, a smile covering her face as she listened to Nema prattling to the cooing baby.

"Won't your grandfather be surprised to find you here this evening, young master? Pleasantly so, I might add. What a fine young man you are…"

Pride filled Elenya's heart when her son smiled at her and kicked his legs in excitement, toppling himself from his seated position in the middle of the large bed. Both Elenya and Nema laughed, which made him laugh when Elenya righted him. He held his hands out to her, sobering instantly when she didn't pick him up. As was usual for him, it didn't last long before he became quickly engrossed in the toys she handed him from the basket she'd placed on the side table.

"You seem ill at ease with your old friend. An unasked *why* hung in the air as the two women stood side-by-side watching the baby.

Elenya sighed. "I don't know, Nema. I think perhaps it's just me." She shrugged, not really wanting to think about Shemek. She didn't want anything to spoil this night with her warrior. Not the fact that it was to be her first night away from her child, or that this night should have brought her sister Denya to the Centrehead to celebrate her inclusion in the Dremis gathering. Denya had gotten ill months ago and although her sister's lengthy recovery had kept her parents from visiting as well, she wasn't upset Denya would not be a party to the frenzy that would be taking place at nightfall. She also refused to let the fear of rejection that kept attempting to unsettle her keep her from the man she loved, and she certainly wouldn't let thoughts of Shemek intrude on what *had* to be a perfect night.

"So, after dinner, Rennie will come back here with me and you'll return to your chambers to prepare for Tahruk to arrive home..." Nema was saying when she pulled herself back from her musings with one last thought. *If he returns tonight.*

Chapter 45

Elenya paced through the rooms she shared with Tahruk, attempting to assure herself that his extended absence meant nothing. Nema's words ran through her mind as a gentle reminder. The older woman knew her warrior better than anyone and Elenya had to believe she could not be wrong where his feelings for her were concerned.

She looked at the wine bottle, deciding to have a small glass to help calm her nerves. The wine of Zanak—she'd learned to drink it, though it had been her enemy those first days, lulling her to sleep before her match made by the marking could be consummated. She was thankful Tahruk had not given up on her completely then, remembering the first time… She closed her eyes, clinched them tightly against the tears. Never had she imagined loving anyone as completely as she did the son of this enemy Drille.

Time clicked by slowly, her body growing weary of the path that led her nowhere. Elenya sat down on the edge of the bed, their bed, with a heavy thud. She let her hands fall limply to her sides, her chin dropping before she pushed herself down, burying her face in the pillows. Her tears fell as silently as her heart broke. He hadn't come to her. He'd known he'd be unable to resist the drive of the Dremis moon, and he'd chosen to stay away. For once, Nema was wrong.

She fell asleep wondering whose bed he'd chosen to grace with his charms. Had he gone to the Dremis gathering seeking a fresh maiden, or had Cerissa won at last? For the first time in a very long time, Elenya's heart longed for home. She wanted to return to the shores of Aleone.

The darkness of the room startled Elenya when she awakened. She had no idea how long she'd slept, though the bed was still empty when she reached to her side. She ran her hand over the empty space. At least she had the memory of what they'd once shared…

"Lady Elenya. Please…"

Becoming so still she could hear her own breathing, Elenya listened. Afraid to close her eyes, she tried to determine if her imagination was playing tricks on her. A scuffing sound in the secret passageway had her upright in the bed, scrambling for the lighting tinder and candle on the bedside table.

"Please. Unlatch the door. There's been an accident. It's Shemek. He needs your help. You have to come…"

"Shemek?" she whispered, quickly kicking her legs over the edge of the bed and slipping into the soft shoes she'd left there. With the candlestick in hand, she pulled back the curtain that shielded the secret passage from view. "Shemek?" she said again, louder though so whoever it was could hear her.

"Yes, my lady. Your friend Shemek… he's been hurt, badly. And he's asking for you. Please. Unlock the door. You have to come with me. We need to hurry."

Her hand poised above the lock, Elenya hesitated. "Who are you? How did you know how to get here?" she called through the heavy wood planks.

"It's Shemek's friend Garin. If you'll open the door…

he gave me something to give to you. Said you would understand. Please, my lady. We need to hurry," he repeated. "I'll explain on the way. If we don't hurry, it's going to be too late."

Plagued with doubt, Elenya cursed the voice of caution that made her wary, knowing if Shemek perished before she could see him it would take her a lifetime to forgive herself. She slid the lock back then pushed on the heavy door, dropping her candlestick and nearly toppling into man's arms when he pulled from the other side.

"Steady, now." He helped her to regain her balance and handed her the rose with its single thorn before pulling the torchiere from its arm on the wall. "He said to give you that as proof, that you'd understand what it meant. Now, come quickly, we have to hurry," he repeated yet again.

Elenya stared at the rose, unsure why warning bells still rung inside her, though Garin didn't leave her any time to contemplate. He grabbed her hand and began pulling her into the hidden passageway.

"Stop," she shrieked, attempting to pull away, then crying out when he tightened his hold. "Please, you're hurting my hand."

"Be quiet!" he told her while continuing to pull her down the passageway. "Stop fighting me. Don't you see, you have to come. There's no choice. I'm doing this for Shemek. It's him you belong with. Not the other."

Fear coursed through her, threatening to empty her stomach of her evening meal.

"Have you forgotten already the kiss you shared on the beach? How many nights have you've stared up at the stars thinking of that night? He never forgot. Did you know that, my lady? Did you know he visited that beach every night after you left, remembered how you felt in his arms, your body molded to his? He told me of the taste of your lips, and your tears…"

"No," she whispered. She shook her head. "He said himself that we could never be."

"No!" he yelled, pushing her back with a hard thrust that had her stumbling to keep from falling. "Being with that warrior released you from the bounds of the marking. You have given Zanak their son… now you're free to be with the man who truly loves you."

Elenya matched Garin's approaching steps with backwards ones, stopping only when she bumped into the passage wall. She looked from side to side, knowing she could never outrun him, at least not within the confines of the tunnels.

"Tell me, my lady. Tell me you don't feel anything for me." He shook his head. "For him, I mean."

Her fear increased at his words, his demented eyes glowing as he looked her over. Pinning her against the wall with his body, his free hand raked into the thickness of her red curls, and with a less than gentle tug, he turned her face up to his. He moistened his own lips while looking at hers. "Your lips tremble, Ya. I see the tears pooled in your eyes. Do you fear me? You needn't be afraid, love."

Elenya quaked. He'd used the name Shemek used for her. Did this man think he was Shemek? Fighting back revulsion for what she had to do, she ran her hands up his torso to rest her palms against his heart. She shook her head. "Oh, my lord," she whispered, praying she was right and her ruse would work. "I mourn now only for lost time. All those months we could have been together after you were released from the infirmary…" She pressed herself up to kiss the hollow of his neck, thankful for the shudder that told her he was beyond logic. "Where are we going?" she asked in a whisper as she pushed up closer to his ear.

She could feel Garin's breath hot and heavy on her neck, her face contorting more with every touch of lips that made her flesh crawl. "Oh, Ya. I knew you cared. I just knew."

The smile she flashed at him when he pulled back must have passed because she found herself suddenly by his side heading deeper into the secret passageway. "Slow down! I know we're in a hurry, but I need to know where you're taking me." She pulled against him, failing to slow him in the least.

Garin laughed. "Does it matter as long as we're together?"

"I suppose not, but… how did you know about the tunnels beneath Zanak and the secret halls within the walls?"

"Shemek, of course. And lord Redahn. We used the tunnels to access the castle a time or two when we were in need of… uh, entertainment."

Redahn. Of course. He'd used the tunnels in search of easy access to the Ladies of the Courts and had breached family security, and that of their King, in the process. And so few knew about the tunnels… a tear slid down her cheek. No one would know she was down here, that any of this was happening.

Elenya knew she had to get away from him. They were close enough to the passage's exit that she could smell the sea air. If she could make it to the outlet before him and gain access to the copse of trees outside, there might be a chance she could make her way back to Zanak, just as she'd run to the Masters' on that night some fifteen months before. She still didn't know if Garin was acting alone. She may well encounter Shemek on the other side. But she knew she couldn't continue to be led along like the proverbial lamb. With that thought, she pushed against him with all her might.

Garin stumbled back letting go, his free arm flailing in the air keeping him upright. She pulled up her skirt and turned to run, only he was much faster than she'd anticipated and had her by the waist before she'd managed to get more than a few steps away.

"Let me go!" She fought him, her nails digging into his arms, her body bucking against him in an attempt to break free.

"Stop it, Ya," he yelled at her, tightening his hold while moving them closer to the passage exit.

"Don't you call me that. You're not Shemek. You're not the man that kissed me on the shores of Aleone and told me my sacrifice was for the future of our Drille. You're not that man. In fact, you're no man at all."

He stopped abruptly and gave her a hard push, thrusting her to the passageway floor. Her breath whooshed out from the force, the taste of blood seeping into her mouth from where she'd bit her lip.

Face down, holding herself up on skinned hands, she contemplated her course of action. Garin stood above her, silent except for his heavy breathing. He emanated a tension filled with violent rage, fueled by… was that resentment? All those negative emotions encompassed them.

Elenya, you are an idiot, she thought. Why had she not simply kept quiet and allowed him to take her outside before fighting him? She'd always known her inability to restrain her tongue would be her downfall. But she'd also been fearful of him pulling her along that outer path. Tears threatened. She blinked them back. This was no time to show weakness.

His boots crushing the debris littering the natural floor of the passageway, Elenya cut her eyes to see him moving away. If she could get up, she could try to run again while he fought to place the torch in one of the holders scattered randomly along the length of the corridor. They weren't that far from the exit… if she could get free before he caught her… Her heartbeat drowning out all other sound, she tried to rise, tripped on her gown, then regained her footing just as he turned back toward her.

He was on her within a few feet, knocking her back to the ground, though she'd made it far enough to see the thick, vine covered branches that covered the end—the door to her freedom. If she could just get to the other side…

Twisting beneath him, she fought with all her might, working against logic to get a sure footing that would allow her to thrust him off. The sting of his palm against her face halted her movements. Shocked, she stared up at him sitting atop her, his hands holding hers to the ground, and for a brief moment she thought she saw the depravity in his dark eyes lift as he took in her tears. It was replaced with a sadness she didn't understand. "Please," she whispered. "Please, let me go."

He looked up, seeming to look beyond the tree covered exit. "We could have made a wonderful life together, Ya." His voice was distant, a higher, airier sound that made her shiver. He looked back at her, through her. "You're Shemek's, you know."

She shook her head, the tears trickling down the sides of her face wetting the hair at her temples. "No. I have always belonged to the Zanak warrior."

He nodded, and Elenya took a short-lived breath of relief before his hands moved to her neck and the air was cut off from her lungs. "I can't let you go. You know that. I can't…"

She resumed fighting, though with his body straddling her torso, his feet hooked over her legs, it left her little room to maneuver, and resistance grew harder with the intensified burning in her lungs. Billowing clouds took over her mind. She stared up at him as her body stilled, attempting to find a spark of reasoning in his brooding eyes. *Please*, she thought. *Dear God, help me one more time.*

The sound of the warriors gathering to leave for battle sounded in her ears, the thunder of a thousand horse hooves lulling her, pulling her into darkness. She felt so light, the hard ground giving way as she floated into nothingness. *I love you.* That one last coherent thought formed, along with a vision of her warrior's face looming above her, right before she closed her eyes.

Chapter 46

A woman shrieked. A man yelled. Elenya gasped as Garin's hands were torn from her throat. She opened her eyes briefly to see Cerissa advancing on her, though her limp limbs thwarting her escape from the woman who wanted everything she had. Was she working with him? If so, who had screamed, and who had removed him from her?

She closed her eyes, too tired to try to make the pieces fit. A coughing spasm overtook her as Cerissa hooked her hands under her arms and pulled her toward the tunnel wall. The other woman sank down, holding her upright until the convulsions passed. She cradled Elenya who tried to force air into her aching lungs through a throat constricted and denied for far too long, now wracked by the bout of coughing.

Again Elenya heard the thunder of horses, the ground beneath them vibrating with the growing sound. She opened her eyes to see her warrior and at least ten other mounted men advancing down the passageway toward her. Tahruk pulled up, stopping beside her and sliding from his mount with the agility of one well-trained. His eyes darted between her and the expanded area before the tunnel's exit. With effort, she tore her gaze from him and turned her head.

The battle between Garin and Redahn was heated, quickly moving toward the vines and limbs that protected the passage from unknowing intruders. Swords clanked, steel against steel, as each man tried to gain the upper hand. Elenya sat forward, pushing away Cerissa's hand, her own discomfort quickly forgotten. She noticed Redahn's arm drop, once then twice, knew he didn't have the strength after his injury to be fighting the madman.

"Help him," she tried to scream, though the sound came out as a screech through her chaffed throat.

"Go! We'll tend to your wife."

Elenya watched, surprised to see her old friend. Her eyes rounded when Shemek placed his palm over Tahruk's heart and nodded his head in the direction of the fighting men. "Remember, we fight on the same side… my friend."

Split second decision making had Shemek dropping down beside Elenya and Tahruk turning toward the end of the tunnel.

"Now!" Tahruk roared. He and the other men charged forward when Garin turned his back on them, the tip of the madman's sword precariously close to Redahn's neck. The latter man, having nowhere to go except through the brush, ducked down just as the others rushed them thrusting Garin toward the branches. His horror-filled scream filled the tunnel causing Elenya to grab her head as she watched Tahruk drop to his knees. She could see him shaking his head, a heavy *no* echoing through the passageway.

The other men backed away—the other men, minus Redahn. Elenya had watched in disbelief as Garin turned and grabbed him, both men toppling through the opening. She crawled to her husband's side, not touching him, not saying anything. Together they just stared at the emptiness.

"Brother." The faint sound of Redahn's voice filled her ears just before a hand pushed through the brush. Startled, she scurried backwards while Tahruk, already in motion, clasped the hand and began trying to pull his brother back through the vined branches. Seconds later, Shemek was at his side, the two of them working together to free Redahn from his trap without releasing him to the same fate as Garin. With one last tug, they freed him, the force unbalancing them all, both brothers and Shemek ended up on their backs, side-by-side on the tunnel floor.

"Hellfire and damnation, Brother, are you trying to give me heart failure?" Tahruk turned his head to look at his younger brother. "How did you manage to avoid the fall?"

Still breathing heavily, Redahn shook his head. "When your body is gone, you have to rely on your other senses. I realized earlier he was trying to force me through, just as I would have done to him given the chance. Only I'd managed to kick the rope over when the scuffle began…"

"The rope?" Shemek interrupted.

"There's a safety rope, to keep those without a stomach for heights from falling." Tahruk nodded and Redahn continued, still breathing heavy between words. "I tried to move when you charged him, but he grabbed my ankle. Luck had me grabbing hold of the rope, though I wasn't sure I could hold on with his added weight. We slid down several feet before I managed to kick him off, and with my arm, it was a bear climbing back up. Next time, consider checking for survivors before you drop in defeat, Brother."

Tahruk frowned, though it was short-lived before he found himself encompassed in a huge bear hug from his brother. The two men, laughing together much as they had as children, climbed to their feet still wrapped around one another.

Redahn broke away and looked at Shemek. With a smile, he helped him up, then pulled him into the circle and the three men laughed heartily for a moment more before they sobered and all turned, scanning their surroundings. Three sets of eyes came to rest on Elenya.

“Is she okay?” Redahn asked, his face bathed with the same concern as the others.

Elenya sat huddled close to Cerissa, her body shaking, even beneath the heavy blanket offered up by one of the warriors who had yet to unpack his gear from the extended training session. The three men hurried to her, Tahruk wrapping her in his arms where she fell against his chest. He held her until the tears subsided.

“How did you know?” she managed to ask, her voice cracking still as she clung to Tahruk, afraid to let him go.

Redahn turned to Cerissa who nodded her head after a few seconds. “Cerissa found the rose on the tunnel floor. The single thorn seemed peculiar enough to alert her senses, especially after she found the dropped candlestick just inside the passage outside your chambers. She looked first for Tahruk, and then came to the Dremis gathering to get me,” Redahn told her. “Thankfully, I was with Shemek who knew exactly what that rose meant.”

Elenya turned to look at the other woman who smiled at her and said, “I’m not your enemy, my lady. I truly am a warrior from Goddai, hired by your father to assure your safety. I was patrolling the passageway when I spotted the rose. Something just felt wrong, which is the only reason I was down here.” She smiled. “Call it woman’s intuition.” They all laughed a bit and she continued. “I tried to find your warrior and learned there’d been a mishap that had kept a group of the already matched elite out longer than expected. That’s when I tracked down Redahn.” She shook her head. “I knew if I tried to fight that madman on my own I would only endanger your life further.”

“But… you tried to take Tahruk from me…”

Cerissa was already shaking her head before Elenya could finish her sentence. “No, my lady. I was merely testing your warrior and assuring he did not stray." She looked at Tahruk and smiled before looking back at Elenya. "I agreed that his nicely filled bed was where he needed to stay." She laughed before adding, "Besides, fending off his brother provided more than enough Sharanis fulfillment to last a lifetime."

The brothers chuckled. Elenya looked at Redahn, attempting a smile through her tears. "You missed your chance for first pick of the unmarked maidens."

Redahn pressed his lips tightly together and nodded his head, trying to look vexed, only he couldn't hold his laughter. "I've heard the maidens don't match up to last year's group, my lady." He winked at her. "Besides, this is only the first night. And it's early. There's still plenty of time to dance."

"Shemek." Elenya turned and held out her hand to her old friend, who took it only after receiving a small nod from Tahruk. "Garin said you'd been hurt. He knew things about you, about us…" New tears streaked down her cheeks. "He… half the time, he thought he was you." She turned her face back into her warrior's chest.

Shemek squeezed the hand he still held. "I'm sorry, Ya. It… it was hard seeing you loving someone else as much as you did your husband." He paused and she looked back at him. "I guess I talked too much about you before I came to terms with the rightness of everything. I knew Garin had trouble with his memory after the last battle. He'd often think we were back on the fields. It's why I kept him close as much as I could, but I never imagined he was dangerous or I'd never have left him within your walls alone. I… I thought tonight he was sleeping off a headache back in our chambers. After we ran into you taking your son to Nema's quarters, he'd grown quiet, claiming he wasn't feeling well. Oh Lord! He was the reason I was in the family wing. One of the servants told me he'd gone down the wrong passage and I'd gone to fetch him. I had no idea… I'm sorry. I should have known."

Elenya shook her head, wishing she could do more to comfort Shemek, but all she could think of was what might have happened if Garin had found her and her son alone. She sucked in hard, her voice rising with emotion as she turned to Tahruk. "Please, take me home. I need to see my son."

Tahruk nodded and helped her to her feet and up into the saddle of his warhorse. Before he mounted behind her, he instructed one of the other men to fetch Doctor Jorian and bring him back to Zanak. He spoke quietly with Redahn, Shemek, and Cerissa for a moment before swinging up into the saddle and leading the way as part of his men rode behind them, taking Tahruk's horse once they were assured the couple had entered the security of Zanak's halls. Guards were to be posted until they could be certain Garin had acted alone. Elenya had already promised herself that she would never unlatch the passage doorway again and that she would learn to trust her gut. She shuddered again thinking about what might have been.

Hours later, assured of Rennie's safety and of Elenya's health, the couple lay alone in their chamber. Thinking her asleep, her back against him, the warrior pushed himself up just enough to see her without disturbing her rest. Twice now, he'd almost lost her and someone else had saved her life. The first time, he'd distanced himself from her, afraid of what might happen should she conceive again through his desire for her. He'd learned tonight there were far greater dangers, especially since Doctor Jorian had told him yet again that she would be all right.

Silently, he cursed himself for pushing her away when

she'd tried to make her desires known. He wouldn't be so foolish again. Once she opened herself up to him, letting him know that she was ready, he would be there, waiting.

With a gentle stroke, he swept her hair back from her face and kissed her cheek, her ear, her temple. He buried his face in her honeyed-cinnamon curls and breathed deeply. Essence of Oleander. The scent fueled his desire, especially when she turned in his arms, a tiny moan sounding in her throat and her arms encircling his waist to pull him closer to her.

"Elenya, my love," he whispered. He knew he should let her rest after all she'd been through, but his need for her surged, every bit as fierce as that first night she'd spent in his bed. As if having a mind of their own, his hands moved over her forming a trail for his mouth to follow, and he tasted every inch of her, searing her, marking her again as his—as a part of him, not some creature to be owned and used. She lay beneath him, her body responding with heightened need when his mouth again found hers. Breathless from the assault of his tongue against hers, she turned her face away, arching her back to press into him.

"Tahruk," she whispered, looking back. "Make love to me."

As the last light of the Dremis moon pierced the darkness of the room, Tahruk once again claimed Elenya, uniting them as one—spirit, soul, and body—in the only union that would ever make either of them whole.

Epilogue

Five year old Rennicus Kahlan Sharanis danced around the deck of the *Petit Cadeau*, holding the hands of his sister, Emylene, almost two years his junior.

"Is it time, Mama?" he asked, picking up the bottle filled with the rolled parchments that carried their dreams. A lover of stories, he had asked his mother over and over again to tell him of the time she'd tossed her bottle of wishes overboard on her maiden trip to the Centrehead and had asked if the family might set free their own dreams on their way to visit Aleone.

Elenya laughed and handed the nearly one year old baby to her husband. The exchange came with a peck and a hug, and Tahruk pulled Elenya back to him before she could step away.

"I have something more for you to add," he told her after kissing her fully. Elenya raised her brows in surprise. He'd been reluctant to participate when she and Rennie had scribbled their notes for the bottle. Rennie had added notes for each of his sisters and nearly cried when there was none for his father. Elenya had assured him it would be okay, that his father's dreams were safe. *Dreams are not born by words in a bottle*, she'd told him, *but by what you hold dear in your heart*. The little boy had nodded and asked if they might still launch their dreams. Elenya smiled, thinking more of her romantic notions had ended up in her son than might be fitting for the future leader of the King's Elite Guard—not that his father hadn't done well in that position with a romantic side all his own.

She took the rolled up parchment Tahruk pulled from behind his back. "Would you like to read it?" he asked.

Elenya hesitated. "Do you wish me to?" Tahruk nodded. Carefully, she slid the leather tie from the roll and let it fall open to find it was actually two sheets. The first appeared to be a copy of a decree from the new King. She fought back tears with thoughts of Andorak, whose companionship she'd grown to love, especially as they'd sparred verbally over matters left unspoken by most women. They'd talked of battle, and families, of her feelings about the markings—and his. She'd questioned their need for such a ritual and he'd considered her words. It was an uncanny relationship that both had enjoyed.

She scanned the page, starting with a cursory glance at the signature and date at the bottom then read again, more slowly, from the top. In his final moments, King Andorak had demanded an abolishment of the act of marking. Elenya's mouth fell open, her heart hammering. King Shenai had acted out his father's wish, adding that he understood there were still those whose blood serum had already been administered to another and that arrangements would have to be made to see to their unions—a better plan for uniting the young couples. Elenya felt tears welling and offered silent thanks to Shenai. The new King, Andorak's third son, had often been present during Elenya's visits to the old King. She thought about later visits when she'd taken Rennie. Both men seemed to enjoy the boy's antics as well as Elenya's company. She imagined watching her son had been a soothing assurance to Andorak that his bloodline was strong and would continue with future generations. It was a pity his body gave out well before his mind. Elenya was so thankful for the time she'd had with him and hoped Rennie would turn out to be even half the man his great, great, grandfather had been.

She remembered the day Andorak had apologized for the fact that the throne would be passed to his oldest living son instead of the Sharanis family, even though honor and their system demanded him to act as he did. Elenya knew Shenai would make an excellent leader. Her only concern had been Renaine. She'd been unsure how he would receive his removal from the direct passing of the throne, though she needn't have worried. Renaine seemed more at ease now than ever before, taking the time to enjoy his grandchildren in a way he'd never been able to do with his own children. The weight of two kingdoms had been lifted from his shoulders, at least for the time being, and he'd morphed into the man only Nema had known before. The kingdom changes and the last battle had changed him. Even now he was overseeing the final details to assure the Avenille home was completely ready for Elenya's family. She felt her heart soar at the thought of them moving to the Centrehead, returning with the couple and their children when they left the shores of Aleone.

Not bothering to suppress her smile, Elenya continued reading the document in hand. King Shenai was asking her to come and talk to him once she returned. He'd like to hear her views on how they might best deal with the already paired couples and their families, how they might ease the unions when their times came. Her mind was already working, thinking how Daruh and the other Masters would have to go through the sealed records to find the matches and contact those involved. The blood serum not yet administered would also need to be destroyed.

Elenya looked at her own son whose blood had been ceremonially drawn when he was three. Did it already run through the veins of another, binding him to an unknown woman? His wife might well be the last lady marked.

She looked at Tahruk. Had the marking been abolished before her birth, would she have ever known this man that made her who she was? And if she had met him, without the marking, would she have fallen in love with him so completely? She liked to think she would have. Life with him was everything she'd ever imagined it could be. Not perfect by any means, but he'd still been the answer to all she'd written and placed in her bottle of dreams.

She pulled the first sheet away to look at the second page and glanced up at him with a frown before looking back down. "It's blank, my lord." When her eyes finally found their way back to his, her frown collapsed. There was no way she could help but smile at his huge grin.

"Of course it's blank," Tahruk told her. "How could I ask for more than I already have?" He reached out to caress her cheek, his thumb catching a tear. "All my dreams came true the day you turned three—that moment when we became one for the first time."

The End.....for now!

And what became of Redahn?
In Nema's words, that's a story for another day…

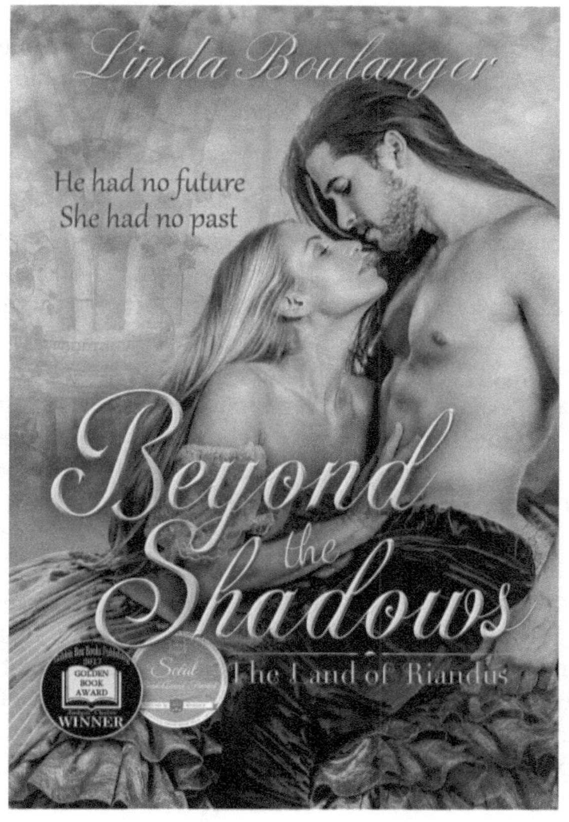

Beyond the Shadows

In a time when men fought for their king, protected him and their families with might and sword, Redahn Sharanis questions his self-worth after losing strength in his arm due to a battle injury and botched surgery. He grows hard, maintaining a facade of bitterness and cynicism that only begins to chip away after he meets a woman at the annual gathering of the maidens who is smothered by her own shadows.

Eighteen year old Mahryn's innocence is tarnished by the baggage of her past and now she's been thrown into the pool of beautiful maidens, whose sole purpose is to provide pleasure to the King's warriors. Knowing she was sent by her father when he could have made a good match for her opens a floodgate of questionable memories from her past. And if that wasn't enough, she manages to attract the attention of a man fighting his own battles—a warrior who had been second only to his older brother, the King's finest, before he was wounded.

But there's more to both of them. Lord Redahn is fiercely loyal and bound by his own code of honor... traits that Mahryn's presence brings out. She's stronger than any woman Redahn has ever known, which comes to light when her true past is exposed. Together they begin to help one another fit the puzzle pieces of their lives back into their right places, though the picture that results isn't something everyone wants to see.

Author Note

Thank you for walking into the *Land of Riandus* with me. As the first in the series, *Dance with the Enemy* will always have a special place in my heart. Beginning as a short story, these characters opened a whole new world for me when one thought loomed in my mind. That was *the scent of a woman*. Yes, I know that is a movie, but that thought kept running through my head until I had to answer the question: *what if?* Those are words that lead to new worlds in the mind of an author.

If you're just jumping into this fantasy land, be sure to grab a copy of *Beyond the Shadows*, Redahn and Mahryn's story. It's currently available only on Amazon, and while each book is a complete story in itself, you can never go wrong with getting to know the characters from a perspective all their own.

Joining my Facebook Group is a great way to stay informed and enjoy the one on one that comes from being a part of an interactive group. Just look up Linda's Dragon Guardians. We'd love to see you there!

Until the next story…
Thank you for being a part of my dream,
~Linda

Acknowledgments

Books are not written by a single person. It takes the cooperation of many and *Dance With the Enemy* is no exception. If it had not been for my four children and one husband—who is a much better housewife than I ever dreamed of being, I feel certain this book would still be only partially written. Thank you all for stepping in to pick up the slack around our always overly busy household.

Along that same route: A HUGE thank you to Patricia Green for lovingly cracking her whip and demanding chapter after chapter until I was finally able to write *The End*! on the first draft.

To Kristina Haecker whose love of my characters brought me back to make them the best I could. And to the world's best first round beta reading team: Cindy, Schuerr, Kerri Wood, Gayla Catrett, Patricia Green, Nissie Lambert, Myrna Gamble... Your encouragement means more to me than any of you will ever know. When Kerri emailed me and said she was ready for the next book RIGHT NOW, I knew we had a story to share. I hope each of you know that *Enemy* would not be the story it is without you. I'd like to add for the revision that Kristina Haecker's Personal Assistant duties have saved my sanity. She is top-notch, and has a lot to offer. And an additional thank you to Krissy Smith for her proofreading services. Between her eyes and Kristina's, I know I have a much cleaner (typographically speaking) version of this story to put in your hands.

Special thanks to Andrew E. Kaufman who has served as a source of great encouragement as I've watched him go from having just published his first book, to consistently climbing to the top of Amazon's top 100—I've seen the magic key through him… HARD work, and writing really well. His stories are amazing. And he's also been a great friend that I'm grateful to for so much more than I have time to list out here.

To Pat Sipperly, the very best *video guy* I've ever known. His talents are unequalled. I also appreciate his encouragement to keep at it until I was done. I wouldn't be writing this acknowledgment if he hadn't given me that push I needed way back when, and held my hand as we walked into the published world together.

Landshark—Violet says thank you for always believing in her. Once upon a time in her wildest dreams… Glad you came back to be a part of this dream.

To Judi Violette and Dixie Wiggins for not only having awesome "home libraries" but also for giving me a free pass to read book after book without overdue fines. Love you both for opening up my world. (*note: Dixie has since passed from the original writing of this acknowledgment. Her presence will be forever missed, her marks left on the world are indelible).

Jaimey Grant/Laura J. Miller and Rachel Rossano, thank you two for putting up with me while I made tweak after tiny little tweak to my cover and other visuals surrounding this book. You also answered all my silly questions concerning life in historical times. Your advice, encouragement, and knowledge pools were invaluable. Jaimey/Laura… you made a comment to me way back when I started writing this book and let you read a little to see if it was viable. Do you remember what it was? Something about a particular line making you lightheaded. I LOVED that comment! It spurred me forward.

I especially want to thank my mom and siblings who have supported me and my love of writing for a long, long, long time. Mom, Jackie, Bobbi… thank you seems so little for all you've done, but it's all I have. I love you guys with all my heart.

If you read the dedication of this book, you know we lost two of our family members during the writing of this book. This story would have made my sister Leigh SMILE. My brother Dean… he would have loved the woman on the cover and been *tickled pink* for me getting it done!

And finally, to those of you who encouraged me to continue on with this story after reading the original short on *Clever Fiction*—you're the reason *Enemy* continued to grow in my head and expand well beyond those initial 1,152 words. You have no idea how many times I went back and re-read your wonderful comments. Because of you, this novel version of *Dance with the Enemy* was given life.

I saw a plaque that said *Dream Big, Little One*. It made me smile because that's what Tahruk calls Elenya and I saw it just days after I finished the final edits. It seemed funny that I should see it when I did, so I decided to accept that it was a message to me. *Dream Big*. I do! Thank you for being a part of my dream.

About Linda Boulanger

Linda Boulanger is a happily-ever-after author, wife, and mother of four human children and two fur babies. She has an eclectic mix of published books, numerous story singles and short stories in a few group anthologies, plus a slew of always evolving works in progress.

Along with being an author, she designs book covers for herself and others through *Tell~Tale Book Covers* and *TreasureLine Designs*, all from her desk just north of Tulsa, Oklahoma.

Other place to find Linda:

Website
LindaBoulangerBooks.com

Blog
writersshelflife.blogspot.com

Facebook
www.facebook.com/TheShelfLifeOfLindaBoulanger

Facebook Group
www.facebook.com/groups/664151640414859

Email
lindaboulangerbooks@gmail.com

Amazon Author Page
www.amazon.com/Linda-Boulanger/e/B002NPYDC6

Linda's Writing

Novels/Novellas
On Wings of Time
On Wings of Fire
A Leap of Faith
Stirring Up Some Love
Dance With the Enemy
Beyond the Shadows
Arms of an Angel

Mini-Novella
Makinna's Secret
A Warrior's Christmas Gift

Anthologies
Echoed Heartbeats
Time Out on a Roller Coaster
Becoming…
Whispered Beginnings

Color Illustrated Children's Book
When Sadie Learned to S.M.I.L.E.

Short Story Trios and Singles
Up To Bat / Center Stage / Best Friend Rules
Face of an Angel / Life Changes / Talk With Me
Secret Shame

www.ingramcontent.com/pod-product-compliance
Lightning Source LLC
Chambersburg PA
CBHW030423180626
46812CB00005B/2153

* 9 7 8 1 6 1 7 5 2 1 5 9 1 *